For Joe, quite possibly the kindest and
wisest man I've ever known.

# IN TRUTH AND CLAW

# IN TRUTH AND CLAW

## CLAW

### A MICK OBERON JOB

## ARI MARMELL

**TITAN** BOOKS

In Truth and Claw
Print edition ISBN: 9781785658891
E-Book edition ISBN: 9781785658907

Published by Titan Books
A division of Titan Publishing Group Ltd
144 Southwark Street, London SE1 0UP

First edition: August 2018
1 3 5 7 9 10 8 6 4 2

A CIP catalogue record for this title is available from the British Library.

Printed and bound in the United States.

Did you enjoy this book? We love to hear from our readers.
Please email us at readerfeedback@titanemail.com
or write to us at Reader Feedback at the above address.

To receive advance information, news, competitions, and exclusive offers
online, please sign up for the Titan newsletter on our website:
**www.titanbooks.com**

# A BRIEF WORD ON LANGUAGE

Throughout the Mick Oberon novels, I've done my best to ensure that most of the 30s-era slang can be picked up from context, rather than trying to include what would become a massive (and, no matter how careful I was, likely incomplete) dictionary. So over the course of reading, it shouldn't be difficult to pick up on the fact that "lamps" and "peepers" are eyes, "choppers" and "Chicago typewriters" are Tommy guns, and so forth.

But there are two terms I do want to address, due primarily to how they appear to modern readers.

"Bird," when used as slang in some areas today, almost always refers to a woman. In the 1930s, however, it was just another word for "man" or "guy."

"Gink" sounds like it should be a racial epithet to modern ears (and indeed, though rare, I've been told that it is used as such in a few regions). In the 30s, the term was, again, just a word for "man," though it has a somewhat condescending connotation to it. (That is, you wouldn't use it to refer to anyone you liked or respected.) It's in this fashion that I've used it throughout the novels.

# CHAPTER ONE

It started the same way it was all gonna end: in the snow.

You birds ain't ever seen anything like an Elphame winter. A quilt of the brightest white over absolutely everything, and I do mean *white*. The slop you pump into the sky from your factories and your flivvers and who knows what else make your own winters sorta plague-gray, but even your cleanest, freshest snow don't compare. I told ya before about the colors here, how they're more'n just hues and shades. Entities unto themselves. Our snow? It's like the gods just forgot to paint it in. It's the shine of everything and nothing. Hurts to look at, but too pure to look away.

Like the cold. Sharper'n the chill of your world. You feel it more, but it bothers you less.

And through it all, a constant spatter of browns and golds and reds—and I mean *gold* and *red*, not those off-browns of your world—where tree branches and leaves'd shaken off their coats of snow. A couple flowers that'd forgotten they were supposed to be bunking for the season, or maybe they just had insomnia. Little islands where toadstools peeped up through the snow, mostly alive'n awake because the pixies liked 'em that way.

Me, I'd seen it a million times before. Pete'd seen it before more'n a few times, too, which is why he'd already dusted out, headin' deeper into the wilderness for his hairy weekend. Funny thing: the prints he left in the snow were wolf tracks even though he wouldn't be changing for a few hours yet.

But Pete wasn't my only guest.

"Oh, Mick, it's beautiful!"

"Yeah, sister. It really is," I answered, more 'cause I figured she expected an answer, not because I was much for admiring the scenery. I was too busy givin' her the up and down, even though I guessed I wouldn't see anything new.

Adalina looked same as she'd looked for more'n a year now. Massive peepers spaced way too wide across her face, skin paler'n a worm with the runs, and just overall... fishy. She'd started comin' along when I stepped Sideways with Pete every month, somethin' I'd allowed in hopes of learnin' more about her. I mean, I look different here than I do in your world. Shorter, a touch less human. Thought maybe she would, too.

So far, I got squat. I knew nothin' more about her than I had the day she woke up, the day she'd spouted off some nonsense in half a dozen languages—a few of 'em deader'n the mummy who'd helped revive her. She seemed to have no memory of any of that, and her parents and I had decided it wasn't anything we needed to tell her about.

I had a whole lot I hadn't told her about. Or them, for that matter. Hadn't yet figured how.

Old Gaelic. Old Polish. Old East Norse, not to mention several others, all muddled together in her initial disorientation. Somethin' about that combination nagged at me, chewing at the back of my head like a persistent louse, but I just couldn't figure why.

If she was at all steamed that she hadn't died that day in the burnt-down church, when she'd walked into her grandma's spell in despair over becomin' a "monster," she never said. In fact, in the months she'd been awake, she hadn't talked much about those days at all, and Orsola's name never once passed her lips.

Mine, either. Like I said, there were some yarns I hadn't spun for any of the family yet.

Anyway, point is, I hadn't uncovered a damn thing I didn't already know. Bringin' Adalina to the Otherworld hadn't worked. I'd spent some time nosing around Chicago—our Chicago, I mean, not yours—and that'd turned up bupkis, too. On the square, I'd run outta places to dig.

Well, no, that ain't entirely true. I still had some people I could ask, but… Well, that'd mean talking about Adalina to ginks I wasn't so sure I wanted knowin' about her. Or, at least, knowin' she might be important.

By now, I didn't really have any good reason to keep taking her along when I brought Pete here on the full moon, but I didn't really have good reason to refuse, either. She loved these trips, and Fino and Bianca loved anything that made their little changeling happy.

And if I was good'n sick of her wide-eyed "Everything's so beautiful and amazing and *ooh* and *aah*" routine, well, it was a burden I could shoulder.

Besides, this was the first time she'd really seen *our* snow. I thought she was gonna break her neck, tryin' to take it all in at once. "It's the same snow in all directions, doll."

"It's like something out of Wonderland!"

*So you've said, more'n a couple times.* "Yeah, maybe."

"There still aren't any shadows."

"Never are on the Seelie side of the joint. I told you that."

She shrugged as she turned. "I know, it's just… Against all that white? It seems like there should be shadows." She stopped mid-turn, then looked at a small copse of trees over my shoulder, and actually *squealed*. "It *is* like Wonderland!"

My turn to, uh, turn. "What's that, now?"

"You never told me the Cheshire Cat was real, Mick!"

I peered into the branches. Sure enough, big eyes, big ears, even bigger grin.

"Sorry, Adalina, but it ain't."

"What's that, then?"

"That," I said, sighing, "is a friggin' pixie with good hearing, too much time on its hands, and a lousy sense of humor."

The image vanished with a moist *pop*, leaving a tiny naked figure with dragonfly wings and filthy, scraggly hair. Scrawny, too; sharp-featured, and not in a pretty way.

"Fuck you, Oberon!"

You ever hear a pixie try to come off hard? Sounds like a teamster made of marmots.

"Ah, buzz off, you little gink! Your momma was a woodpecker."

Tiny bastard flew off, shrieking something unprintable— and I don't mean "obscene," I mean there literally ain't letters in any mortal language to convey those sounds—and we were alone again.

"Sorry," I said.

Adalina just sorta blinked at me. Lamps that big, I'm surprised I couldn't feel a breeze. "Why would it…?"

"Like I said. Lousy sense of humor, the whole lot of 'em. Frankly, you got lucky. That was just a dumb joke. I've seen people kick off or even lose their families over what some of those creeps think is funny."

*Lucky.* That reminded me…

I pulled a pinch of salt from my coat pocket and tossed it over a shoulder. Even after all these months, I was still suffering those occasional strokes of bad luck. (I told you about 'em back during the whole mess with Tsura and the mummy, Nessumontu, and so far I'd had about as much luck findin' the woman I was pretty sure was behind it as I'd had in uncovering any more about Adalina.) Odds were mortal magics wouldn't hit me too hard here in the Otherworld— but on the other hand, it was just possible, if the magic was powerful or pervasive enough, it'd be worse. So yeah, I was still wearin' various charms and taking steps.

If Adalina wondered why the hell I'd just seasoned the snow

behind me, she chose not to ask.

Me, though, much as I'm more comfortable here away from all the hissing and snapping and itching technology of your world, I was about done with the place. "So, you ready to go back?"

"We just got here!"

"Yeah, but you know how it is. I don't care to—"

"I want to see the city, Mick."

Yeah, I knew this was comin' eventually. No way was her curiosity gonna be satisfied with a couple square miles of wilderness forever.

"Adalina, we talked about this…"

We had, too. Wasn't the first time she'd asked, and wasn't the first time she was gonna get the "it's way too dangerous" spiel. We'd gone through the whole rigmarole as early as our second trip.

And the third.

And the fourth.

She'd skipped it last time, but yeah, it was gonna come up again sooner or later. Just thought maybe I'd had more time.

So we went through it all again. You'll have to live with me skippin' the details. Wasn't real fun the first time, let alone the fourth; I sure as hell ain't eager to repeat it for you.

But you know what? After about ten minutes of this hooey, I gave in.

Sure, I didn't want anyone in the Seelie Court—let alone out of it—gettin' wise to why she was important to me, that she was a mystery even I couldn't crack. *Definitely* didn't want anyone gettin' the bright idea that she might be useful, or powerful. And even in Elphame, or at least the civilized parts, she was gonna stand out a bit.

She wasn't gonna let it go, though. Here we had someone with no idea what she was, where she belonged. Also, adolescent and hormonal.

She didn't have a lot back home. Can't really go to school or go cuttin' a rug or whatever else kids do when you look like an eel. Her family loved her well enough, and did what they could, but she was a pariah and a shut-in. Wasn't much made her happy except these monthly trips, so what happened when the shine rubbed off 'em?

So, fine. Okay. All right already.

"I got some ground— Hey!" I tried again when she was done jumping and squealing and all around trying to hug me into oatmeal. "I got some ground rules if we're gonna do this, Adalina. You so much as bend one of 'em, and we scram so fast it'll be an hour before your own name catches up to you."

All ears, then, with that same serious expression I was more used to her wearin'. Frankly, much as I liked to see it, "happy" still didn't sit quite natural on her. "I'm listening," she promised.

"You don't go *anywhere* without me, and I mean not even across the street. You follow my lead, always. You curtsy when I bow, you avoid who I avoid, you don't breathe a peep unless I tell you to talk. And… look, doll, you know I don't much like tellin' you to do this, but you keep your hat pulled low and your scarf wrapped high, you dig?"

That brought out a deep sigh—guess she'd hoped that wouldn't be necessary away from the humans—but she set about arranging everything just so. Wouldn't hide that she wasn't human, but it might make it harder for anyone to tell that, even for us, she was an odd one.

And then I'd run outta excuses to delay, so we set off.

Ankled it the whole way, too, even though we hadda cross the brass railroad tracks to get there. We coulda hopped the train, I suppose; it's what I did, more often than not. And I'm sure she'd have been real taken by the experience, seein' the brass and bronze and gold, maybe even peekin' down below to see the goblin rowers who kept the wheels turning.

Thing is, hoppin' aboard while the dingus is rumbling along ain't exactly a piece of cake. I know I can do it; wasn't so sure she could, slight as she was. Giving it a shot and failing coulda got her hurt, bad, and you might remember that a hurt here in

Elphame ain't something we can shrug off so easy.

Plus, I wanted to tire her out much as I could on the walk. Try to encourage her to spend a little less time playing tourist in the big city, see?

Don't gimme that. I was tryin' to keep her happy *and* safe. Ain't as if that's easy even with *human* children now, is it?

Besides, she had a lot to see on the walk. Icicles hangin' from tree branches, so clear they magnified whatever was behind 'em—and this bein' the Otherworld, sometimes they did even more than magnify. Look through one just right, in the right moment, you might see the tree behind it spinning and dancing; look *around* it, though, and it was just another stiff and motionless trunk. Some of 'em gathered in clusters of varying heights, so that if you knew just the angle to get a good slant, and you happened to know the old tongues, you could read the lyrics to ancient songs. She heard the calls and the cries and the poetry of those beasts and birds that hadn't taken the run out soon as the snows started to fall, and she exchanged waves with a few lonely passersby. Not anything *too* peculiar. A few kobolds, marchin' to work come rain or shine or snow; a white-frosted *ghillie dhu* who musta had somewhere important to be, to be out'n about with his bark and his leaves near frozen. And of course, a few more pixies, who knew what was good for 'em enough to keep their distance.

We did spot a silhouette in the distance speedin' along atop the snow, and damn me if it didn't look to be a *harbegazi*, icy beard whipping in the wind, skiing on those big honkin' hocks they laughably call "feet." Couldn't imagine what one of 'em would be doin' here in the Chicago area—or at this altitude, or even on this continent—but then, I never did understand those mugs too well.

Hell, maybe he was just a tourist, too. What do I know?

Right. We took a walk. We saw some things. A few even bordered on interesting.

And then we were there.

Adalina'd seen some of the taller buildings from a distance before, but that hadn't prepared her. The trees, bigger'n she'd ever seen, with doors built into the trunks at every height, buildings constructed on the branches. The gleaming skyscrapers of glass and bronze with support columns made of more trees, towering but spindly. White marble and black granite. Streets cobbled and walls constructed of bricks from every building that had ever burned or collapsed in your Chicago.

Fae in suits and fancy dresses, in slacks and suspenders, a few holdouts in the fashions of past centuries. Carriages pulled by horses, or giants, or wing-clipped griffons, or, occasionally, humans. Countless human workers and servants, more of 'em than there ever could be of us. The whistle of the winter wind. Words that blended into a chorus of song, and songs made up of nothing resembling words.

Chicago. *Our* Chicago.

Damn it felt good to be here, and I couldn't wait to leave.

So we did the rounds, and I pointed out the sights. City Hall, where the local Seelie Court pretended they were mayors and police and aldermen and were more serious and dour and dangerous in their playacting than you lugs are with the real deal. The nearby establishment, half castle and half office building and all marble, where King Sien Bheara and Queen Laurelline—sorry, that's "Judge" Sien Bheara and "Police Chief" Laurelline, because, gods, the whole lot of us are dippy—lived and threw their shindigs and everything else the royalty does when they weren't holding court at City Hall. Pointed out our own police station, which was an ugly hunk of granite that was more a barracks and an armory.

And, of course, the giant stone serpent that wound its way around the fanciest public joint in the place, the Lambton Worm.

"Is that real?" Adalina asked, breathless.

"It's real stone."

Okay, maybe that was a bit short. But we'd been wandering

around for a couple hours now, and I was startin' to get real, *real* nervous.

A few strange looks? Those I'd expected. Like I said, Adalina's "disguise" wasn't exactly a paragon of the craft. Your average Joe might not get a good slant on her, probably couldn't begin to describe her, but he could tell that she didn't entirely fit in, even here. Fact that she was gawping at everything like a hick off the farm wasn't doing us much good, either.

But here, unusual still ain't that unusual. So yeah, I'd expected some stares, but nothin' else. Even if anyone important *had* come over curious, it wouldn't be polite to just walk up to us and start digging. They'd make a note to pump me for information later, and I'm real good at avoiding that sorta thing.

For the past hour or so, though, I'd seen a lot more'n "some stares." It was starting to feel as though *everyone* was giving us the once-over.

And the thing was… I been doing what I do a long time, and, occasionally, I'm even good at it. So, while it might seem paranoid to say, when I had Adalina right beside me, I was really feelin' more and more that those curious blinkers weren't pointed her way, but mine.

I coulda just snatched one of the bums right there off the street, put the screws to him until he told me what it was everybody suddenly found so fascinating about me. Gotta figure, though, if I wasn't already in hot water, that'd dunk me in it pretty good. That kinda direct roughness wasn't the done thing. Wouldn't be polite.

Besides, wasn't as though I didn't have friends here I could go chin with, maybe get some answers. I didn't have a *lotta* friends here, mind, but not none.

Probably.

"Hey, Adalina. How'd you like to go see the Lambton Worm up close?"

If anyone was gonna have the rap I needed, and might just

like me well enough to actually spill it, it'd be Ielveith, owner of the Lambton, *sidhe* about town, and the closest thing I really had to a pal in this burgh.

Also a dame I already owed more'n a couple favors, and here I was about to ask for her help. Real wise head, me.

Still, good idea or bad, end of the day it made no nevermind one way or the other. Adalina'n me reached the big marble columns that even the Ancient Greeks woulda thought were overcompensation, the shining glass façade, the brass-framed revolving door—and that's as far as we got.

A huge bushy red beard, with a vestigial person attached to its backside, stepped up to block our path. "Don't need the trouble, Mr. Oberon."

"You serious, Slachaun? Find a new dance. This one's gotten real worn out."

The Lambton's hotel dick puffed up his chest, literally. The spriggan was just a little over my height right now, which meant he'd grown far enough to look down at me, but not so big that he was *really* expectin' trouble. He opened his yap, and I was all set for the usual bluster and threats and all the other pleasantries me'n him tossed at each other every time we met…

And just that quickly, he deflated. All the way back to his normal size, which is about chest-high on me when I'm in the Otherworld.

"Look here. I'm just tryin' to keep the boss outta dutch. It's my job, remember? Mrs. Ielveith seems fond o' ye, fer reasons that beggar understandin'. She's lent ye a hand when ye were needin' one. Seems like the least ye could do in return would be to keep yer messes to yer own self."

Okay, the little lug was being *way* too polite about all this. This wasn't his usual beef with me, wasn't just that he didn't want me popping in to jaw a spell. Something specific had happened.

Or was still happening.

"You tell me what sorta mess you think I'm bringing down on Ielveith…" I started.

"That's Mrs. Ielveith to you, boyo!" It was a reflex; his heart wasn't in it.

"...and maybe I don't *need* to talk to her anymore."

Slachaun's glare packs almost as big a wallop as his fists, which pack almost as big a wallop as his personality, but for all his bark and bristle, his loyalty to his employer's stronger'n anything else, even his anger and resentment. The idea of helping me out mighta caused him physical pain, but he'd do it if it meant helping her, too.

"Áebinn's gunnin' for ye, Oberon. Haven't the foggiest why, an' I can't say as I care. But she's been to the Lambton three times already. That sorta attention, Mrs. Ielveith and me don't need. Ye get me?"

"I get you. Thanks, Slachaun."

"Don't be thankin' me, boyo, just deal with it." He stepped back a pace and vanished into the revolving door. Pretty sure he was holding it from the other side, too, just in case I decided to push past and try meeting with Ielveith anyway.

"Adalina, we're going home."

"But who's—?"

"*Now.*"

No bunny, that girl. Whatever she heard in my voice, she kept her head shut and followed me.

Good thing, too. I'd have to answer some of Adalina's questions eventually, sure, but for right now I was in no mood for explaining.

*Áebinn*. Shit.

You remember Áebinn, yeah? *Bean sidhe* from the old country. The bloodline she was tied to died out, so she found herself a new purpose working as a detective for the Seelie Court. Comes in real handy in that job, her power to sense death comin'.

I'd crossed paths with her a few times, most recently during the fiasco with the Spear of Lugh, and frankly I wasn't real eager to do it again. We didn't exactly drink outta the same bottle, if you get my drift.

Yeah, I know. *Lotta* Fae don't seem to care for me much. Whaddaya want from me?

Point is, whether she was nosin' around after me on an assignment from the Court, or for more personal reasons, it wasn't good news for me either way. I couldn't know if it was important enough that she'd come lookin' in the mortal world, but I wasn't about to hang around here and make it easy on her.

We didn't exactly run back to the Path that'd take us back to my office in the basement of a dirty graystone in the middle of Pilsen, but it sure was a much brisker walk than we'd taken on our way in.

The tunnel of wet loam, rainbow molds, and twisting strands that mighta been roots or worms or somethin' else entirely led us back to the little niche in my office. You know the one: where other folks mighta had a refrigerator or a cupboard, I had empty space with mildew in the corners for just this reason.

Adalina'd been pretty patient with me, considering how bad the curiosity musta been burning her, and it was right as we stepped back into my place that she finally demanded, "So who's this Áebinn person, anyway?"

It was also right as we stepped back into my place that Franky stood up from the chair by my desk and said, "So, Mick, that witch thing you wanted me to dig into…"

They both stopped and blinked at one another, which did me just fine, since it gave me half a moment of silence to think, and quick.

"Witch thing?" Adalina asked. "What witch thing?" She did a pretty fine job of keepin' her voice steady, but I still heard the quiver she wasn't lettin' out. No surprise; given her grandma, it hadda be a sensitive topic.

"No witch thing. *Which* thing. He's lookin' into a whole *heap* of things for me, ain't you, Franky?"

"Uh, sure, Mick."

"But that's not what he—"

"Yeah, it is. Franky, this is Adalina Ottati. You mighta heard me mention her a time or two. Adalina, 'Four-Leaf' Franky Donovan. Ain't ever mentioned him to you. Sorry to break that streak."

"Hey!" Franky protested. And then, "Wait a minute, what about Áebinn, now?"

"Nothin'. Nothin' about nobody."

"But—" she said.

"Hush."

"But—" he said.

"*Hush!*"

I tossed my flogger over one arm of the rack, took Adalina's coat and scarf and hung 'em a lot more neatly from another. Then I passed her a nickel.

"You know where the blower is, doll. Why don'tcha let your parents know we're back and they can come get you?"

"I still want to know about… Um. I'll just go call them, then."

I made myself break whatever expression'd changed her tune with a smile. She slipped into the hall, leaving the door open just wide enough to eavesdrop. I stepped over, pulled it shut, poured myself a glass of milk from the lukewarm icebox, and then flopped into my chair. Franky sank back down across from me.

He musta either been on his way to, or comin' from, an important meet. He had on his best gold chains—well, best of the latest lot—and those ugly green glad rags of his looked as though they might actually have spent some time in the same room as soap and an ironing board.

Took a big gulp of milk, and then, "I'm almost positive I locked my office door before steppin' Sideways, Franky."

"Aw, c'mon. I know you didn't mean that lock for *me*."

"Really? And where'd you get *that* notion?"

"If you had, you'd have gotten a better one."

Worth a courtesy chuckle, I guess. Followed by another

few gulps that finished off the glass. I decided it wasn't worth gettin' up for a second helping.

"So, that's Adalina, huh? You're right. She doesn't look like anything *I* recognize. Maybe a *little* like a *bagiennik*, but…"

"But only a little, yeah."

"So whatcha think—?"

"Franky, if you got news for me, I really do appreciate it, but you didn't come here to talk about Adalina."

"No, sure didn't. You first, though."

"Me? You came to—"

"What's this about Áebinn, Mick?"

I really wanted to sigh, but that was a fair question. He had plenty of good reasons not to wanna run into her anymore'n I did.

"Not a lot to spill," I admitted. "She's lookin' for me. Dunno why. Plan to do my damnedest not to find out."

"That's it?"

"That's—"

Door clicked open and Adalina stepped back inside. "They're on the way."

"Good. Grab a…" Huh. My place only has the two chairs. I hopped up, shoved mine her way with a foot—didn't scoot too far, but I guess the intent was clear—then pushed the typewriter aside and perched my keister on the edge of the desk.

Yeah, before you ask, *that* typewriter. The one that croaked a man. And no, before you ask, I still ain't telling that story.

"Um…" Franky said.

I smiled, real friendly, and said, "You know I can't talk client business in front of a guest."

By which I meant, *Keep your trap shut or I'll nail it closed for you.* Franky seemed to understand me fine, since his lips clamed tighter'n a vampire with lockjaw.

If the three of us had just sat there studying one another, though, it mighta gotten awkward. So, not havin' much else to bump gums about, I wound up telling Franky about Adalina's first experience in the Otherworld Chicago. She piped in with her own observations, and Franky started tellin' embarrassing yarns about this Fae or that.

He'd just finished the one about a minor *sidhe* noble, name of Kileagh, and the night he'd gotten completely lit on ambrosia and mistaken one of the *ghillie dhu* for a compost heap, when a quick rap on the office door announced some new visitors.

Bianca Ottati, dark of hair and burgundy of dress and wife of Fino "the Shark"; and Archie Caristo in his tan suit, Fino's lieutenant and, so far as I'd ever been able to make out, best friend—and nothin' more—to Bianca.

"Hello, Mick," Bianca greeted me, warm enough to melt the snow we'd just recently come from.

"Oberon," Archie added. He wasn't really payin' me much mind, though. Only had attention for the stranger in the same room as Bianca and Adalina. He didn't twitch so much as an inch toward the bulge in his coat, but it was still crystal clear he was thinkin' about it.

"Nothin' to worry about, Archie. This is Franky. He's good people."

"Good people, huh?"

"Actually, he ain't *either*, but he's no threat."

Franky's gaze kept flickering between the two of us. Archie just gave him a last sideways slant, and then actually cracked a small grin.

"Y'know, Oberon, before I met you, bein' told somebody ain't 'people' woulda seemed hinky."

"That's me. Opening people's horizons."

"Opening horizons. Right."

Bianca had already crossed the office and wrapped an arm around Adalina. Didn't show the slightest sign that she was at all bugged by one of her daughters bein' all fishy. One of these days, I was actually gonna have to get around to askin' how a woman like her'd wound up hitched to a mobster, anyway. She'd never struck me as the type.

"How was the trip, sweetie?"

Adalina immediately launched into a repetition of everything she'd been raving to Franky about, only more so—and without a peep about anyone hunting me. I'd have to thank her for that later.

Over the girl's running monologue, Bianca and Archie pretty much had to nod and wave their goodbyes, since nobody was gettin' a word in edgewise any time soon, and it wasn't until the outer door of Mr. Soucek's basement shut behind 'em that Adalina's voice finally went silent.

"That guy always repeat what you say to him?" Franky asked.

"They don't call him 'Echoes' without reason."

"Uh-huh. And did you have a *reason* for tellin' him I'm not human?"

Got myself more milk, since I was up anyway, and returned to the chair I'd lent out. "Because you get in trouble with *everyone*, Franky. I'm honestly surprised you haven't run into the Shark's crew already. One of these days, you're gonna wind up owing them money, and when that happens, we're both gonna be a lot happier if they come to me insteada tryin' to deal with you like any other mook."

"Hrm."

"Now, then… Milk?"

"Nah. That's the great thing about being part human. I never touch anything as natural as milk."

"Fine." I took a sip, wondered if I was stalling. If I was nervous at the idea of finally having an answer.

Half a year. I'd been lookin' for the better part of half a year, pounding the pavement, examining the ether, paying out more kale and minor favors than I could easily afford convincing Franky and my other contacts to keep their peepers wide. And I'd spent all that time keeping mum about every bit of it to the Ottatis, partly 'cause the truth would hurt 'em and scare 'em big time…

And partly 'cause, at least with Fino, I wasn't so sure whose side he'd be on, not once he got wise she was still alive.

Lunatic witch. One of the *benandanti* gone bad. And where the Shark was concerned, dear momma.

Orsola Maldera.

I knew how she'd faked her death; figured that much out even before I found the *phouka* bones in her coffin. I was a lot less sure how she'd survived in the first place, since, witch or no witch, a quarter-drum's worth of Tommy gun ain't healthy for *anyone*.

But more important than that, I hadn't the first notion of where she was or what she was up to, other'n having put a bad luck hex on me at some point. And it was drivin' me batty.

If Franky'd finally found her…

"So spill, Franky."

"I… *might* have found her."

Because God frickin' forbid I get a straight answer on anything, ever.

"Grapevine has it," he continued, "that there's a gathering coming up. Handful of Chicago's up-and-coming, hedge witches, amateur warlocks and the like."

I wanted to chuck my milk glass at his head. Or my typewriter. Or maybe my desk. "Franky…"

He raised both hands, palms out, squirming in his seat. "I know, I know, but lemme finish!"

"All right. Still listening."

"So, yeah, the broad you got us all watching for is pretty much the opposite of an amateur, wouldn't be caught dead joining up with any such group. That more or less where you were going?"

Guess my flat stare was as good as a nod, 'cause he went on. "Now, what if I told you the entire point of this sit-down was to meet with another witch—a *much* more powerful one?"

Now *that* had some potential. I found myself leaning forward over my desk. "Why?"

Franky's smile turned sheepish (which is actually one of its natural states). "I couldn't tell you, Mick. Only so much you can pick up from third-hand rumors. Some kinda trade? You teach us, we do favors for you? Or the big witch wants something from the baby witches? I dunno."

Frustrating, but fair. "And that's also why you dunno for sure if it's Orsola or not."

"You got it. Word was 'powerful witch,' and we don't have too many of those here in Chicago, so I'd say it's a good chance, but…" He ended with a shrug.

"I'll take 'a good chance' over the bupkis I've found so far. You got a date and time for this witchy wingding?"

That smile got even more sheepish, until I expected him to sprout a wool mustache, and his eyes flickered down at his suit.

I groaned. "You're puttin' me on. *Tonight?*"

"Came to you as soon as I heard, Mick," he protested. "I tried calling earlier, but you didn't answer the horn." He waved at the mildewed nook. "Guess you were already out."

"And you thought it was worth your time to tidy up for the occasion?"

Another shrug. "I tell you I don't wanna go, I can just give you directions. You insist on me coming along, to make sure you find the place. I argue that I might wanna work with one of these people in the future. You demand I come anyway. There, I just saved us five minutes."

Well, he *does* know me pretty well. "Okay, but—"

"I thought I'd at least try to make a solid first impression."

Nothin' to say to that. I stood up, reached for my overcoat…

Huh. Adalina'd been so excited and caught up in tellin' Bianca about everything she'd seen in Elphame, she'd left her scarf. Musta missed it when she grabbed her coat. Well, I'd get it back to 'em later.

And if you're wondering whether her forgettin' that was just coincidence or more of that weird Fae luck kickin' in, for good or bad, well, so was I. I ain't *that* big a bunny. But since

I had no way to tell, I didn't spend too much time worrying over it.

"Okay, Franky, let's—"

"Uh, Mick." He coughed once.

Oh. Right. Deal's a deal, and he *had* come through with something worth digging into. I dug a double sawbuck out of a billfold and handed it over.

"This is… more than you promised."

"That musta hurt to admit."

"I do feel a little faint, yeah."

I chuckled, slipped on the coat, and double-checked my shoulder holster. Luchtaine & Goodfellow Model 1592, sittin' right where it should. No reason it wouldn't have been, but even with my precautions, I couldn't be sure when and how that runnin' bad luck would dry-gulch me. And if we *were* crashin' Orsola's party, I sure as hell wanted my wand with me.

"The extra's hazardous duty pay," I told him.

"Oh. Um. Can I give it back?"

"Sure, if you want. You're still comin' with me, though."

"I knew you were gonna say that." Franky sighed, then squared his shoulders. "All right. Let's go aggravate some witches."

# CHAPTER TWO

So, what're you expecting? Witches' coven in black hoods, meeting out in the late autumn woods? Fallen leaves, twisted branches, maybe a full moon behind the racing clouds?

Horsefeathers.

This is still Chicago, modern city. Swanky suits and slinky dresses were the order of the day, and your average witch and warlock about town traveled by train or tin can, not by broom.

(They actually never traveled by broom, but you get what I mean.)

And whoever was throwin' this soiree, Orsola or no, wasn't too shy to go fancy. Table for ten at the College Inn might not break the bank, but it'd sure put a heavy beating on it. Place is supposed to be worth every dime, too. I almost wanted to try the chicken à la King myself, except for the whole bit about me not eating in your world.

It wasn't snowin' your side of Chicago yet—autumn and winter were still slugging it out—but the wind was already a lot colder'n I like my milk. Newspapers chased leaves in short circles and around corners, while hems pressed against ankles and calves, maybe wishin' they could join the game.

Nowhere near cold or windy enough to keep you lot from your evening entertainments, though. Me'n Franky made our way down Randolph, exchangin' nods and friendly how d'ya dos with plenty of other early nighttime goers. More'n a few were even headed for the same place we were—we were both a little underdressed, honestly, in our cheap suits, but not so bad we were likely to get the bum's rush; just a few frosty sneers—and we just sorta got buffeted along with the small crowd constantly coming and going through the Sherman House doors.

Yeah. The College Inn, which is a restaurant, is located inside the Sherman House, which is a hotel. Whaddaya want from me, it's *you* lugs who name these things. If you don't understand, how the hell am *I* supposed to?

Anyway, Sherman House. Statuary and arches decorating the roof, white and red brickwork, all real ritzy, but what always gets me ain't the style. It's the size.

Place is *huge*. I mean, I been around a while, and I spent a lot of my early years watchin' humans living in *towns* smaller'n this. Well over a thousand guest rooms, banquet hall big enough for elephants to play hide-and-seek. I'm glad Nessumontu never saw anyplace like this when he was in town. All the trouble he'n his people went through to build their fancy tombs, this woulda given him insecurities.

Woulda been fun to show Tsura, though.

Between a couple thousand voices in hundreds of conversations, a few more ordering the staff this way and that, and the jazz slinking outta the College Inn, the din was enough to sour a guy on the whole notion of ears. Franky got my attention with some shouts and dramatic gestures, long enough for me to focus on him through the ruckus.

Not that I was a real big fan of what he had to say.

"Whaddaya mean 'I'll be waiting over there'?"

"Look, Mick, if there's any trouble, or you can't find who you're looking for, you just wave me on over. I won't leave you in the lurch. But I'm not walking in there if I don't absolutely have to."

It woulda been more effort than it was worth to argue with him. "You know what? Fine! See if I pay you extra again!"

I didn't bother to tell him that if he *did* run off and leave me, he'd better hope Orsola rubbed me out, or he'd be in a bad way. I didn't have to.

Also, it'd be insulting. Franky ain't the most reliable mug, but he wouldn't just outright abandon me like that.

Probably.

So he pushed through the arriving throng one way, and I went the other.

And as big as the Sherman House is, and as packed as it was, it wasn't really unlikely that I bumped into someone else I know. We were goin' to the same place, after all.

"Evening, Gina."

She stopped cold, dropping her fancy furs just before the coatroom attendant could close his mitts on them. Even from behind, I could see her steel herself before she turned my way.

"Mr. Oberon."

She'd cut her hair in a short'n stylish bob since I'd last seen her, but other'n that and the evening getup, she was the same witch I remembered: a little sweeter'n was good for her, given the company she kept, and way too eager to learn secrets and lore she was better off without.

"So," I asked, mostly because she was goin' almost stiff trying hard not to fidget, "how's Bumpy?"

She twisted around, almost panicked.

"Relax, sister. Anyone around here who don't already know you're tied to a mob crew ain't anybody who's likely to care, either."

It'd be a gross exaggeration to say she relaxed any, but she at least stopped tryin' to make like an owl.

"You know Mr. Scola doesn't like it when just anyone calls him that," she said.

"I won't tell if you won't."

It all came out in a single sharp breath. "Why'reyouhere

MisterOberon?" Guess she was afraid of the answer.

"I think you know. And I think you should probably go home. Tell 'em you came over with a headache or something."

For a couple heartbeats, her eyes went near wide as Adalina's and her fingertips trembled. And then she straightened.

"No."

"Sorry, that was the deaf side of my head. Come again?"

"I said no." Any paler and she coulda vanished into a moonbeam, and she was gonna take half her lip clean off if she bit down any harder, but damn if she wasn't really tryin' to stare me down.

It'd be a pretty big fib even for one of the Fae if I said I wasn't impressed. Especially since she knew full well what I was, and that her magics wouldn't like to much more'n tickle me.

"You can't just keep walking into my world and telling me what to do," she went on. I think she mighta actually practiced for this. "We've worked together, and I don't want to be enemies, but I've got my own studies and my own *life*, and—"

"Gina. Stop."

She froze. Probably toeing the edge of her courage right there. I coulda just gotten into her conk, told her to leave in a way she couldn't refuse, but I didn't care for that idea. I'd never disliked the girl, and she'd earned a little respect tonight.

"This ain't about you or your life, except that I'd rather see you hang onto it. I dunno exactly who you're meeting here, but if it's who I *think* it is, we got some seriously nasty beef between us. You really wanna be around when a *real* witch and me decide to settle our scores?"

She bristled a bit at "real witch," but she was no bunny. She knelt down to pick up her fallen fur coat, brushed it off, and made tracks.

And if you're thinkin', *Hey, Mick, ya boob, you coulda asked her who she was sittin' down with, and why,* well, congratulations. You got there a few seconds before I did. I was too busy patting myself on the back for gettin' her gone without magic.

Those few seconds were long enough for Gina to vanish into the crowd well enough that I'da wasted more time hunting her down than just sticking my schnozzle into the restaurant and seeing what I could see.

Sometimes I wonder how I've lived this long.

The College Inn was as nice a joint as you'd expect in the Sherman House. Sorta abstract ivy designs on the paneling and the ceiling, a whole array of fancy dishware displayed up on a ledge of molding, and of course tuxedo-wrapped waiters slipping between the tables, doin' that weird "dignified scurry" that only the most swanky service staff can pull off. I could smell and even hear the roasting chickens and boiling lobsters and rising breads, and it probably woulda been real appetizing to anyone else.

"How may I assist you, sir?"

That's somethin' else the highfalutin' waiters are real good at: Sneering at my clothes and generally tellin' me I'm in the wrong joint without a bit of it actually leaking into their words or their expression. It's a nifty trick.

"Don't worry about it, bo. I'm just meetin' someone. They oughta be here already."

"Very good, sir," by which he meant there was nothin' good about it whatsoever. "Perhaps you'd be more comfortable if you left your coat with the attendant?" By which he meant *Please at least drop off that worn and tattered piece of wrinkle before too many of the* quality *patrons have to suffer being subjected to it.*

"Nah." I moved around him and started wandering around the edges of the main room, giving the whole place a good up-and-down.

Nothing there, but I hadn't figured there would be. Orsola—or whoever—probably woulda preferred a more private table in one of the smaller nooks.

It was in the second of the side rooms where I found 'em, and it wasn't Orsola Maldera who'd called this sit-down at all.

Tricky as I knew it'd prove to deal with her in public, I kinda wished that it had been.

I stared across the table, over the noggins of a half-dozen or so witches and warlocks, at the most gorgeous redhead I'd ever seen. Even after everything that'd happened, my pump skipped a beat or two. If I hadn't spent so much effort shielding myself from her power—her presence—in the past, I'da felt she was here the instant I walked into the restaurant.

"I gotta say, Ramona, you… ain't who I was expecting."

She stood, runnin' her hands down a deep-emerald silk number in a move unconsciously sensual enough to give a bishop apoplexy. "I could say the same, Mr. Oberon."

*Mr. Oberon*, huh? Chilly. I wondered if that was her playin' to the audience, or 'cause of the way we'd left off.

Me'n her hadn't ended the mess with Nessumontu on real good terms, if you remember. The couple times we'd bumped into each other since hadn't really given us the opportunity to make good, either.

Assumin' we even wanted to. I still wasn't real sure what *I* wanted, much less what she did.

"Ladies and gentlemen," she said, never takin' her blinkers off me, "I'm afraid we're going to have to reschedule. I'll be in touch. Don't worry about the bill; I'll handle it before I go."

A few muttered protests—nothin' too serious, this lot seemed pretty keen on jumpin' at her every command—and the table cleared out. She sat, sorta half-waved for me to do the same.

"So, we doin' this all formal-like, *Miss Webb*?"

"I see no reason not to. I'm only casual with my friends."

Ouch.

"I helped you kill a rival succubus who wanted to drag you back home to torture you!"

"By using me as *bait*! And keeping me from doing my job!"

"Oh, yeah, your 'job.' How *is* dear old Assistant State's Attorney Baskin, anyway?"

She caught herself before glancing around to make sure

nobody heard, but I spotted the instinct nonetheless.

"So, what're you doin' having a chin-wag with a whole gaggle of witches, anyway?"

She leaned back, tapping a fingernail on the table, and kept her head closed.

"All right. Wouldn't be hard for you to convince 'em you had something to teach. You don't, of course. Your magic's innate, same as mine. Ain't somethin' you can pass on to a mortal, but you could put on a good enough show to make 'em *think* you were a witch like them. But that's how, not why."

I gotta admit, I was enjoyin' this a little, and I think maybe she was, too. The pair of us, we'd always been fond of watchin' each other work.

"Lookin' for a loophole in your contract with Baskin? Nah," I went on before she could answer, "you've got less than a decade to go on that. Wouldn't be worth the hassle. And even if it was, you wouldn't be lookin' to these amateurs for a hand."

Tap. Tap. Tap.

No, she wasn't here for herself. Didn't track. For Baskin, then, but why? That bastard was always lookin' to grow his collection of grimoires and mystical dinguses, but, again, he wasn't gonna get anything worth a wooden nickel from these nobodies.

Did he need help with some ritual? That was possible, but the fact that Gina was on the guest list made it unlikely. Pretty sure he'da made a point of avoiding anyone mobbed up or otherwise connected with...

Hang on.

"Oh, for the Dagda's sake, Ramona! Are you frickin' *under cover* for Baskin?"

Still she said nada, but the tapping stopped.

"You are! For the love of..."

Wasn't a coincidence Gina had been on the guest list. And I knew, if I looked into 'em, that at least a couple of the others would also be linked to an Outfit crew, or someone else in organized crime.

Guess it made sense, in a twisted sorta way. If you got a handful of gangsters wise to magic, and you got your own pet Fae—or demon, dependin' on who you believe—maybe it makes sense to try to get to 'em through their witches.

You know what else it was, though? Unrelated to anything that had squat to do with me. My chair thumped against some mug eatin' at the table behind me as I stood up, making him splash a spoonful of soup over his glad rags.

"What about you, Mick?" Ramona asked, rising along with me. "Who were you looking for here?"

Maybe it was brusque. Rude, even. But I was scrambled from bumping into her unexpectedly. I'd been braced for a fight all evening, and I was steamed that, after all this, I still wasn't any closer to finding Orsola.

So yeah, I was probably outta line when I answered with, "Work it out, Miss Webb. You just watched me do it, so I'm sure you can figure out how."

I was long gone before I let myself regret what I'd said.

Next day dawned just as chilly and windy and gray as the last one ended. Cloudy skies and flurries of old newspaper.

I'd spent the whole night slouched at my desk, chugging milk, and staring at the filing cabinet. That's the problem with needing to sleep so much less'n you mugs do: It means I sleep so much less'n you mugs do.

Worrying over Adalina. Worrying over how I'd left things with Ramona, *again*. Worrying I wouldn't find Orsola. Worrying Áebinn *would* find *me*, since any mess big enough that she'd subject herself to your world wasn't anythin' I wanted to do with.

Hell with this. I hadda get out, do something. And since I didn't have any pressing cases, or anything more urgent to do for the couple days until it was time to go fetch Pete home, I tugged Adalina's scarf off the coat rack and headed out to pay a call on Shark and family.

By now, I'd taken this same route on the L enough times I'm surprised the benches didn't know me by name. The usual background itch and buzz went to work in my conk as the train rumbled and groused its way along the track, a bit worse'n usual today.

Lookin' back, I think I was concentrating on it instead of trying to ignore it. Letting the pain come. Guess I was feelin' low about how I'd handled my run-in with Ramona.

Wandered off the train, wandered up Calumet. The wind was just right to give me a snootful of fumes from the passing flivvers, which was fine. Suited the mood. A few mechanical roars, the clop-clop and clatter-clatter of a horse-drawn milk wagon, a few more mechanical roars. Another day on another street in Chicago.

I trudged past the same nobby redbrick homes, the same manicured lawns, all the usual. Swanky as houses can get while still being anonymous, or maybe as anonymous as they could get while still being swanky. All that appeals to the well-to-do and self-respecting mobster.

Maybe it was just my mood, but I was kinda sick of the whole thing. I ankled up Fino's block and actually gave some thought to flagging down the milk wagon comin' my way, seeing if I could buy a bottle off the driver and…

Wait. Another milk wagon on the same route? Less than ten minutes apart?

No, not another. Took a hard minute of thinking back, since I hadn't been payin' anything much mind, but this was the *same* wagon. Same mottled nag pullin' the contraption. Same scratches on the dirty white paint, same chips in the wheel.

And now I was close enough, same odor of milk long-curdled, hidden from mortal senses by a cheap glamour, but not *quite* from mine.

Every god damn it to every imaginable hell.

Quick tug on the strings of fortune trailin' from the folks passing by in their flivvers, not much from any one of 'em, gave me enough luck and magic to see through the illusion as well as smell through it. The horse was still a horse, the wagon was still a wagon. The driver, though, he was a hunched mass of leathery skin and gnarled muscle in a shabby suit and a hat the color of old blood.

Mostly because it was covered in old blood.

Redcaps. I've always hated redcaps—which suited everyone just fine, since they'd always hated me—and after Grangullie's schemes nearly got a whole bunch of people rubbed out last year, me included, I hated 'em even more.

I'd seen this particular setup before. Redcaps in a milk wagon, I mean. Hadn't been more'n a few blocks from here. In fact, it was entirely possible that this gink *was* one of the same redcaps I'd run into back then.

Didn't figure they were after me—they knew where I worked, wouldn't hafta sit on the Ottati's place and hope I showed—so what were they *doin'* here?

He had his beady little peepers glued to me, definitely knew who I was, but I didn't figure he knew I'd seen through his glamour yet. Me, I kept on walkin' like I hadn't a care in two worlds, and tried to work out how I was gonna handle this. Not a lot of humans around on the street, but enough driving or ankling by on occasion, plus however many might decide to look out a window if things got loud. Lots of opportunity for people to get hurt, or see more'n was good for 'em.

Also, coulda been any number of Unseelie in the back of that wagon. Hmm.

I waited until I'd right about drawn even with the driver, then spun and gave him my best glare from across the street, yankin' the L&G from its holster.

He shot to his feet, hand goin' for his own piece. It looked to be a .38—Elphame-made, seein' as how it was brass.

"This is for Grangullie, you fuck!" he shouted. Speak of the devil.

That was okay, though. Using the wand to magnify it a couple dozen times over, I brought some of my oldest fears to mind—not the *worst* ones, since that woulda killed the poor creature, but bad enough—and shoved 'em all into the horse's noggin.

Screaming like you've never heard, eyes rolling and mouth foaming, the creature tore off down the street, yanking the wagon to speed as though it weighed nothin' at all. The redcap driver was thrown from his hocks by the sudden start, bouncing off the seat before tumbling to the roadway. The wagon wheel just missed him as it rumbled past, and then the wagon was gone faster'n a Dizzy Dean fastball. I heard screeching tires and car horns and angry shouts.

Me, I was already sprinting across the street. I landed on the fallen redcap, knee in his stomach, and jammed the L&G hard into his throat, hard enough to have crushed a man's windpipe. For this little shit, that just meant it hurt a lot.

"And this is for you," I told him, pickin' up where he'd left off. "Who'dya think's gonna get his delivery first?"

Oh, he was angry. It roared off him, near hot enough to burn. He was smart enough not to move or grab for his fallen roscoe, though.

I reached out and pushed it away with my other mitt, far enough he couldn't reach it if he tried, just to be sure.

"One fuckin' day, Oberon…" he growled.

"Yeah, probably. When that day comes, though? It still ain't gonna be you."

His teeth sounded like grinding rocks—and probably *coulda* ground rocks, frankly.

I hadda make this quick. I'm sure we were already drawing curious eyes, and I really didn't need someone callin' the bulls because all they saw was some crazy mook beatin' up on a milkman.

Didn't figure Fino'd appreciate the police runnin' up and down on his street, either.

So I dragged the bastard off behind someone's hedge before demanding, "What's your business here, you little shit?"

Got an ugly, jagged grin for my troubles. Redcaps are *tough* bastards, and even if he hadn't been ordered to keep his yap shut, he'd stay mum just outta spite. I could probably get into his thoughts and *make* him tell me, but it'd take time I didn't guess I had. Couldn't threaten him with much, either; nothin' I could do in public would hurt him too bad, and popping him now he wasn't an active threat would get me in serious dutch with people I really didn't need gunning for me.

I stood up, makin' sure to snatch up the heater he'd dropped. "Get gone. I see you or any of yours around here again, redcap, you're dead and nuts to the consequences. Savvy?"

He said nothin', but that hideous smile fallin' into an equally hideous snarl told me as good as a nod that he understood and believed. He climbed upright, tossed me one more glare for good measure, and stomped off along the sidewalk.

*Probably* he'n his buddies would report back to whoever they answered to—hopefully not Eudeagh, "Queen Mob" herself, or this was gonna get even more complicated—before takin' any further steps. On the other hand, it wasn't outta the question that he was goin' to fetch those buddies before comin' right back and trying to introduce me to the underside of some off-season daisies. I decided gettin' inside off the street was today's "better part of valor" special.

It was, of course, only then that I realized I'd lost my grip on Adalina's scarf when I'd jumped the damn redcap. Gods only knew where the Windy City's autumn gusts had taken it.

Random misfortune? Or another manifestation of that bad luck curse that even my best precautions still couldn't entirely cancel out?

Either way, fuck.

Didn't have to knock at the Ottatis' door; Fino's boys, always on guard for trouble, had seen the whole scuffle through the windows. They opened up for me soon as I stepped onto the porch and ushered me inside.

Fino "the Shark" himself met me in the hall. "What the fuck was *that* about?"

"Ehm. Fino, why don't we talk somewhere a bit more private? Might wanna bring the wife and kids in on it, too."

Saw his shoulders slump under his coat. Fino knew "You're about to have some Fae-related difficulties" when he heard it. He ordered a couple of his people to bring drinks to Bianca's sitting room—including a glass of milk—and led the way. I'd been here enough times that the boys were no longer confused when he cut them out of a sit-down but invited his family, though I'm sure they still guessed and gossiped about what went on behind those doors.

I felt the usual faint itch of the wards he kept around the place, meant to protect against my kind. Weak and basically useless, but they made him feel better.

His mother, now *there* was someone who knew how to inscribe a ward. I'd been happier when I thought she was dead.

I still didn't say anything to him about her.


"All right." I put the empty milk glass down on the table. I was sittin' on that same old sofa, in that same overstuffed room with *way* too many crucifixes and votary candles. Bianca held a rosary in her fingers, had since before she'd walked into the room. Adalina was curled up small and tight on the seat beside her, Celia—Adalina's sister, sorta; it's quicker'n saying "the daughter who was taken away when Adalina the changeling was left in her stead"—standing behind, hands on the back of the chair. Fino leaned forward in his own chair like he was gonna lunge out any second, one mitt wrapped around a glass of whisky, the other clenched tighter'n a *leprechaun's* coin purse.

"Um." Now I was here, I found myself oddly reluctant to get into it—in part because I was feelin' a little guilty over the mess they were in. "So, how's business, Fino?"

"You really here to talk about my fuckin' business, Mick?"

"Pretend I am so we can all stay happy for a few more minutes, yeah?"

"Anyone in this fuckin' room look fuckin' happy to you?"

"What, that's not your laughing face?"

Fino sighed. "Business is okay. Not great. We're all still figurin' out where to refocus and how to divvy up operations now Prohibition's winding down. There. You fuckin' satisfied?"

"No." Then, before he could pop a blood vessel, "But we'll get on with it anyhow. Friends, you got problems. Unseelie problems."

Didn't take much time to go over what'd gone down. *What* wasn't the part that really interested the Ottatis, anyway. The first big question was...

"Why?" Celia was the one who asked what they all hadda be thinking. She sounded put out as much as worried, as though frustrated that she hadda deal with this new bullshit in her life. Save me from pouty teenaged children.

"Can't say for certain." I turned to look at the other girl, the one clearly not human. "But I think we gotta be square and admit it's most likely you they're after."

Adalina sorta squeaked from her little ball of knees and elbows, and tightened up even harder, until the chair creaked.

Nobody here needed reminding that the Unseelie'd made a go of snatching her once before, back after I'd made a real unfortunate bargain with 'em to help find and retrieve Celia. At the time, best I was ever able to figure, they did it just 'cause she was hinky, bit of an unknown quantity that they thought they might be able to exploit. That was before Orsola's magics had revealed she was even weirder than we'd thought. And also before she'd just about died and gone all Sleeping Beauty for a year.

But if they didn't know she was more'n she'd seemed, why bother tryin' again? And if they did, why wait? She'd been lyin' there ripe for the picking for a good while, and been up and about for months now.

"It's just possible," I admitted, even though I really didn't care to and hoped I was wrong, "that it was our little trip into the other Chicago that tipped 'em off. The Courts have eyes and ears in each other's territory, and even with you keepin' your face hidden, someone mighta put two and two together."

I shook my head at Fino before he could explode. "I said possible, and if it's so, I already said everything to myself you're about to yell at me. But it ain't *probable*. We were just there yesterday. For word to get back to Eudeagh or one of the other bosses, and them to figure out who Adalina was, and then get someone to sit on your place? Think it'd take more'n a day to set up. And it still wouldn't tell us what their interest is in the first place."

"Can you poke around, Mick?" Bianca asked, rosary goin' click-click-click. "I know you don't have much to do with the Unseelie, but you must have contacts?"

"I... can do a little digging, but not as much as any of us'd prefer. I gotta be careful." I was answering her, but I made sure to catch Fino's gaze. "I got... certain debts that could put us *all* behind the eight-ball if the wrong Unseelie took an interest."

He nodded, thinkin' he understood, and I let him go on believing that. Fae oaths make mob debts look like a kid's IOU, and the one I owed Eudeagh was a doozy. If she called in that marker and just flat-out told me to turn over Adalina... Well, I cared for the girl, and most of her family, but they weren't worth my soul. Sorry, they just weren't.

So I hadda make sure it never came to that. I'd offered up that marker for the sake of one Ottati daughter. I didn't mean for it to cost us the other.

"I intend to learn how this all figures," I told them. "What it is they want—with Adalina or the rest of you or whatever this is about. Why it's goin' down now. All of it. But that ain't the first priority."

Which brought us to the second big question, and it was Bianca who asked it. "What do we do?"

"I know what to do," Fino admitted, though the low growl said pretty clear that he wasn't thrilled.

"You do?"

"He does," I said. "Fino'n me, we talked about this a while ago."

Bianca's rosary stopped clicking. "Without me?"

"Oh, *Maddon'*! We'd just gotten both girls back, dollface," he protested. "You were happy. I didn't want nothin' to mess that up, but..." He sorta petered out, hands waving.

I wasn't about to let this argument happen, not now. No time. "You go to the mattresses," I said. "You lie dormy as though you were target number one in the biggest mob war you ever imagined, and you *stay* there. You give your orders to Archie over the blower, you don't let *anybody* know where you are. You have what you need delivered, under fake names, from different shops. You disappear outta your lives so fast and so completely your own goddamn dreams can't find you."

Celia opened her trap to protest, clapped it shut when she saw the looks me'n her father both gave her. More pouting, then, but at least she also had one hand holdin' Adalina's shoulder.

Fino turned back my way. "You know what you're fuckin' asking, Mick? You know how hard it is to run a fuckin' business that way? Plus Celia's fuckin' school, and—"

"You know the alternative, Fino."

"Fuck! Yeah, I know. I just... We really there already? No other options?"

"Yeah, I think we are, and no, none I can see."

"Fuck!"

"Think you mighta mentioned that already."

He started to pace, waving his empty glass like a weapon. "I don't care what kinda fuckin' monster he is or what it takes to kill him, I ever fuckin' find whatever *stronzo* is behind all this, he's fuckin' *dead*!"

*You better hope for your sake you don't, Fino.*

"Times like this, I wish momma was alive. For everythin' she did, she woulda known how to protect us from this."

I almost bit through my tongue. Judging by their expressions, nobody else in the room was real happy to be reminded of Orsola, either, if not for all the same reasons.

"Okay," he said finally. "Okay. We'll be packed and out in an hour. We'll go to—"

"No!" Then, at the shock on every one of their mugs, "Sorry. It's just a lot safer if even I am in the dark about where you are."

"You wouldn't betray us, Mick!" Bianca protested.

*Oath I made, I might not have a choice.* But what I said was, "If the Unseelie are desperate enough, they got ways to make other Fae hurt. A *lot*. Probably they wouldn't go that far, but until I'm wise to what they want, and why, I can't be sure. Better if I just don't have the beans to spill."

They were even less happy now than they had been, but they bought it, which was the important part. Me, I hung around long enough to see 'em off, make sure nobody and nothing turned up to shadow them, and then I hoofed it back toward the L.

Unseelie watching the Ottatis. The Seelie Court's pet banshee gunning for me. Orsola still lurking out there somewhere, workin' who-knew-what kinda magics.

Connected? Coincidence? Some of each?

Lot to ponder on, lot to do. *But at least,* way I figured it, *nobody's in any* immediate *danger.*

Adorable, wasn't I?

# CHAPTER THREE

So, in the "How long did it take for Mick to learn what an optimistic twit he was being" pool, who had their money on three days? Congrats. You win.

They'd been quiet days, for the most part. I wrapped up the paperwork on a few small jobs, went to fetch Pete from Elphame once the full moon was passed, got a quick ring from the Ottatis lettin' me know they were settling in, though I still wouldn't let them tell me where, and otherwise sat around twiddling my thumbs.

Well, no. Otherwise kept diggin' around trying learn anything new about what Orsola or the Unseelie or Áebinn mighta been up to, but since I came up with zilch, the results were the same either way.

Mighta had more luck if I'd been willin' to do any poking around in the other Chicago, but I had plenty good reason not to show my mug there. But at least I was startin' to figure that Áebinn wouldn't be bothering me here in your world; I mean, if she was plannin' to show here, she'da done it already, right?

Yeah. See above, regardin' me being a twit.

So, three days. Weather'd gotten a little crisper, skies a little grayer, just enough rain to keep everything chilly and damp without actually washing any of your factory- and flivver-pumped crap out of the air.

Miserable, basically.

I was kickin' around the office, avoiding workin' on anything big by avoiding work on anything small, when the ameche out in the hallway rang.

On the square, I gave real thought to ignoring it. I *hate* that contraption, and I was preoccupied worrying over everything going on already. Still, it coulda been related, and if it wasn't, well, even a stiff like me's gotta work on occasion. I shuffled out my door, glowered at the dingus hopin' I could scare it into a shutting up, and then answered.

"Hello, Mick?"

I already had the familiar itching in my ear and my head that comes with usin' a telephone, but I had no trouble hearing him. He was already talking pretty loud, over the hubbub around him. I was used to the police station's noise, and this was worse.

"Busy day down there, Pete?" I said.

"You got no idea. That's kinda why I'm calling, actually. Any chance you can come down? They've got... Hang on. *Will ya pipe down! I'm trying to talk here!* Sorry. Got a job for you, some lighter stuff they want taken off their hands."

I allowed myself a petulant grumble about the timing, but I wasn't gonna say no. I made a good chunk of my folding green from the police department, and funds had gotten lower than I liked. Wouldn't do me any good to run out of milk—or palm-grease—while out hunting Orsola or tracking redcaps.

"Okay, Pete. Lemme pin my diapers on and I'll be there."

How many times have I described the ride on the L, or the squatting brick of a building that was the clubhouse, or the constant in-and-out stream of bulls and people with a complaint for the bulls and mugs nabbed by the bulls? I'm not sure either, but point is, I ain't doin' it again. I headed there, I got there, I went in.

Place was a zoo. Well, if you swapped cigarette smoke for zebra dung. Citizens were packed into the waiting area up front, standing room only. A lot of 'em had been waiting for hours, to judge by what they were yellin' at the beleaguered desk sergeant—the parts that weren't profanity, anyway. Sarge didn't even cast me his usual evil eye as I stepped past him without signing in, so I *knew* he was havin' a bad day of it.

Detectives pushed this way and that through the desks, calling to each other, and a lotta uniforms who shoulda been out walkin' the beat were loitering here instead. Waiting for instructions, maybe? Pete was one of 'em, but no way could he have heard me if I'd tried shoutin' across the room, and anyway he was currently busy being harangued by Detective Shaugnessy over something or other.

I also recognized a few other local PIs, jerked them a nod in greeting. Looked like the department was pullin' out all the stops on this one, whatever this one was.

Kevin Keenan, homicide detective and a friend of Pete's—and maybe of mine? Acquaintance, anyway—finally waved me over to his desk. It was covered in layers of creased, coffee-stained papers deep enough to bury a body, and had definitely looked better.

He'd looked better, too; the sweat stains on his shirt had probably permanently set the wrinkles, and he had a sorta wild, sleep-deprived edge to his blinkers.

"Slow day, Keenan? Least the peace and quiet's nice."

He started to say somethin', then glared as the cigarette he'd forgotten was hangin' from his lip tumbled to the floor in a spray of embers. He dug into the coat draped over his chair for a pack of Luckies, pulled one out, and stuck it in his mouth without lighting it.

"Sorry," he said in a tone that made it sound very much like *fuck you*. "We're swamped."

"I hadn't noticed. Guess you're the better detective."

"You want the job or not, Oberon?"

"All right, sorry. Don't blow your wig. Why don'tcha tell me what it is, and then I can give you an answer."

"Couple of assault cases, all in the same tenement. Nothing *too* serious, but some people got cut up. On any normal day, we'd just assign a junior police detective, but…"

"Yeah. But. What's up with all this, anyway? What's going on?"

"Can't tell you. Chief wants it kept hushed for now."

Thought about pushing further—or, y'know, *pushing*—but the poor sap was already a mess, and it wasn't as though I really *needed* to know.

And if I decided I did, I had other methods, anyway.

"Okay, I'll give it a good once-over, see what I can find."

"Thanks." He was already movin' on to other issues, digging through the stack of forms and reports for something or other. "I'll have Pete show you to the scene. Talk to Sarge up front, he'll arrange the usual vouchers for the usual amounts."

I glanced back at the desk sergeant, who was screamin' himself hoarse at the crowd of angry people who were screamin' back in turn, until there wasn't a chance in hell that any of 'em heard a single word of what anyone else was saying.

If I was human, I'da sighed. Me'n Pete weren't going to be on our way any time soon.


"So, what's going on? What's got everyone so worked up?"

Pete didn't exactly frown, but he didn't exactly not frown, either. "I'm not really supposed to say anything about that, Mick."

"I'm not really supposed to exist, so I'm still one up on you."

The not-frown deepened, and he checked behind to make sure nobody was listening to us, even though I'd waited until the station was a couple blocks behind us before I'd asked. Then, finally, "I don't know a lot in the way of details. Something to do with a couple murders. Real bad ones. The kind the newspapers would have a field day with if they found out, and would probably cause genuine panic."

Wow. They *musta* been somethin' else. Chicago ain't a squeamish city.

We walked on. Pete tilted his cap down to keep the drizzle offa his face. Me, I wasn't wearing my hat—I don't care for how it chafes my ears, even if most of you lugs don't see 'em properly—so I settled for squinting.

We were maybe one more block from the train station when I got my first of the day's reminders that I was, in fact, a twit.

"We meet again, Oberon."

I stopped cold, made a real big point of *not* movin' my hands or clenching my fists or anything that mighta landed in even the general neighborhood of hostile; since our kind don't tend to fidget, she'da taken any such move as prelude to an attack. "Most people just say hello these days, doll."

"I am not most people." Even at her coldest, her tone was musical, as much an instrument as a voice. *Bean sidhe* are like that. "Most people these days also say 'doll.' When speaking to me, I suggest you not be most people, either."

"Right." Still not moving, "Pete, what do you see when you look at her?"

"Uh. Dame in a man's suit. It's kinda weird, but nothin' more."

I finally turned around, and yep, she had a glamour up if that's all he saw. I mean, she *was* wearing a man's suit. She also had whiskey-gold hair reachin' down to her knees, and—rather more alarming—eye sockets gaping emptier than a snake's conscience.

"How're you doin', Áebinn? I didn't know you were in town."

"Did you not? Or did you just hope I wasn't?"

"Those ain't mutually exclusive."

"Indeed. I've been seeking you for some time, Oberon."

A few pedestrians wandered by, absently steppin' aside without ever breaking conversation or even seeming to notice. Whatever glamour she was wearin', it was impacting others even more'n it was Pete. Was that deliberate on her part, I wondered? Or somethin' to do with his… condition?

"I ain't hard to dig up. My office is listed in the phone book."

"It... took some time to convince the necessary people that this was important enough for me to pursue outside Elphame," she admitted.

"Ah. So you *are* workin' on behalf of the Court, not on your own."

"Everything I do is for the Seelie Court."

That wasn't exactly a confirmation, I noticed. But with Áebinn, it was more likely she was bein' pompous than deliberately cagey, and I really didn't need her aggravated, so I didn't press.

"Well, you found me. Congratulations. Whaddaya want?"

I'm not entirely positive how to describe what she did next. You know how, when you're talkin' to somebody and they get *real* intent about somethin'? Excited, obsessive, to the point where they're more preachin' at you than jawing with you? Their eyes get wide, kinda bright, maybe even look a bit like they're gonna bug outta their heads?

Yeah. She did that, only without any eyes.

"There is death in this city, Oberon."

"This is Chicago, sweetheart. Death's a tax-paying resident."

"Do not play the fool with me!"

"What makes you think he's pla—?"

"Probably not right now, Pete."

Áebinn ignored him completely, which was absolutely the best possible option. "I'm not speaking of a few paltry mortals perishing! I mean something potent, a true power of decay, dissolution. Corrupt and far-reaching."

Well, she had my attention. Áebinn wasn't one to panic too easy, and sensing the coming of death was her bailiwick. If this had her worked up, it was nothin' to be sneezed at.

"There were those murders..." Pete began.

"Silence your pet, Oberon, or I will."

"Look here, sister..."

"I just said this goes beyond a few humans! I don't know

yet what we're dealing with, but it could be dangerous to *us*."

I'da almost been more comfortable if she'd flailed or paced or somethin', the way one of you woulda. But, like me, she lacked a lotta human mannerisms unless she was actively thinkin' about 'em. Between that and the missing peepers, it was like listening to a real agitated mannequin.

"I hear you. Dangerous. Important. But why come lookin' for me specifically? It ain't just for my knowledge of human Chicago, you never had any real respect for—"

"It's touched you, Oberon."

For a few seconds, until I could get the words out, I swear every sound of the city faded away, until there was nothin' in my ears but the light drumming of the rain.

"It's what, now?"

Good thing I took my time thinkin' that one up.

"I don't fully understand how or when, but it's touched you. Or you're connected to it. I had a sense of you even in my earliest premonitions, and I can smell it on you now."

Lovely. Just fuckin' swell. This, I didn't need.

Orsola? Was it her bad luck curse Áebinn was "smelling"? If so, what in the name of everything holy or even just vaguely pleasant was the old witch up to that had a *bean sidhe* ready to throw an ing-bing? Or what if—?

"Obviously," she said, training her empty sockets on Pete as though she'd just piped him for the first time, "I'm going to have to question all your associates, intently. We'll start with this one here, and then you can provide me a list. We'll bring them to your office, or go to—"

"Slow it down, doll." I figured that'd get her attention, even as I stepped between her and Pete. There was plenty room, since he'd wisely started backpedaling as soon as she'd turned his way.

"Out of my way, Oberon!"

"Not happenin'. You wanted my attention, you got it. You want my help, you got that, too, but *my* way. I'll definitely be keepin' a lookout for any trouble, anything hinky. You wanna tell me how to reach you, I'll put you wise the minute I tumble anything relevant.

"But you wanna put the screws on any of my people, you come through me to do it. *Capisce?*"

That face swiveled back my way, and I won't fib, a chill went through me. Those sockets seemed deeper now, darker, and I heard somethin' in her throat, a second, sonorous tone behind her voice.

"Do you believe I couldn't, *Mick*? Or that your relation to the *real* Oberon would stop me?"

"First, sister, I'm real as he is. And forget about him; he's only my second cousin. He wouldn't even notice if anything happened to me, and I don't need protection in his name."

I took a step toward her, straightening. The rain around us went colder, almost icy, though it stayed liquid. On the street behind her, a couple cars sputtered to a halt, engines pouring smoke, headlights popping like cheap balloons.

"And second, Áebinn, maybe you could go through me if you tried." The people gathered around the broken-down flivvers jumped back, crying out, as a radiator burst open, vapor shooting from a maw of suddenly twisted metal. "Then again, when it's my friends you're threatening, maybe you couldn't." The whistle of the steam grew higher, first like a teapot, then a siren, then a horrified, breathless shriek. "You wanna find out?"

It woulda been more dramatic if we'd gone for the full stare-down after that, but she shook her head almost immediately. Her mug was normal again, or as normal as it could be with those empty pits. I was normal again, too. The various bits and dinguses in the cars went silent, and they'd probably worked just fine again if they hadn't, y'know, twisted themselves apart.

"Conflict between us serves no one," she said. Was that really why she'd backed down? Or was she saving face? Who knew, with her? "No, there is no good way for you to reach me, but I will check in with you. You share any information you've uncovered, and I shall do the same. Keep alert, Oberon."

Didn't even wait for me to agree to her terms, just walked away. Not real courteous of her.

Pete's own peepers were about as saucer-sized as I'd ever seen 'em. "What…" He waved helplessly at the cars. "What was *that*?"

"Chest-beating. Nothin' to worry about."

"Think maybe I'll worry a little bit, anyway."

On the square, I was worried a little, too. I know I've told you about those episodes before, times where I get steamed enough I lose control. Thing is, they didn't use to happen this often; I'd had more in the past couple years than the past few decades. Gettin' stronger, too. Used to be a few light bulbs might flicker or burst. This, with the cars? This was new.

It *mighta* just been, in part, Orsola's hex. I really *hoped* it was Orsola's hex.

I only realized we'd walked another half block in silence when Pete spoke again. "Hey, Mick?"

"Yeah?"

"Isn't it *third* cousin?"

I stopped. "What?"

"I've heard your spiel before. About King Oberon. He's your third cousin on your mother's side."

"Yeah. So?"

"So back there. You said second cousin."

"Huh."

*Huh.*

"She had me rattled," I admitted. "Musta misspoke."

I think Pete almost even believed that.

I wasn't sure that I did.

The rumbling, rattling, skull-itching L carried us over to Englewood, which is a real prosperous part of the Windy City except for the really poor sections of it—or the other way around, if you prefer. You got real successful department stores almost-but-not-quite within sight of tenements so cheap they won't even provide decent-quality rats; you gotta import your own.

Hey, guess which parts were mostly Irish, Italian, and Polish, and which parts were mostly good old-fashioned "proper" American white? I'll wait while you puzzle it through.

We passed a couple of sidewalk vendors right near the border between one sort of neighborhood and the other, with apron-clad shopkeepers callin' out these wares or those. Pete tossed one of 'em a penny and collected an apple from the table. And yes, it was out of season; most of the fruit I saw here was.

That wasn't the hinky part. Chicago's got enough well-to-do who want what they want when they want it, and are willin' to pay to either have it shipped in or for a few farmers to grow the goods indoors.

If they were sellin' *here*, though? This was either a bad lot, or it'd waited around too long, and they were movin' it on the cheap.

"How is it?" I asked.

Not that I had to. It hadn't *crunched* so much as caved in when Pete took his first bite. He chewed once, then actually froze, his face twisted in a pretty close relative of horror.

"That good, huh?"

"I don't think this apple is made out of apple," he said around a mouthful of… well, not-apple, according to him.

He took a minute to recover, and we went on. He ditched the thing in the nearest gutter, and we both agreed to swear up and down we knew nothin' about it if it grew into something monstrous.

Still, the vendors were doin' brisk business. When you're poor enough, you buy what you can afford and find a way to *make* it palatable. Pies, maybe, or jams. Or fermentation.

An intersection, a left turn, another intersection, and Pete checked his notebook for an address. "I know it's one of the nearby tenements…"

"Hey, I'm just guessin' here, Pete, but maybe it's the one with the cops loitering out front?"

He looked up from his notes, down the block, and then at me. "You think you're *so* much smarter'n me, don't you?"

"Well, it ain't like you make it challenging…"

Place didn't stand out much. Just another gray brick building, three stories high, dirty and startin' to get run down and full of people who couldn't afford better. Just… there.

We ran through quick introductions with the bulls who'd been sittin' on the place, whose names I won't even pretend to remember. I had no real interest in becomin' pals, and they were just as happy to be on their way.

"Seven victims," one rattled off before he dusted, followed by more names I don't remember and four apartment numbers. "All of 'em were woken up by slashing wounds to arms or legs, but said they never saw an attacker. Whoever'd done it was gone by the time they finished thrashing around and got to the lights. Doors were still locked. Good luck. Bye."

Helpful lot, these guys.

And fulla bunk, besides. They hadn't even given me the story right, probably because they were only half listening when they heard it.

I'm sure the fact that most of the victims were Italian, and a couple were black, had nothin' to do with that.

So Pete'n me went around to the different apartments. Poor saps were all waitin' in the hall, had been for hours. The bulls had told 'em not to go back in until we'd come by to give the place a thorough up'n down. A lot of 'em had bloody bandages wrapped around arms, legs, or both.

Most sang more or less the same song, but one older guy, he told the story different. He hadn't been the victim, least not initially. Said he'd woken up and heard a scream from the other room, where his daughter sleeps. He'd gone runnin' in there with a knockoff Louisville Slugger and smashed the place up pretty good, tryin' to protect his girl. No lights, so he'd never gotten a good view of what'd attacked her, but he swore to me it was some sorta animal.

"If your bosses called me in here after a raccoon," I told Pete, "I'm never gonna let them, or you, live it down."

That's when the old man yanked the bandage from his arm. Injury wasn't gonna kill him, probably wouldn't even cost him any strength in the arm as long as he took proper care, but that was sure no raccoon.

The wound was too thick to be the claws of any kinda animal I was familiar with—at least any animal small as what the fella was describing—and way too ragged to be a blade. I'd almost have figured it was some sorta carpentry tool or a trowel or what have you, but not too many stray animals carry those, even in the big city.

Even weirder, the wound had a smell to it. I mean, beyond blood and sweat and the rags he'd used to bandage it. Faint, too faint for even me to identify it, but it nagged at me. It definitely didn't belong, but more'n that, it was somehow familiar...

I decided we'd try his apartment first.

Ankled down the hall, stepped inside, shut the door behind us 'cause we didn't want anyone following us in and trying to be "helpful"...

And stopped.

Nothing happened, not a flicker or a spark, when Pete flipped the light switch. Mighta been the middle of the day, but between the autumn overcast and the next tenement over blockin' most of the window, it was darker'n a *dullahan*'s neck-hole in here. Pools of shadow and general shapes to my senses; Pete musta been all but blind.

I did notice a sorta sweet aroma, not floral.

I reached into my coat, brushed a finger over the wand and wove a little ambient luck into my aura. Not enough to gum things up for Pete or change the room's general auspices, just a tiny extra oomph. I could tell ya it was to help me hunt for clues, and that'd be part of the truth, but mostly I just didn't wanna bump into anything while blundering around and embarrass myself in front of the mortal. Pete's a pal, but I got my pride.

So, what'd we have? A busted lamp, for one thing—looked to have been one of the first casualties of the baseball bat—which explained why the switch on the wall did bupkis. A sofa with blankets and a few extra pillows, now heaped in a pile on the floor, where I guess the girl'd been bunking. Curtains, hanging unevenly where the rod had been partly pulled down. Table, undamaged, lying on its side. An array of scattered and partly smashed fruit: couple apples, a partly squished cantaloupe, a watermelon with a big honkin' gash in one side. Least I knew where that smell was comin' from.

This was just the one room, too. Still hadda half-sized kitchen and a closet-sized bedroom to check after here.

Well, since nothin' interesting had jumped out at me, I figured I'd start with the sofa. I knelt down, idly pokin' at the sheets to see if anything'd gotten wrapped up in 'em...

And somethin' interesting *did* jump out at me.

No clue what it was. Something slammed, hard, into the calf I was resting on. Quick, tearing pain raced up my leg; my whole body tensed, from surprise as much as the hurt, and I felt blood pooling, sticky and wet, in the ripped leg of my trousers.

"Mick!" I could make out from his silhouette in the gloom that Pete had skinned his revolver, but all he could really do was sorta wave it around. No way he could see well enough to even have the faintest notion where to shoot, let alone actually hit a target. "Mick, what the hell's going on?"

I stumbled upright, hissing at the pain in my leg, and drew the L&G. "I dunno! Get your back to something solid! I—"

Something tore the hem of my flogger—I go through more coats!—and I half-stepped, half-fell forward, yankin' myself from the grip of whatever it was. The table thumped as something careened into it before vanishing back into the darkened corners.

Dark, but no longer silent.

A wet, trilling noise—a sorta *brrl! brrl!*—like a cooing dove and a purring cat makin' whoopee on a rip-saw.

It was movin' again, I could tell that much. I put myself in front of Pete, not knowin' what else to do, and I caught *just* enough of a glimpse through the shadows to realize what I was tusslin' with.

"You have *got* to be—"

I probably woulda finished that up with *kidding me* or somethin' equally clichéd, but I went with a pained shout instead as the thing smashed into my foot and proceeded to chew on me through my Oxfords.

I kicked it away, just a few paces, and then dropped to my knees, stabbin' at it with the L&G, not only piercing it physically but ripping away some of the animating power from its aura. It slipped from my grasp—*brrl! brrl!*—and started to slide away.

"Oh, no, you don't!"

I jumped up, stomped on it—and it was, despite the holes I'd just put in it, still a lot harder'n I expected. It went spinning one way and I toppled the other, crackin' my noggin against the wall before landing in a heap.

The momentum of that stomp propelled it into the kitchen, where it bounced off the counter and came right back at me.

*What had I heard about killing these things? Dump it in boiling water and then... brush it? With an old broom?*

Nuts to *that*!

I shot back upright, wand gripped in my teeth. I reached down, lifted the fallen table by its legs, and—shoutin' past the hardwood of the L&G—toppled forward onto the thing right as it neared me, tabletop first. We rolled for just a heartbeat and then it gave, bursting under the surface with a gooey *splat*.

I just lay there for a spell, waiting for the bleeding to stop. Pete came over, and I think I'da preferred panic or confusion to the plain blank mask he was showin' me. "Should we check?"

"I fpupofe…" I took the wand from my trap, reholstered it, and tried again. "I suppose we'd better."

Now, look. I know what some of you are gonna think. I get it. I've told you some *real* weird stuff before, but nothin' as whacky as this. I mean, I'd heard the legend, but even with all I've seen, I didn't suppose for one second it was real. You wanna figure this is all bunk, that I'm pullin' your leg, I can't blame you. But it's what happened. Whaddaya want from me?

Gingerly, we lifted the table, and examined the red pulp and green rind smashed into paste beneath it.

"Mick?"

"No."

"You don't know what I was gonna ask!"

"Doesn't matter. The answer to every possible question is no."

"Were you… just attacked by a watermelon?"

"N—actually, yeah. Yeah, I was. Vampiric, if you gotta know."

"What?"

"Look, there's folklore about it. Among one particular bunch of Romani in, uh, somewhere in Serbia. Vampiric watermelons. And pumpkins."

Damn, I was glad it hadn't been pumpkins. I got a bit of a problem with pumpkins, since your Revolutionary War—first time I ever came to this continent—and that whole nightmarish mess with the Jack-o'-Lantern Gate…

Sorry. Rambling. And yes, I know you're just as disbelieving as Pete, and yes, you can look the damn stories up for yourself if you want. I ain't makin' this up.

And yes, this means that "gash" I'd seen in the rind was where it'd split into "teeth" to slash at people's skin so it could feed itself. Have I mentioned that I'd never for an instant considered the possibility that these things were real?

As for Pete, he'd gone from slack as empty suspenders to laughing so hard I thought his fool head was gonna pop off and go rollin' around in the mush.

I'da glared, but he wouldn't have seen it. "You about done?"

"I gotta tell you, Mick," he began, struggling to breathe.

"You really don't, and I can't say I recommend it."

That just set him off again. I wondered if slapping him would help.

I thought about doing it even if it wouldn't.

"Whaddaya think?" he finally asked, still chucklin'. "Blood-sucking fruit. This the big deathly danger your friend was yammering about?"

I knew he was joshing, but… "No. It's connected, though."

That sobered him. "It is? How do you know?"

"Because in thousands of years, I ain't ever seen this before."

"I don't follow."

I moved forward with deliberate steps, until we were damn near beak to beak. "Because I just fought a vampiric watermelon. A vampiric frickin' watermelon, Pete!"

"Uh, yeah?"

"And even in *my* absurd life, I refuse to entertain the notion that a fight with a vampiric frickin' watermelon is a *goddamn coincidence*!"

With that, and what tiny slivers of dignity this whole damn affair had left me, I made for the door.


I can only imagine what the small crowd gathered in the hallway musta thought when I stepped out, covered in blood and various sticky juices, trousers and coat torn all to hell. They drew breath in unison to start shoutin' questions, and deflated in unison when I raised a finger, backed up by the meanest glower I could muster.

"Not. One. Word."

Then, when I was sure the nice peace'n quiet wasn't gonna burst any time soon, "Pete, gimme your nightstick."

"Mick, you know I can't just—"

"Nightstick."

He sighed and handed it over.

Now that I knew what I was dealin' with, and had time to draw a lot more luck my way before gettin' into it, the other lurking, uh, *enemies* weren't too tough to handle. Billy club in one hand and wand in the other, it only took me a few minutes to go through the other crime-scene apartments and deal with the lot.

Turned out one of 'em *was* a pumpkin, but I handled it.

"You're safe," I told the starin' victims as I wiped the club clean on my flogger—might as well, I was gonna have to replace it anyway—before passin' it back to Pete. "Don't ask questions. Just accept it. If you really *gotta* know, feel free to request an official police incident report."

"Gee, thanks," Pete groused as we headed back downstairs. "How the hell am I supposed to write this up?"

"Say it was a raccoon."

"Mick…"

"Whaddaya want from me? I solved the damn case, and got nothin' to show for it. Nothin' I can say that anyone's gonna buy. You think I'm gonna get paid for this? I'll be lucky if I can squeeze a few 'expense' bucks out of the department for dry cleaning. Today was a bust, so if I'm a little short on sympathy, you're just gonna have to put up with it."

*Was* it a bust, though? I'd been serious when I told Pete this hadda be connected with whatever Áebinn was investigating. The timing was just too hinky not to be, and so was the nature of the situation. Even if the tainted spiritual essence that'd been drawn here had taken a human corpse instead of, uh, bad produce, had become a genuine vampire… Well, Chicago woulda been in for a bad time, but it probably wouldn't be nasty enough to have snagged the *bean sidhe*'s attention. But they *were* spirits of corruption and death, like she'd said, so there *hadda* be a link, right?

Too many questions. They gave me somethin' to ponder

on the L, which was a nice distraction from the stares I was attractin' with my new bloody hobo fashion, but they stubbornly refused to match up with any answers.

# CHAPTER FOUR

I was ruminatin' over all of it, and still no closer to connecting bloodthirsty ground fruit to Áebinn's worries, when the blower rang.

Again. Two days in a row. I coulda done without that.

"Yeah, what?" Maybe not the most courteous greeting I coulda led with, but between the itching and the general frustration, it was all I had in me.

"You say hello to all your pals that way, *amico*?"

I actually stopped to think on it. "Yeah, I really do. What's the rumble, Fino?"

"Figured we'd let you know we got settled, finally. And give you the number here. I wanna know what's what every step of the—"

"Fer cryin' out loud, we been through this! I can't know anything about where you are!"

"It's a new fuckin' line, Mick. Nobody knows nothin' about who it belongs to or where it's hooked up."

"The exchange tells me what part of the city you're in, *babbo*!" Maybe if I threw some Italian back at him, he'd start payin' attention.

"We'll chance it," he answered, stubborn and just a little cold. "I wanna be kept in the know if you learn anything about my daughter or the fuckin' Unseelie, and that means you gotta be able to fuckin' reach us, *capisce*?"

I gave some consideration to just hangin' up on him, but… The Ottatis were only half-convinced that hidin' out was the right play as it was. If I isolated them, kept 'em in the dark, or didn't give a little here and there, Fino was just mule-headed enough to throw the whole idea over and try somethin' dippy.

I tried one last time, though. "You know this ain't just the Uptown Boys or Bumpy's crew you're hidin' from, right? That these bastards already got ways to dig you up that nobody else—"

"Yeah, I got it already!"

Wasn't sure whether the blossoming headache was more from the phone or from him. "Fine. Gimme the number." Maybe I'd even bother remembering it.

He rattled it off, I repeated it back. "Got it. Nothin' to tell you so far, though. Lot goin' down, but I ain't tumbled how much of it's connected to Adalina or the Unseelie. If any." Then, really more outta habit than anythin', "How *is* Adalina, anyway? Handlin' the excitement okay?"

"She's… fine."

"Fino?"

"Yeah?"

"You know I can *hear* it when you hesitate like that."

He growled a whole string of Italian that I ain't gonna bother translatin', mostly because half of it was variations on the word fuck. "I don't wanna pester you with nothin' while you're trying to find out what the fuckin' *stronzi* want with her…"

"Why don'tcha spill, and let me decide if it's nothin'."

"I… Yeah, okay. She was all right the first night, but since then? She's been havin' nightmares, bad fuckin' nightmares. Wakes up screamin'. Just the thought of goin' to sleep's got her crying, now."

Not good. I mean, sure, it coulda just been bad dreams, girl had plenty of bad on her mind to dream about. Or it coulda been more of her turnin' into whatever it was she was turnin' into. But when she'd been completely unconscious, she'd still sensed that the Spear of Lugh was in town. Whatever she was—oracular, psychic, what have you—you don't ignore the dreams of someone, something, like that.

Besides, even if it *was* just a young girl or a young Fae havin' night terrors, maybe I could help.

"I'll talk to her," I said.

"Appreciate that, Mick. You want I should put her on the horn, or—?"

"No! Uh, that is, I don't think that's a great idea. You know it makes me uncomfortable, it probably don't feel too great for her, either, and I can't really see her reactions or get into her head if I gotta… No, bring her by. Just make sure—"

"Make sure we ain't shadowed, yeah, yeah. I've done this before, you know."

Figured it'd take some time, even if they left immediately. I got my coat—then remembered what shape it was in, tossed it across the room, and pulled a far more worn and generally uglier one from the back of the rack. I think the original hue had been a sorta rich brown. Now it was just old-colored.

If things were gonna keep up the way they'd gone the last couple years, I needed to start buyin' in bulk.

Moseyed outside far enough to pick up a rag from the newsie on the corner, then ducked back in before the rain soaked it through. Dropped back into my seat, tossed my heels up onto the desk, unfolded the paper…

Huh. Wondered if that was one of the murders the coppers had been tryin' to keep outta the press. If so, there'd be a lot of steam and profanity at the clubhouse today.

The story didn't have a lotta detail, since they'd never gotten close to the stiff and so far everyone who needed to stay clammed up *had* stayed clammed up, so they hadda go real salacious with what they could. In other words, I couldn't tell just how nasty or messy the crime mighta been, only that it was ugly and violent. Mostly, it was a whole bunch of alarm about the possibility of this bein' the start of another gang conflict, with a lot of implied "Buy the evening edition or tomorrow's paper and hopefully we'll have found out by then!"

And yes, despite what Áebinn said about "mere" mortal deaths, I was wonderin' if this was linked to what she'd been sensing. I'm not *completely* dippy; you dangle somethin' like that in front of me, I'm gonna question it.

Nothin' I could do from here, though, so I kept on flippin' pages and reading until, finally, I heard a heavy knock on the office door.

"It's open!"

Adalina, I was expectin', but I'd thought it'd be one of her folks accompanying her. Instead, Archie walked through the doorway beside her.

"Oberon. How've you been?"

"Fine. Fighting watermelons. You?"

"Fighting wat— What?"

You know, I don't recall ever stoppin' him cold in the middle of one of his "echoes" like that before. Couldn't help but smirk.

Only lasted a second, though. "Please tell me Fino didn't tell you—"

"Get a load of this guy!" Archie barked at Adalina. Guess he'd decided not to follow up on the watermelon. "C'mon, Oberon. Whaddaya take us for?"

*Uh, humans?*

"Boss knew you were gonna blow your wig about this. He called me up. We met on a random street corner. I got no more idea where they're holed up than you do."

"Huh. All right. So how come Fino or Bianca didn't play taxi for Adalina? Not that I ain't overjoyed to see you as always, of course."

"Overjoyed to see me. Right." He shrugged. "Boss's got a lot on his plate, tryin' to run a business entirely over the blower. Besides, he figured, anyone's keepin' watch on your office for him or Mrs. Ottati, they're a lot less likely to recognize me."

Well. I guess Fino *did* have some idea how to lie dormy when necessary.

So, that rigmarole over with, I hung up chairs and offered coats—or somethin' similar, anyway—and went for the milk. Archie passed, as always, but Adalina accepted a glass. She was quiet as a sleepin' snail, and her hands were even clammier than usual. Those nightmares had her shook up bad.

And then Archie surprised me. He snatched the newspaper off my desk, announced that he'd be out in the hall if we needed him, and vamoosed. Dunno if that was his own idea or if he'd been told to give us some privacy, but it was a stand-up gesture either way.

"Okay, doll. Let's hear it."

"I don't... I don't want to talk about it, Mick." If she'd fiddled any harder with the crease in her skirt, she was gonna rip the fabric. Funny that she even fidgeted at all, come to think; guess it was 'cause she was raised human. "I'm only here because Papa said I should be."

"He's right. You know you can talk to me. Maybe I can help."

"I don't *want to*!" She was real near to the full waterworks, those huge fishy peepers shimmering in the lamplight.

I waited, just watchin'. She fidgeted some more, sobbed once. Stood up, wandered around the office, absently sliding drawers open and closed. I let her work through it, though I'd have had to stop her if she'd gotten near my drawer of special knickknacks and doodads. Some things are private.

She was waitin' for me to argue, I figured. If I'd given her a fight, she coulda focused on that, dragged her feet. But I didn't, and finally the silence got to her.

"Death." She dropped back into the chair, so limp I'm surprised she didn't slide right off to the floor. "I've been dreaming about death."

Nuts. Any hopes I had that this *wasn't* connected to Áebinn's premonitions were suckin' in their last gasps.

"Tell me."

She told me. The images themselves weren't all *that* awful. I mean, they weren't fun; bloody fights, putrefied carcasses, the graves of loved ones, Adalina herself wielding a gore-stained knife. Pretty nightmarish stuff, literally, but I've heard worse from humans and Fae both. More'n enough to ruin your beauty sleep, especially a couple nights in a row, but accordin' to Adalina, that wasn't the worst of it.

Which brought me to the obvious question. "So what was?"

And she clammed up again. No amount of waitin', no convincing or cajoling, would drag it outta her. She just sat in her chair, starin' at her lap, and cried.

Yeah, I coulda forced the issue, gotten into her thoughts and *made* her tell me. It's harder with Fae than mortals, impossible with some, but she had no teaching, no knowledge how to block me. I coulda pulled it off.

No way I would, though. I was tryin' to help her, not make it worse, and not leave her betrayed by the only person she could really talk to.

Instead… "Adalina?"

She sniffled twice, looked up.

"These may not just be bad dreams."

I swear to you, I worried for a split second she mighta just up and died on me, pale as she got. "What do you mean?" Voice was tiny as a mouse's sigh, but I still heard, *tasted*, the panic beneath the surface.

Maybe I shouldn'ta said anything, but I couldn't leave it there now.

"I've heard from Áebinn. You remember? The one who was tryin' to find me in Elphame?"

She nodded.

"She's felt somethin' in Chicago, somethin' bad. And sensing the coming of death is basically her whole shtick. I think you may be pickin' up on it, too, in your dreams. Like I told you you did with the Spear of Lugh."

Adalina's gaze went so intent, I thought for a moment she was tryin' to mess with *my* noggin. "And that could explain the nightmares? I'm having them because I'm feeling this... this other horrible thing?"

"Could well be, yeah."

She sobbed again—in relief. I felt, and I mean literally, a huge weight of tension, of stark terror, leave the room. "Thank you, Mick. Thank you for telling me."

"Uh... Yeah. Always glad to be of help." I was pretty sure I'd missed an ingredient when baking this conversation.

"So, listen, Adalina... If these dreams *are* because you're sensin' something, you may be able to help me out. If they keep comin', and you start to see a lot of anywhere or anyone you know, anywhere or anyone real, you gimme a shout."

"I will, absolutely."

"Swell. Let's get Archie back in here and get you home."

She about floated to her feet, and she was around the desk to wrap me in a hug before I'd even stood up. I let it go on for a few, then gently disentangled myself and made for the coat rack.

I was *really* itchin' to know just what it was she hadn't told me, what burden or worry I'd taken off her shoulders. Maybe later, when this was done, she'd be more inclined to spill.

Adalina popped her head out the door to tell Archie she was ready to scram, and went to collect her stuff.

"I got some of the boys keepin' a slant on the boss's house, even though the boss ain't stayin' there," he told me while she was shrugging her way into her coat. "We ain't got the vision to see through those, whaddaya call, glamours, so I dunno if they're human or not, but *someone's* sittin' on the place."

"Good to know. Just don't let 'em tumble to you. And—"

"Yeah, yeah, and be careful. Change the record already, bo. I even told the guys to carry some iron pipes or prybars, just in case they gotta mix it up with the faeries."

"Huh. That's actually pretty sharp thinking, Archie."

"You gotta sound that surprised about it?"

"I don't *gotta*, but it does come naturally."

"Comes naturally. Cute."

He started to go, but… "Hey, Archie?"

"Yeah?"

"How'd you explain it to 'em? The iron?"

"Heh. Told 'em I'd go into it later. Hope I think of somethin' by then."

I snorted. "Good luck."

"Good luck. Right."

He nodded. I nodded. They left. I didn't.

I was alone with my thoughts, and they were lousy company.

Didn't much care for the notion, but I hadda stop treatin' this as a distraction, just another chore to check off my list. Whatever it was that Áebinn—and probably Adalina—were sensing, it needed my full attention. Or at least a pretty solid portion of it.

So, put my ongoing search for Orsola Maldera aside? That didn't sit right. Then again, I'd been workin' that angle on and off for months, and had squat to show for it.

Then again *again*, depending on what she had cooking, the witch might well be exactly what Áebinn had felt, or at least connected to it.

But maybe…

Nuts. My head hurt.

So, fine. Nobody knew from nothin' about Orsola, so I'd abandon that trail for now. But my people might know somethin' that could lead me to this "deathly power" from a different angle. Time for more of that shoe-leather and gum-bumping and huntin' down my various contacts that you love hearin' about almost as much as I love doin' it.

Normally Four-Leaf Franky'd be my first stop, but when we'd parted ways the other night, he'd promised to shout if he learned anythin' interesting—about Orsola *or* Áebinn. Yeah, he wasn't listenin' specifically for anything about this thing of corruption and death, whatever that meant, but… Well, much as I give him a hard time, and for all he gets himself into hot water more often than the city's entire supply of lobster, Franky's no bunny. Between the *bean sidhe* and the witch, if he'd tumbled to anythin' in the way of unnatural deaths, he'd drop me a dime.

So I hadda dig up one of the others.

Gaullman had escaped from his latest nuthouse and blown town. He'd be back soon enough, always was, but that didn't do me any good now. Took me a day to track down Pink Paddy, and he was so completely over the edge with the rams on scotch and curdled milk that, even pushin' my will into his head and tryin' to get him to sober up did nothin' but get me a slurred diatribe on how much better the hooch tasted back when it was illegal.

Lenai wouldn't even open her door for me, and told me in no uncertain terms which parts of me she'd remove with garden shears if I threatened to break it down like I had last time, and how she'd prepare 'em before makin' me eat 'em.

"I heard," she told me through the door, "that some of the mojo-humpers—" that'd be her term for any of the Fae-blooded denizens of the Second City with more magic'n she had "—headed for the hills, or at least pulled up the welcome mats and triple-locked their doors. Why don't you go bug them instead of pestering an old woman, you jackass?"

Seemed as good a lead as any, and definitely the best I was gonna get from her, so I set out to do just that.

And she was right. The "mojo-humpers" had gone to ground, the lot of 'em. I spent a couple more days diggin' around, and came up with nada. I was just wonderin' if I was desperate enough to go banging on Dan Baskin's door, see if he or Ramona had any wisdom to share, when I finally got lucky.

Well, lucky may not be the right word. Wasn't exactly how I'd wanted things to turn out, and it sure wasn't how *he* woulda.

Can't say I ever knew his real name. Hell, I ain't even sure *he* knew his real name. We all just called him the L King.

Old, craggy hobo, lived mostly in and around the train yards, shoutin' prophecies at passersby and pigeons, both of whom paid him about as much notice. He wasn't exactly an oracle, far as accuracy went, but he was right just a mite more often than you could chock up to random chance. And between all the yappin', he kept an ear to the ground and discovered a lot more of what was happenin' nearby than most gave him credit for.

But he never saw or heard *this* comin', I guess.

It was the pigeons that led me to him. I'd just dusted from one of the stations where he sometimes loitered and was racking my noodle tryin' to figure where else to look when I spotted 'em a ways off, circlin' like vultures or raptors do, and very much like pigeons don't.

Took me some while to get there, since I hadda climb through some alleys, over a few fences and scattered junk, and across some mostly bare, autumn-stiffened scrub. I tumbled to where I was goin' once I stumbled across the tracks—painfully, what with the iron—but they led me right to a small opening in a hillside. Entrance to one of the underground freight and postal railway tunnels that run through parts of Chicago like an oversized anthill.

More pigeons were gathered at the opening, standing way too still. Almost at attention. Maybe they *had* listened to some of those prophecies.

The fetor of days-old rot was gathered pretty thick out here, too. Even if I hadn't already figured what I was gonna find, that woulda told me all I needed.

The L King was only a few paces inside, sloppily dumped right around the first bend. Whoever'd left him here'd done the bare minimum to keep the body from bein' *too* obvious, but clearly didn't care all that much about secrecy. The old man was a heap of meat, no longer stiff. His clothes were another matter, starched not just with the usual filth and sweat, but blood. It covered his chin, his shoulders, his chest, a flaky brown shawl that wasn't ever gonna catch on in the fashion industry.

The smell was gone this close, of course. That'd always been one of the hinkiest things about the L King: You'd smell him coming from down the block, even upwind and with the worst cold in your life, but the air was always clear within a few feet of him. Like his stink didn't start until you were well outta arm's reach.

As I said, not entirely human.

I stood over him, feelin' like I oughta say somethin' but lacking the words. We'd never been what I'd call pals, never drunk outta the same bottle, but he'd been a useful fella to know. He'd been harmless. And he'd been one of mine.

Somebody was gonna have a mighty bad day when I learned who did this to him.

Or *what*.

See, the body was pretty badly mangled, the throat torn almost totally apart, so I didn't have enough to be sure. And even if it'd given me more to go on, this wasn't a conclusion I wanted to jump to based on a single corpse.

But everything I *could* see pointed to the possibility of...

Well, remember when I said Chicago might be in for a real bad time if we'd had ourselves a genuine vampire, instead of some corrupted fruit?

It was lookin' like Chicago was in for a real bad time.


Called the nearest clubhouse, left an anonymous report of the body—figured I'd let the bulls handle it, and even if a few of 'em noticed the hinkiness with the smell, it ain't as if they'd suss out why—and went back to pestering my contacts.

Still nobody would talk to me.

I mean, it don't take a detective to figure that if you're dealin' with a vampire—or even if it's some other kinda killer beastie—and you got one vicious, bloody murder on your hands, first place you go hunt for clues is in the *other* recent vicious, bloody murders. Genius, no?

But the press still hadn't sniffed out anything helpful in the way of further detail. Keenan still wasn't "authorized" to talk to me. Pete still didn't know from nothin'. Baskin and Ramona wouldn't return my calls, and the idea of payin' my not-so-favorite Assistant State's Attorney a visit, confronting Ramona mug to mug, appealed to me about as much as a dental drill suppository.

I even faced the dreaded contraption at the end of the hall yet again, and dredged up the number Fino'd given me, so I could ask him if the killings might be mob-related, and if he'd heard anything about 'em. He hadn't, said he'd nose around a little, but that he was pretty sure they had nothin' to do with his "business." He'd almost certainly have caught wind of something if they were. I asked him to take an extra close look at Saul Fleischer, the gangster-Kabbalist I'd locked horns with some months back, just in case.

I retraced my steps and went back to all my usual contacts, but nobody'd heard anything new in the last couple days, and most of 'em just locked up even tighter, or pulled their burrows in after 'em, when I even got near the word "vampire." Mighta been better for me if I hadn't spilled that particular tidbit, but I ain't *that* big of a crumb. They hadda right to know and to take steps, especially since we don't necessarily have the same protections from the nosferatu that you mortals do.

Fine, then. I'd tried to do it the polite and unintrusive way, but it was time for tougher measures.

"C'mon, Keenan." His desk was, if anythin', even more of a disaster area than it had been the other day. So was the good detective; if he'd looked any more all in from lack of sleep, I'd probably have heaved garlic at him or shoved a stake through *his* pump, just to be certain. "It's a good deal."

"How many times, Oberon? We all got strict orders about—"

"You know I'm good at my job." *Well, when I'm able to actually* tell *you how I solved a case, like when it don't involve bloodthirsty melons.* "You know I can keep my head closed around a secret. You need all the people you can get on this before it blows wide open. And I'm willin' to completely forego my *per diem* unless I actually dig up somethin' useful. I don't deliver, the department don't owe me a dime. What's to lose?"

It *was* a solid argument, under the circumstances, and he knew it. That just made it easier. When he drew breath to answer, I caught his gaze, slipped in behind his thoughts. All I hadda do was bump up his desperation a little, tamp down his concern about following orders to the letter. It really didn't take much; he was plenty desperate as it was.

"All right, Oberon," he said, shakin' his head as if he'd just remembered where he was. "I still gotta get the captain to sign off, but I think I can bring him around."

*And if not, I can always get you to let me jaw with him and convince him myself.* "Sounds good. I'll wait."

A short while later I was sittin' in an empty interrogation room, filling out some of the usual forms, and a couple of unusual ones, so I could look into the case all official and proper.

"Oberon."

I looked up as Detective Driscoll Shaugnessy poked his noggin into the room. I'd known it was him before he spoke, or even gotten to the doorway; the guy's hair damn near glows orange in the dark. I knew he meant business, too, 'cause his shirt-sleeves were rolled up even tighter'n usual.

"What's up, Shaun?"

"That's 'Detective Shaugnessy' to you until I says otherwise, pally!"

"Your moniker, your decision, I suppose."

"Damn right!"

"But why would you *want* people callin' you 'Otherwise'?"

His mouth stuck wide open and did this sorta weird twitchy thing on one side. Also…

"Your face is goin' red, detective." Don't get the wrong idea, me 'n Shaun have no beef, other'n him bein' just your generally unfriendly sort. He's fun to wind up, though. "You blushin'?

Was it something I said? Or are those freckles just annexing—"

"I dunno what sorta hot water you got yourself into this time, Mickey." Guess he was determined to get to his point—but I gotta admit, that point ain't at all one I saw comin'. "But whatever it is, get a handle on it. I don't need the fucking Bureau bargin' in here and gummin' up our day when we got our own messes to clean up!"

I carefully put down the pencil next to the form I'd been filling in and stood up. "Play that for me again, startin' with the first verse."

"You heard me, you—"

He was more interested in yellin' at me than explaining what the hell he'd meant, so back through the eyes and into the brain I went.

Turned out an agent from the Bureau of Investigation had been in here yesterday, pokin' around about me. Well, no, not investigatin' me personally; he'd made a big point of assuring everyone of that. No, he wanted information on who my connections were, who I was chummy with. "Known associates," as they say in the trade. Especially interested in anything new or changed in the recent past. He'd read up on Franky Donovan (what, you didn't think Four-Leaf Franky of all guys had a record?), Fino Ottati and family, Pete's service file. Even dug into Vince Scola and Saul Fleischer, two mobsters I've run into a few times but never once palled around with. Honestly, nobody from the Bureau shoulda been wise that I had any connection with 'em at all.

But then, I hadn't bought for one second the notion that this had been a real agent.

She'd done this before, you remember? Last year, though she'd been more specific, come in as part of the Bureau of Prohibition division. Basically the same glamour, though. No reason anyone here woulda tried to see through it, even if they could.

So, Áebinn was still lookin' into my contacts. Well, let her. I mean, yeah, I'd prefer she keep her schnozzle focused elsewhere, but as long as she was just reading and watching, probably no harm to be done. And it wasn't as if I could stop her anyway, not without sparkin' a conflagration we neither of us needed or wanted just now.

I didn't think she was gonna learn much, though. Pretty sure none of the people with files here were likely the source of whatever nastiness she'd sensed. Now, Orsola, maybe Baskin and his collection of mystical gewgaws he didn't know near enough about... Those mighta led her somewhere useful.

Maybe I'd even mention that, if we crossed paths again. *Bean sidhe* might have more luck finding the old witch than I did.

Shaugnessy had wandered off, probably to snarl at someone else, and I'd planted my keister back at the table, but the form was still half empty, my mitt near frozen around the pencil. Thoughts kept chasin' each other around in my brain like amorous squirrels, and I was too distracted to focus on the paperwork.

Orsola, Baskin, maybe even Ramona herself, with her hellish background... Who else? It itched at me, like a telephone or power line but all inside. I was missin' something. I knew it, felt it, picked and prodded and tried to grab, but it wouldn't come. A link I wasn't seeing or a detail I'd forgotten, something I *shoulda* had in front of me plain as day, and it *wouldn't come*. *Why* couldn't I bring it to mind?

The bulb in the lamp, the one they swing around and shine in ginks' faces when they're sweatin' em, was the first to go. It shattered with a sharp *pop*, almost like a tiny round goin' off. The one overhead that actually lit the room started to dim, and I heard half a dozen blowers out in the bullpen ring at once, all just slightly outta synch. The windows of the room fogged over, rivulets drippin' down to draw funny shapes in the condensation, even though the temperature hadn't changed a single degree.

This... was *not* good.

I clamped down, breakin' the pencil, and it all stopped

as quick as it started. I heard the buzz of voices across the clubhouse come over confused, takin' wild guesses about power surges in the lines and whatnot, worryin' if anything had been damaged.

Me, I had bigger concerns. Yeah, like I mentioned, that'd been happenin' more often in the past few months, maybe last couple years. But always, *always* when I was beyond furious, blood boilin' to the point where I teetered right on the edge of losin' control.

Not now. Sure, I'd been frustrated, but mostly I'd just been bewildered. And other'n that slight bit of aggravation, I'd been absolutely, completely calm. I'd been in total control.

And it happened anyway.

Rest of the paperwork was gonna have to wait. I hadda get gone, away from the precinct, get myself on the trail of whatever it was I was chasing.

Then hope to every heaven and hell that finding it and stopping it—Orsola's hex, the influence of death, *whatever*—was enough to put right whatever was goin' wrong with me, too.

# CHAPTER FIVE

Pete wasn't available, and I was in no mood to wait, so I let some random bull—Officer Netley, if I recall correctly, and I don't much care if I don't—play escort.

I mighta chosen differently if I'd known he was gonna drive us instead of takin' the L, but by the time I tumbled to that little fact, we were already on our way. No real good reason I could come up with to refuse, and I was too rattled over what'd just happened in the clubhouse to wanna fiddle with his mind if I didn't have to.

Nothin' for it then but to climb into his radio car, brace myself against what was comin', and muddle through it best I could.

He tossed me a queer look when I clambered into the back seat. "Occasional motion sicknesses" was the only answer I gave him, partly because I didn't figure "I'm allergic to the damn engine and I wanna be as far from it as possible" would go over real well.

We drove. It itched and hurt and burned, like it always does. I managed.

You seen one hospital you've seen 'em all, so I ain't gonna give you a full play-by-play of Cook County. It was all the usual; doctors and nurses in white, sick people in pain, smell of cleansers and soaps waging trench warfare against the stink of sweat and vomit and blood. I mean, don't get me wrong, it's mostly good folks tryin' hard, and it's a lot better'n facing a broken bone or flu without help, but that don't make it a playground, savvy?

Anyway, the hospital proper wasn't our destination. No, my buddy in blue flashed a badge here and there, and we made our way down.

Cook County Morgue.

Now this? This was *not* a good place.

I could yammer about the stark lighting, the cold tile and the colder steel drawers, the flat tables and ugly tools. Or maybe about the atmosphere, the pungent chemicals that made the hospital overhead into a fragrant patch of flowers in comparison. The artificial cold of the refrigeration? The lifeless eyes and limp flesh of the poor souls bein' worked on, sawed open, and stitched up all across the broad room?

Nah. See, all that's nothin', just what *you'd* notice. You're luckier'n me.

Death hung his hat in this room. Constant, unending death; sometimes violent, sometimes sickly, and far, far too often just plain ugly. The walls marinated in it; it bubbled and swirled in the drains. I could feel the ghosts, damn near couldn't move against the throng of 'em. Unhappy spirits, grieving or enraged, the kind who might, given time, grow corrupt from gnawing on their own fury until they slipped Sideways to add to the flocks of the *sluagh*. Or worse.

A bad place. An Unseelie place.

The coroner himself was part of the reason for that. A goddamn elected official, more concerned with holding onto his job than gettin' the pathology right; with makin' the cops happy than with truth or answers or justice. Good way to *really* enrage a whole mess of ghosts already on short fuses. Fortunately, he wasn't there at the time, which meant I didn't have to exercise self-control I wasn't sure I had to keep from sluggin' him.

One of the assistants, after a few minutes of whining argument with Netley about revisiting the same stiff *again*, and whether or not I was allowed to be there, shuffled to the stacked rows of drawers and listlessly waved us over to join him. The metal slab slid out with a dull rumble and a brief but angry squeak.

I'd insisted my police chauffeur tell me all the details of the case on the drive over; gave me somethin' to focus on besides the Hellspawned-toaster-on-wheels I was stuck in. Among those details was the fact that the body we were goin' to see was the seventh the cops attributed to this same killer or killers. They hadn't managed to stop word of the crimes from leakin' to the press, but they'd at least kept the extent of the problem under their hats for now. No sense, Netley had said, in sensationalizing it or causing a panic, especially when they weren't *positive* the deaths were all related. Same cause of death and same bloody mess, but no evidence that the victims had shared any other connection.

Yeah, I didn't buy it either.

Point is, the poor sap I was lookin' down at now was number seven, and if the others really had all been killed the same way, our problem was even bigger'n I thought.

See, unlike with the L King, this body'd been cleaned up, so I had a real clear view of the wound. His throat looked like he'd made a genuine effort at starting a new fashion trend of barbed-wire neckties.

No more question about it, no more dithering, no more hoping. We had a vampire. Hell, I could just about still feel the spiritual rot wafting off the corpse.

But I'd pretty much expected that. No, the problem was seven victims over the course of less than a few weeks. Savage and feral as they are, the nosferatu ain't stupid. They don't wanna attract attention, human or otherwise, anymore'n most creatures of the Otherworld.

Seven dead, so close together?

Odds were that was the work of more than just one vampire.

I stayed for a while, flipped through some other reports and checked a couple more bodies, just to compare wounds and make sure I was on the right track. Not fun, and ultimately not all that helpful. I couldn't really even use the crime scenes to try'n pinpoint the vampires' lair, not when dealin' with hunters who can turn into bats and fog and feed however far from home they damn well please in the course of a night. Yeah, I ruled out the edges, but it still left me with well over half the city.

Like I said, not real helpful.

Sun was makin' for bed by the time I moseyed my way outta there. I took the train back to my office, after politely but firmly refusing another ride in the torture box. I mean, the L ain't a barrel of laughs either, but after the flivver, it might as well've been a gentle massage.

Plus, it gave me time to think, though I didn't come up with much. Knowing for sure that I was dealin' with what I'd already *suspected* I was dealin' with was a nice bit of confirmation, but it didn't help at all with either the "why" or the "what to do about it."

Then I got back to my place and the time for thinkin' was over.

It washed over me soon as I stepped through the door, not even a wave but an avalanche. The cold, loamy smell of the grave. The stench of rotting meat. More than scents, they were emotions, a spiritual essence of corruption: the desperation of a suicide, the blood-wet heat of murder, the ache of famine and the dispassionate joy of a patient hunter.

Death and decay and terror and primal violation, draped over bone and wrapped in skin, squatting in a withered shell where a soul once shone.

*Vampire.*

I've always had plenty of swift, but I'm not sure I've ever drawn my wand fast as I did in that moment. I dove outta the doorway, hit the thin, trampled carpet and rolled back to my feet. I already had a slant on it, draped in shadow, waiting in the corner beside the filing cabinet. I sucked up what ambient luck I could manage in that split second of tumbling across the room and then I lunged, the L&G held underhand to stab, like a dagger.

Like a stake.

It ain't exactly sharp, but it's near unbreakable and I'm pretty strong. Maybe it woulda been enough. Maybe, if I'd had the time to draw on more luck than I did, or to pull that luck straight from the creature itself insteada the room around us, the blow woulda landed at all.

But I hadn't, and it didn't. The damned thing was fast, *so* fast. And a lot stronger'n me. The back of its hand hit me right below the wrist and my whole arm near went numb from the shock. I swear I felt bone *bend* a little, and the L&G flew from my fist to clatter against the wall before falling with a soft thump.

The vampire'd already moved, just a step or two, putting itself between me'n the wand, but I was headed another direction. I let myself fall backward to avoid the return blow I was expecting, but never actually came, and then rolled back to my feet once again. The dead thing was only a pace behind me, but it jumped away—more instinct, I figure, than actual worry—when I grabbed the edge of the Murphy bed, folded up against the wall, and hurled it down with a rattle and a crash right where my dance partner had been.

That gave me a second to reach inside the hollow behind the bed and pull out my trusty rapier. Steel wouldn't paralyze the vampire the way wood, uh, would, but with a little luck (well, okay, a lot of luck), I could cut him up bad enough to keep him down until I could get my mitts on the wand again.

My first thrust sank deep into the meat of the vampire's left arm, which earned me a hiss of dead breath ripe with the wet stench of a slaughterhouse. Unfortunately, I didn't get a chance for a second; its right hand came up, a hammer of cold flesh, and the Damascus steel blade that'd served me so well for a couple centuries snapped like a goddamn lollipop stick.

Oh, *now* I was steamed! I stared into its blinkers, tryin' to work fast; it ain't near as easy to get into the mind of another Fae as it is a human, let alone one of the dead, let alone one who's got its own mental whammy to throw back, but if I was quick *enough*...

It jumped back, clear across the office and only just missing the ceiling, before I could so much as tickle an idea. When it landed, it stared back at me but focused just past my left ear, not *quite* makin' eye contact. No bunny, this one. I tightened my grip on the hilt of the broken sword, ready to throw it and then make a dash for the L&G...

"Oberon, stop." Its voice was hoarse, the gravelly rasp of a thing speaking through stiff and shriveled vocal chords. "I do not come here for fight."

And I *did* stop, mostly outta shock. Vampires ain't unintelligent, but they're savage. Beasts. Ravening hunger and burning fury and cold hatred. Many of 'em don't speak at all, and I never heard of one actually talkin', or doing much of anything other'n killing or fleeing, once somebody'd started a scrap.

I studied its mug, bein' just as careful not to look into its eyes as it was bein' about mine. It was wan, gaunt, same as all its repulsive kind. Flakes of old, dried blood stained the creases of its mouth, spotted its yellowed collar, from gods knew how long ago. No fangs, not the way you're thinkin'; not the two neat little canines like Lugosi. No, every filthy, bloodstained tooth in its maw was jagged and broken, perfect for tearing skin and tissue. Not really any longer'n human teeth, but they looked it, since the gums had receded and the lips had shriveled, just as they would on any other corpse.

It looked, in short, not like some Eastern European nobleman or corporate high pillow, but like what it really was. What *all* vampires looked like.

A stiff that dragged itself outta the earth to drink people's blood.

And apparently it wanted to jaw with me. Swell.

"You broke my rapier."

"You stabbed me with rapier."

"I... Yeah, okay. Fair." I mean, I *did* make the first move. Sure, I'd had good reason to figure attacking was my best play—namely, that it was a *friggin' vampire*—but I hadda give it that.

Still watchin' for the tiniest funny move, I edged around the room to collect the Luchtaine & Goodfellow. Then, after makin' a deliberate point of *not* holstering the thing, I leaned back against the wall.

"So, if you ain't here to try'n rub me out, why *are* you here?"

"I am called Varujan." It—he; I guess if we were at the point of tradin' names and chinning like normal folk, I oughta go with *he*—also settled back against the wall, pretty much mirroring my stance across the room. "I come here to seek your assistance."

All right, then. If I'd had a list of possible answers in the order I was expecting 'em, that woulda been somewhere around page never, right before "Will you marry me?"

So, bein' the sharp private dick that I am, I replied with, "What?"

"I know of you, Mick Oberon, and what you do. You know this city, you know ways of both worlds, and you are detective. You are man to assist me."

Oy. This was gonna be one of those days where I really wished I drank more than milk.

I wasn't ready to believe so much as a word of it, but then, I was still thrown by the fact that I was *hearin'* a word of it.

"Before we even get into this," I said, partly because I needed to know, sure, but also stallin' for time to think, "tell me why I shouldn't just put my wand through your heart and saw your damn conk off with a shaving razor? There are *eight people dead*!"

"Eight is not so many." Then, before I could blow up, "But I kill none of them."

"Fuckin' horse feathers!"

"No, is truth, Oberon. I am in Chicago only short while. Here, I do not yet feed."

If the undead bastard's plan was to make me trust anything he said, he was way, *way* off track.

"I'm not swallowing that, bo." Yeah, maybe not the *best* expression to use with the nosferatu. Whaddaya want from me? "You walkin' corpses ain't exactly numerous. Even if I believe there's more'n one of you in Chicago, you're gonna find it real tough convincing me you ain't all part of the same pack."

I dunno, maybe I was lookin' to pick a fight. There's nothin' about vampires that ain't evil, unnatural. It *felt* wrong, made everything and everyone around it grimy with suffering and death. I was near choking on the rot in its aura. I'd be doin' not just myself, but the whole world a favor if I put the damn thing down.

And then...

"But you have already encountered another. A vampire, but not of my kind. Not of my 'pack.' I smell this, a smear on your... essence. Yes?"

He wasn't wrong. I'd just about blown it off, it was so ludicrous, but I hadn't forgotten.

"It was bad fruit. A friggin' watermelon."

"You have met many vampires who hunt with watermelons beside them, Oberon?"

I shook off the image of a bunch of nosferatu creeping through the woods with melons on leashes, like rolling green bloodhounds. I wasn't ready to accept it as coincidence, them all appearing within days of each other, but I hadda at least consider the possibility that they weren't all together, either.

"Fine. Spin me a yarn, Varujan."

"Yes."

He paused there, and the room went silent as... Well, you know. I mean, neither of us tensed, paced, fidgeted, even blinked. The undead gink didn't even have a heartbeat.

"It begins some days ago," he finally continued. "I am on freighter, crossing Lake Michigan. I have fed before boarding, so crew has no reason to suspect I am aboard. And I wish to keep it this way, yes? If they learn of me, or suspect anything amiss, this will be inconvenient."

Oh, well. Glad to know he's capable of choosing not to murder if it's *inconvenient*.

"But after a time, I begin to hear... I am not sure how to say. A call. A *summons*. But it is not so much a sound at all. I hear in head, not in ears."

He had my attention, now. If this was goin' where I suspected it was, combined with everything Áebinn had been yammering about, we were *all* in dutch.

"I think, I can ignore this. The call, it is not so strong. But I have never felt anything like this before, and now I am curious. Obviously, I cannot leave the boat on my own..."

Interesting. Not that he couldn't just cross the lake by himself; running water, vampires, all that. No, it's that he just assumed I was already wise to the limitations of his kind.

"...so I cannot leave the crew alone anymore. The captain, he is easy to convince, and so we follow the call. And it brings us here, to Chicago."

"And did you kill the captain after mesmerizing him?" I tried to keep my tone nice and friendly, but I won't pretend I succeeded.

"This would draw attention I do not wish. I tell the captain to forget me."

Well, that was nice to—

"I feed instead on one of the deckhands. The crew will wonder what happened to him, but not so much attention as the captain. Less attention in the city, also, if I do not need to feed for a time."

The L&G was startin' to hurt my fingers, they were clenched so hard.

"I find nothing useful. The call is faint. Hard to locate, like a sound you can barely hear, yes? But many people speak to me, tell me truths they might wish to hide, and never remember me. From them, I hear of you. Mick Oberon, exiled lord of the *sidhe*. A detective who knows the Otherworld and this one. This man, I think, can track down the call. He can satisfy my curiosity; more, he can tell me if this poses any danger to me or my kind. And so, I am here."

"There are magics," I told him, "incantations in old grimoires, necromancies mortal and Fae both, that can summon vampires…"

Varujan was already shaking his head, an oddly human gesture. "I am old, though not so old as you. I have felt these spells before. This call is different. Weaker, and yet… Deeper? More… maybe best word is 'primal'?" He shrugged, which looked as out of place as the nod. "I do not truly know how to say."

"Figure out how to say this, instead. Why the hell should I help you?"

The bastard smiled, showing those awful jagged teeth, and *that* looked perfectly natural on him. "Because already you investigate this. You try to find this murderer, and you already think maybe he is another like me, drawn by the same summons. In addition, you look into a magic or power reeking of death, and you wonder if that, also, is related to what I have told you. You will keep doing what you do and tell me what you find, and I will assist where I can."

Well, shit. Who *had* he been talking to? Clearly he'd tracked his way back to at least one of my nonhuman contacts. No real sense gettin' steamed at 'em for spilling; if he'd put the whammy on 'em, it ain't as if they had a choice, or would even remember doing it. Still, I wasn't thrilled with how much he'd dug up.

He wasn't wrong about where my own train of thought had gone, either. But while he mighta guessed the questions I was pondering, he had no way of figuring that I was already working on a theory that could answer 'em.

Wasn't about to tell him that, though.

"Well, I got good news and bad news for ya, sport. The good is, yeah, this ties in with everything I'm already diggin' into. I can promise you I'll do my best to suss it out, and assuming I do, you got nothin' more to worry about."

"And this bad news?"

"The bad news is, no fucking way I'm working with, for, or even near one of your kind. You've made an effort not to kill in my town, and you came to me, so I'll let you walk or flap or waft out that door. But listen good, pal. You be outta Chicago before time comes for you to feed again, because if you hurt one soul in this city, I will find you and I will put you back underground so deep you'll have to climb to reach Hell."

I was all set for him to blow his wig. He'd already shown about a million times more patience than any other nosferatu I'd known. He was gonna erupt in a burst of rotted fury, come at me tooth and nail. I had the L&G set to go, I'd gathered my will to draw as much luck and power from him as I could in a single blast...

Nope. All he did was smile one more time. "You think this now, Oberon. Soon you will think otherwise. Then, we will speak again."

One second he was there. The next the doorway was clouded with a chill mist that poured into the hall like water, flowed out past the phone, and was gone.

Guess it wouldn't be nearly melodramatic enough for him to just walk out the damn door. But at least the room didn't make me feel as if I was chokin' on worms and grave dirt anymore.

I took a few moments to enjoy the usual stench of the city leakin' into my office. Spent longer at it than I should, frankly; needed the time to wind down. I'd been steelin' for a squabble with the undead, after all. It ain't duck soup comin' down from that kinda anger—or fear, if I'm bein' completely square.

Wasn't until I finally stood up that I realized I was still clutchin' the L&G, either. I stuck that back in the holster, finally took off my coat, and then collected the broken blade of my rapier.

Spent another few minutes just starin' at it. I'd carried that sword a long time, and it'd seen me through a lotta different fights and more'n a couple actual wars.

Fuckin' vampire.

I went to my drawer of oddities and stuck the two broken halves in there, alongside the various other meaningful or mystical dinguses I'd collected over the years. This wasn't one of my weird instincts, where I feel like somethin's gonna be important down the road. I just didn't wanna get rid of it.

When I started to feel the urge to empty out the whole drawer so I could organize and catalog the whole assortment, I knew I was stalling. I had a trip to make, and I wasn't too eager to get going.

I shut the drawer, stepped to the filing cabinet, and rolled up my shirtsleeves. Like I said, I'm stronger'n most of you, but not by *that* much. This was gonna be tough.

Took a few minutes of shoving and rocking the stupid thing back and forth—woulda been a lotta grunting and sweating and cursing, too, if… Well, you know—but I finally scooted the damn cabinet far enough over for me to squeeze in behind it.

Moving it revealed a hole I'd knocked in the wall the day I'd first moved into Mr. Soucek's building. My own little hiding spot, a hollow where I'd stuck a few odds and ends I'd hoped never to need but knew better'n to throw away. What I was after—a long, thin bundle wrapped in rags—was right on top, so I shouldn't have to dig through any of the…

Except it wasn't right on top, not quite. Sitting on it was a small sliver of wood, maybe two inches long. It was a sorta shimmery white in color; naturally, I mean, not with paint or cause of age or anything.

How in the Dagda's name had *that* gotten there? That cabinet hadn't been moved in years. Had I dropped it in there myself? If so, why, and why the hell couldn't I rememb—

The electric fan squeaked once and started slowly rotating backwards. Out in the hall, the blower gave off a single half-ring, and over in the bathroom, the mirror cracked loud as a .22. Above me—you guessed it—the light bulb flickered and dimmed.

*Calm. Calm, Mick. Settle down. Calm...*

One last stutter, and the bulb steadied back to normal. The fan slowed and stopped. And I was left gawping like an idiot, piece of wood in my hand.

Twice, now. Twice that'd happened when I wasn't angry or on the verge of losing control. What was *happening* to me? No way this was just a product of that bad luck hex I'd been battling, was it?

I hated to put it aside, hated not having answers, but I wasn't gonna dig up any right now, and ruminating on it was like as not to cause more problems. Bein' real careful not to think too much about it, I put the chunk of wood back in the hole and retrieved the parcel I'd been goin' for in the first place. Setting it on the desk, I went back to my supplies and gathered up a few things.

Whether the hex was Orsola's or not, whether it was responsible for those "episodes" or not, I'd only held it at bay by taking the proper steps. Probably time to renew those, just in case.

So I swept the room, widdershins (that's counterclockwise to you), then whisked the dust and carpet fibers out the door. Filled a pocket with acorns, saved from spring, and tossed salt over my left shoulder in four different directions. And so forth.

Hopefully, what'd happened with the mirror didn't properly count as *me* breaking it. That'd be an extra dollop of misfortune I didn't need.

All that rigmarole taken care of, I shoved the filing cabinet back where it was supposed to be (more or less), and finally, after one last minute of procrastination, unwrapped the parcel on my desk.

One of my last heirlooms of home. I mean my *first* home.

It was shorter than the rapier by a fair bit, but broader—at the base, yeah, but especially near the tip, where it flared out in almost a leaf-shape. Didn't have much of a cross-guard, just a horseshoe shape marginally thicker than the blade itself. Not a bit of steel in it, or even iron (not that I'd be wielding an iron weapon anyway); iron hadn't even been discovered when this was forged. Pure bronze, except for the wooden hilt, but with enough Fae enchantments worked in to make it sharper and stronger than modern steel.

Students of Celtic history woulda had a field day with this. Me, given the memories attached to it—not just of what I'd done with it, so long ago, but who I'd been—I'd hoped never to see it again.

I gave it a quick once-over, even though I knew the magics woulda protected it from damage even after so long, then shoved it back in the scabbard and strapped it on under my coat. Double-checked the L&G in its own holster, and then there was nothin' else but to do it.

I walked over to the mildew-cornered nook on the other side of the office and stepped Sideways.

# CHAPTER SIX

And here I was again, one of my least favorite places in two worlds.

Wasn't *quite* as crowded as last time I'd visited, thanks to the heavy snows, but that just meant the din was deafening as opposed to lethal. A lot of the throng was mortal, their expressions just a bit slack, living in the semi-dreamworld Elphame becomes for most humans dippy enough to eat or drink anything they're offered. They hauled crates or ran messages or undertook whatever menial tasks their Fae "masters" couldn't be bothered with.

Good number of Fae here, too, though. Joint like this had too much importance to leave most of it up to slaves. (No, the folks here don't much care for it when you call their mortal pets "slaves." Can't say I much care what they care for.) Fae of every imaginable type and size, from twelve inches to twelve feet; two legs or four; hands and tails and wings; skin and hair and fur and leaves; speaking and shouting and singing.

All Seelie, though, except for a few important prisoners.

Everything you'd expect from Chicago's City Hall.

Well, *our* Chicago's City Hall.

And in all that hubbub, all that crowd, all that mix of the weird and the wild and the beautiful and the hideous, take a wild guess at who got the most stares.

No, really. Guess.

Don't get me wrong, it ain't like my reputation is so widespread that *everyone* here knew me. Just enough of 'em to make me downright conspicuous.

That was just swell, though. For once, I wanted to be noticed.

I stood at a massive mahogany desk in the entry chamber, facing off with City Hall's receptionist. A leprechaun in dapper glad rags and gold-rimmed specs, she was either the same secretary I'd bumped up against last time I was here, or looked enough like her they could be sisters.

Assumin' I could judge by the look of utter revulsion that flickered behind her glasses, the sorta expression normally reserved for finding a dead roach or pixie in your omelet, I was gonna take a stab at the former.

"Heya, doll."

"No. Please leave."

"You ain't even heard my question."

She sighed—which I knew was a deliberate show of contempt since, like us *sidhe*, leprechauns don't normally do that—and folded her hands real neat atop the desk. "Very well, Mr. Oberon. Ask."

"Any chance of me seein' either Judge Sien Bheara or Chief Laurelline? I know it's usually months to get an audience, but this is pretty urgent."

"And that's your full request?"

"Uh, yeah?"

"So, may I answer now?"

"Yes. It'd be expected, even."

"No. Please leave."

Well, I walked right into that, didn't I?

And this was why I didn't so much mind having drawn attention on the way in. Last time I'd needed to visit with one of the high'n mighty of Chicago's Seelie Court, I'd basically caused enough of a ruckus to bully my way in. No reason not to give it another shot.

Sure, last time I'd been tryin' to see one of the lower judges, not their Majesties themselves, but then, this time I had more'n just my own charming self to work with.

"Look, sister..."

"Am I going to have to call security, Mr. Oberon?"

"They're gonna want to see me." I wasn't shoutin', but I made no effort to keep my voice down, either. I knew, even in the din, that a good chunk of the room around us could hear me just fine. "It's about Áebinn's investigation. That's a big deal, ain't it? They put their best dick on it, even sent her to the mortal world. Surely they wanna know what I've learned."

"Mr. Oberon—"

"And I gotta figure, they want it kept hush-hush, since they sent *only* her and not a whole team, like last time. They're bein' subtle—for them, anyway."

"Mr. Oberon!"

"Or, I dunno, maybe they *didn't* send her. Maybe the great Detective Áebinn's gone rogue, and the Court don't know from nothin'. Gotta figure *that'd* be embarrassing, if it got out. But hey, we can keep on jawing about it. Every soul here can be trusted, right? Ain't as though anyone could possibly have any political motivations to wanna take their Majesties down a peg or..."

I felt 'em looming behind me before any of 'em said a word.

"...two." I turned, slow and careful.

One was a spriggan, like Slachaun over at the Lambton Worm, only this gink was bulkier and kept his wildwood of a beard under better control. Slightly. Currently, he was at or near his full size, towerin' over me by close to four feet.

The other was shorter'n me, half the spriggan's current height. He wore a hood, but I saw just the tip of a long nose and a thick beard pokin' outta the shadow, and even though he hadn't laid a finger on me, somethin' about him just felt... hard. Solid. Like he was just the visible protrusion of something mostly spiritual and far weightier than you could even imagine.

*Haltija*. More specifically one of the *vuoren väki*, the folk of the mountain, a guardian of the hills and the stone. Probably the specific stone used to construct City Hall, in this case, which woulda made him somebody I could probably handle without too much trouble anywhere else, but not someone I wanted to tussle with right here.

"Right. I'll just shove off, then," I said.

"Indeed," the receptionist said, and she wasn't enough of a pro—or she just didn't care—to hide the gloating in her tone. "These gentlemen will accompany you in case you need any help... shoving."

They continued not sayin' a word, just shadowed me to the revolving door and watched as I stepped back out into the gentle snowfall. And then they *kept* watchin', I guess to make sure I kept on ankling. No real chance of slipping back in around 'em, and even if I had, I wasn't sure what good it'd do. Looked like I hadda come up with something a lot more subtle than the direct approach.

Maybe tryin' to take this to Sien Bheara or Laurelline wasn't even the smart move, but I couldn't figure a better one. I needed someone with *real* deep knowledge of magic and history both to tell me if I was even on the right path, or if this whole line of investigation was a trip for biscuits. The notion I'd come up with was downright ludicrous, but... Varujan's mysterious summons, the presence of other vampires all at once, the damn watermelons... Nothin' else fit. I *hadda* know if it was even feasible.

No way in hell I was goin' to the Unseelie with it, not without knowing how they were already wrapped up in this, not when I already owed Eudeagh. And while a few other Seelie probably had the lowdown I needed, I didn't wanna come outta this owing *them* any debts, either. With the royals, I could at least make the case that we needed to cooperate for the good of the city, wouldn't have to approach it as a personal favor.

But that wasn't gonna fly if I couldn't even get in to see 'em.

I'd gotten maybe half a block and was still ponderin' options when somebody appeared outta the gray and the snow beside me. *Aes sidhe*, like me, but a lot younger. And under his heavy flogger I could see the same formal getup that was common to the fulltime staff and errand-runners of City Hall.

"Follow me, please, Mr. Oberon." The invitation came only after he'd taken a quick glance around, as if he was checkin' to make sure nobody—or at least nobody important—had a slant on us. Since I had nothin' better to do, and he'd piqued my interest, I followed.

He led back in the direction I'd come, or near enough to it. We took a small side street, approaching the Hall from the side. Eventually he stopped before a stretch of marble that looked no different than any other stretch of marble, and traced a pattern in the striations with a fingertip.

Nothin' obvious changed, but he motioned me to follow once more, and then stepped through the stone like it was just a thick mist.

Well, well. I'd guessed there hadda be secret ways in and out of City Hall, but I'd never figured on actually seein' one, let alone usin' it.

But I did, and after a few more passages and twists and turns that ain't worth the words to tell, I found myself in a fancy sitting room. Sofas with goose-down cushions, mahogany table with decanters of gold and silver and crimson fruit juices, bookcases stocked with hand-illuminated tomes dating back longer'n most countries.

Not that I had any time to plop down on my keister and relax, since I wasn't alone in the chamber. "Chief" Laurelline, queen of Chicago's Seelie Court, was waiting for me.

Do I need to tell you she was beautiful? Of course she was. We're Fae, she's royalty, and we don't do anything by halves. Hair of spun sunlight, emerald eyes, willowy but full of strength, blah, blah, blah. You've heard it all in fairy tales.

It was an empty beauty, though, at least to me. Cold. Like a work of art rather'n a person.

Whatever else she was, though, she was old, magical, and wielded more power among the Fae than anyone I'd dealt with since my cousin's own Court. I bowed—deep, with a flourish, and only a tiny bit of it was sarcastic.

"Your Majesty."

She was having none of it.

"I should have you arrested and locked away for three hundred years!" Her voice... Well, it matched her looks.

"Uh, for what?"

"For being an aggravation!" I swear she near hissed as she took a step toward me. "You've spent too long with the mortals, Oberon. Don't forget which world you're in now! We might *prefer* to have a legal reason to imprison you, but we don't actually *need* one!"

Least she actually called me "Oberon." Lotta the high pillows in the Seelie Court don't much like that I took my cousin's name, refuse to use it. Hell, she probably wasn't thrilled with it either, but she always was real big on etiquette.

"Okay, true," I said, "but then you wouldn't learn what I know."

"Oh, you would talk. Eventually."

Wow. She was *really* steamed.

"Maybe. But not anytime soon. And when I did, I wouldn't be in much mood or condition to help you with the situation, would I?"

"We don't need your help, Oberon!"

"Sure. Which is why I'm standin' here in your private meeting room behind the secret passage." Then, before she could *really* blow her wig, "Come on, your Majesty. I ain't part of the Court anymore. I got no pull here, so there's no need to save face with me. Let's cut the hooey and just get to the part where we figure out how to work together."

Laurelline remained still, a scowling statue, for almost half a minute, before… "Fine. Sit. Have a drink, if you wish."

She musta seen something on my mug, a flicker of doubt I couldn't quite hide, or maybe she just caught a whiff of it in my aura, 'cause her scowl deepened. "What do you take me for, Oberon? I am not one of the Unseelie thugs with whom you are far too comfortable keeping company. I do not play such trickster's games."

I couldn't help it. I still hesitated.

Fire flashed in her eyes—and I ain't bein' metaphorical—but she nodded. "Very well. This repast is offered without condition. Eat and drink freely, and owe me nothing in return."

What's that they say? It ain't paranoia if they really are out to get you?

"Thank you, your Majesty." I sat and poured myself a glass of something made from a fruit you never heard of that's been extinct for centuries.

It tasted like apple juice.

I mean, don't get me wrong, really, impossibly *good* apple juice. But still apples.

She, too, took a glass, swirled it around a bit and then took a real dainty sip. Refreshment as theater. I couldn't wait to leave.

I also decided I couldn't wait for her to decide the most dramatic way to start grilling me.

"So, is Áebinn workin' for you on this? Or is she harin' off on her own? I've never known her to work without a team before."

The queen's—sorry, "chief's"—peepers narrowed, and I think she mighta imagined crushing me with her eyelids. "Everything Detective Áebinn does is on behalf of the Seelie Court."

That was not only not an answer, but it was more or less the same not-an-answer I'd gotten from the *bean sidhe* herself. We were off to a roarin' start, here.

"With all respect," I started, "if you're not gonna—"

"You are here to answer *my* questions. Then, if I feel it in everyone's best interests, I may answer yours."

I was startin' to get irate. Was a time even she'd never have talked to me that way, and yeah, I'd given all that up of my volition, but… "That may be why you had your lackey fetch me back, but it ain't why I came."

"Why you came is of no…" She paused, frowned, gently placed the glass on the table. "All right, Oberon. Why *did* you seek me out, specifically? You've involved yourself in Court affairs quite often of late, but you've never demanded a royal audience."

"Because there ain't many people with the know-how to tell me if this wild theory I've come up with is a total load of malarkey, or if there's even the tiniest chance I'm onto something. You or his Majesty were the ones I figured could do it, and not to tie me up in a web of favors in the process."

"I see." Another pause, then, "Tell me everything."

And I did. I mean, I left out the stuff with the Ottatis, but I spilled pretty much everything else. Áebinn and her death visions—which I figured Laurelline probably already knew, but described anyway—along with the other weirdness around town, the bodies, and finishing up with Varujan.

She looked troubled by the time I was done, which was good; she *shoulda* been troubled. None of it could mean anything positive.

"And this theory of yours?" she asked.

This was the tricky bit. If she decided I was nuts, I wasn't gettin' anything more outta her. But I hadda know if it was possible.

"Vampires," I started, "are sorta 'half Fae.' They're the bodies—"

"I know what vampires are, Oberon!"

I raised both hands, palms forward. "I know you do, your Majesty. I don't mean to offend. But please, follow me through this. My notion's pretty much rooted in their nature."

"Fine. Go on."

"Human bodies that die by real emotional violence, particularly suicide, occasionally leave themselves open to inhabitations by a certain kinda Fae spirit. Or bodies killed by other vampires, of course. When that essence inhabits the corpse, that's when it rises, with access to some of the person's memories but a totally new—and completely predatory—soul.

"Now, we know that a rare few necromancers, real powerful ones, have developed rituals to summon or even control vampires. But this ain't one of those. So...

"Is it possible for someone to have developed magics to summon or control the *spirits*? The essence of what would *become* vampires?"

Laurelline stared at me as though I'd just wiped my nose on her unmentionables. "That's insane."

"You sayin' it ain't possible, then?"

"Oberon, those spirits... For all practical purposes, they aren't real! They have no separate, measurable existence, no being, no personality, no power. They are little more than fragments of a larger body of pure etheric essence! You speak of the equivalent of summoning and describing a nightmare before a mortal has even dreamt it! Yes, the potential for that specific nightmare exists in his thoughts, but as a thing unto itself, it doesn't exist yet!"

"I get that it ain't probable, ain't easy. That it's never been done, that we may not have the slightest notion how it *could* be done. But with everything you know of magic, everything you've learned, seen, even heard of, down to the most basic fundamental theories... By the remotest stretch, in the craziest and wildest circumstances, is it *possible*?"

"No! It's..." She trailed into silence. For the first time since I'd walked through that door, her Majesty seemed to shrink just a touch, and for a couple of seconds, she wouldn't meet my gaze. "I honestly don't know."

Well, it meant I didn't have to start all over from the beginning just yet, but tellin' you square? I think I'da been happier if she'd stuck with *no*.

"But even if I concede that such a thing is feasible," she went on, posture and tone both firming up again, "that hardly means you're pursuing a viable lead with this... this fantasy.

It's never been done, there are no known ways of doing it, and it would hardly even accomplish anything! Such magics would still provide the sorcerer no real control over the resulting vampires. What would be the point?"

"I dunno yet. Maybe it's just step one. There are *other* necromancies that offer some influence over vampires, yes? But either way, I don't figure it's near as improbable as you do."

"And why is that?"

"One," I said, ticking 'em off on my fingers, "we got a call that, accordin' to our firsthand witness, only nosferatu can hear, but which ain't strong enough to compel 'em to do anything. Two, we got enough dead bodies to suggest a small handful of vampires in Chicago, but they ain't all part of the same pack, which is pretty near unheard of. Three, watermelons. Vampire friggin' watermelons, your Majesty. Something so damn rare even I thought it was pure hokum, and which is only even a *myth* in one tiny slice of Eastern Europe. And four, whatever spooky death magic your housebroken *bean sidhe*'s been sniffin'. All in Chicago, all in a matter of a couple weeks.

"So maybe it's a spell per se, and maybe it ain't, but I'd say *something's* attracting those pre-vampire spirits in abnormally large numbers, yeah? I can't really see how anything else fits the facts."

Laurelline, prim and proper queen of Chicago, looked as if she wanted to spit. "No," she admitted. "No, I suppose I can't, either."

We each took a few more gulps of our drinks, absorbing what'd been said.

"Very well, detective," she said, dabbing at her lips with a silk— yeah, silk—napkin. "How do you recommend we proceed?"

"Well, it just about goes without saying that we gotta determine who's responsible, and why."

"Yes, it does."

Heh. "To start with, we're probably lookin' for a mortal occultist. I mean, we can't rule out the Fae, and it'd be dippy to make too many assumptions, but just playin' the odds, our bad guy's more likely a human."

"And how did you come to that conclusion?"

"Because, like you said, this ain't ever been done before. And when you're dealin' with a brand-new idea, well…"

All I could do was shrug as she glowered at me. Sure, some individuals are exceptions to the rule, but it ain't any big secret that we Fae, as a whole, are more mimics than innovators. You only gotta look at how we structure our society, the whole ridiculous "municipal government versus organized mobs" setup the Seelie and Unseelie Courts got goin' in Chicago, to see that. Guess maybe it ain't considered polite to openly talk about it, though.

"Presuming that to be the case," Laurelline said coldly, "it would require a mortal with a frighteningly in-depth understanding of mysticism and the occult. Are there truly those on the other side of Chicago so knowledgeable and so powerful?"

"Yeah, some."

Orsola Maldera was my suspect number one, of course. No surprise there. But would her whacky religious notions even let her interact with vampires and dark spirits? She'd all but dismissed *me* as some kinda unholy monstrosity—I mean, even before we started tryin' to croak each other—but I didn't have the first idea how that crazy old dame's mind worked.

But I couldn't let myself get too fixated, and she wasn't the only possibility. Dan Baskin had himself enough old writings and grimoires and potent relics that he coulda stumbled across something dangerous, something he was too much of an amateur to understand he shouldn't mess with. And what about Saul Fleischer? I'd only bumped up against him the once, over Nessumontu. I had no real idea how powerful his Kabbalistic magics were, whether he'd even be capable of somethin' like this.

And nuts, those were just the three I knew about. Coulda been others; *probably* not, but I couldn't rule it out. Or it coulda been a Fae after all, one with a more creative bent than most of us and a penchant for spiritual or death magics...

I was startin' to get a headache.

"What would it take?" I asked. "For someone to pull this off, I mean?"

"Hmm." I let her ponder on it for a spell. Uh, so to speak. "The specific ingredients could vary dramatically, as long as they had potent symbolic connections to death or undeath. Bones, grave dirt, old funerary wrappings. Blood, of course. The list is long."

"So, no way to track someone down based on that, then."

"Unlikely." More pause for thought. "Sacrifice, almost certainly. A human life. Probably multiple lives, actually. I can't say for sure, not knowing precisely how much power a ritual of this sort requires. Also not much help, I fear, unless you believe you can pick out a ritual sacrifice from among all Chicago's violent murders."

"I'm good, your Majesty, but I ain't *that* good."

"Shocking. The location of the rite would also be of significance, I should think. Equally as symbolic as the components. A graveyard would be the most obvious choice, but hardly the only one. A church or other place of religious importance, no longer hallowed, for instance."

I couldn't help but be reminded of the battle with Orsola in the charred ruins of Santa Maria Addolorata. Yeah, I didn't wanna get too caught up in my assumptions, but this was definitely soundin' more and more like her kinda shindig.

Laurelline's tone hadn't changed as we'd gone through the possibilities, but she was gettin' agitated. Talented as she was at suppressing any sign of her inner feelings, I could feel it in her aura.

"What's buggin' you, your Majesty?"

"I keep coming back to the fact that if we're right about what's happening, we are dealing with an occultist not only of great knowledge, but great imagination. Someone willing to attempt magics that have, so far as I know, never been tried. And who is willing to deal with truly dark powers. I greatly dislike the notion of someone like that running unchecked in my city..."

*Your* city?

"...but even more so, I worry a great deal over what might happen if this person makes a mistake."

Oh, now there was a cheery thought.

"There is already," she finished, "enough going on in Chicago that I do not understand."

Was it my imagination or had she peered my way just a bit more intently when she said that? Was she talkin' about something I was involved in?

Was she talkin' about Adalina?

When the hell had my life gotten so complicated?

Since that wasn't a topic I was too eager to pursue, I made up a few more questions to ask about this hypothetical "vampire spirit spell." We tossed around some more notions, built up a few theories, none of which made any notable difference. Bottom line was, we'd hashed out about everything we could. There was nothin' else for it but for me to see if I couldn't dig up some solid dope, try to turn some of these theories into fact and hope that led me to a "who," or at least a "why" and a "what next."

I put down one more drink, made my polite obeisance and farewells, and was halfway to the door when...

"Oberon?"

I stopped, turned. "Your Majesty?"

Hard as she worked to conceal it, hesitation and uncertainty added a bitter tang to her aura. If she'd been human, she'da been clenchin' her mitts, or maybe workin' her jaw without sayin' anything.

"I am... concerned about Áebinn's involvement in this affair."

"How's that? You said she was acting in an official capacity."

"Indeed she is, but she has become, ah, unduly obsessed with this case. It was she who first brought the issue to our attention, first reported the deathly essence she had sensed, and even then her eagerness to pursue it was a bit startling. I felt the same from her when she pressed for permission to pursue the matter into the mortal world. She has been brusque in her communications, and has missed several scheduled reports. It is unlike her, to say the least."

Yeah, I'll say. Normally, when it came to rules and procedure, the *bean sidhe* detective was wound tighter'n a *dvergr*'s pocket watch.

"I appreciate the tip-off, your Majesty. Uh, I think. *Why* are you tipping me off, your Majesty?"

"It's not a decision I make lightly, Oberon. But I've no idea *why* Áebinn is so consumed with this case, and with her in a potentially compromised state—and assuming we're correct in our conjectures—I'm equally uncertain as to how she'll react to an opponent this unpredictable and outside her experience."

"Okay. Sure. I can dig that. But I still don't quite get why you're admitting this to—"

"Because you need to be ready to step in and finish the job if she can't, or to clean up any… residual damage. Now that you've involved yourself in this matter, and now that I've taken the time to assist you with it, I expect you to act on behalf of the Seelie Court should it become necessary."

I didn't figure that "not interested" would go over real well, and it ain't as if she was wrong. I *had* involved myself. So, "Yeah, all right. I'll make sure this doesn't blow back on you guys if I can manage it."

"Good."

I was three-quarters of the way to the door, when…

"Oberon!"

I stopped again, turned again. "Yes, your Majesty?"

Now she was all business, her aura the same cold and near-colorless wall it usually was. "This is twice now that you've bullied and brayed your way into an audience with someone of power and influence in the Court without going through proper channels. That's two more than most are permitted, and it is the *last* that *you* will be permitted. Attempt it again, and I do not care what the circumstances may be, you *will* face the justice of the Court and find yourself imprisoned—at best.

"You may go."

That last was blatantly unnecessary, since I'd already been on my way out, but I didn't guess pointing that out was a wise choice. Didn't much think she was kidding about the consequences if I pulled a stunt like this again, either.

Not having anything else to say that'd do either of us any good, I made for the door a third time and skedaddled.

I was maybe half a mile on from City Hall, head'n shoulders covered in a light dusting of snow, when I saw 'em rumblin' down the street and headed my way.

Black carriage. Tarnished silver trim. Dark-haired and mean-eyed horses that, from what I could tell at this distance, might or might not've been kelpies.

I've mentioned before, it ain't unheard of to find Unseelie in Seelie territory, or vice-versa. Diplomatic missions, or Fae on separate sides doin' business, or even an occasional friendly chat; you find all kinda weird pals and relationships between the two sides. It's rare enough, though, to catch your attention. Especially when you just happen to be in the middle of an investigation that just happens to involve big names in the Court and you also just happen to have tussled with a few redcaps not all that long ago.

I walked faster. The carriage kept closing.

I turned off the main avenue. The carriage turned after me.

Nuts.

It still *coulda* been coincidence. Those tend to follow me around, especially with that hex always lurkin' in the background no matter how thoroughly I'd warded myself against it.

On the other hand—the more probable hand—they coulda been gunnin' for me. No way they'd openly attack me this deep into Seelie turf, but an attack wasn't the scariest possibility.

They mighta been here to call in my marker with Queen Mob.

At best, that meant Eudeagh wanted something big from me, something that I probably wouldn't wanna do and that'd take me away from this mess with Áebinn and the vampires longer'n I could afford to be away.

At worst? She wanted me to help her out on something to do *with* the case—or with Adalina. And no matter the consequences, I'd hafta do it, or make myself oath-breaker.

Real, *real* nasty things happen to Fae who violate a sworn oath. Nasty enough that, if I hadda choose... I might just do anything, including handing the poor changeling girl over, to avoid it.

Think less of me for that, if you want. You got no idea. You truly don't.

Fortunately, that still left me one option.

I ran.

I ran like I couldn't remember ever running, churnin' up a spray of snow behind me. I ducked down every narrow alley, anything I thought was tight enough that the carriage couldn't follow. I made wild, random turns; jumped a few fences, clambered in a couple windows. I even burst through the back door of some poor brounie's apartment, knockin' over his dinner table, and then out through the front. His *cu sidhe* buddy chased me a few blocks, barkin' his schnozzle off, before he decided it wasn't worth the cold on his paws.

I felt... I ain't sure how to describe it. A cold drag on my soul, like a chill breeze tuggin' at me instead of blowin', and I shivered. Even just trying to avoid letting them call in the oath this way was dangerous, could just maybe draw the attention of the nightmarish things that would inevitably follow if I actually broke my word.

But I kept on goin', and it faded after a few.

Maybe the Unseelie just hadn't planned on me lamming off that way and I'd caught 'em by surprise, or maybe they didn't know where to find the toadstool ring that marked the Path back to my office in the mortal world. (I hoped it was the latter. I made a point of tryin' to keep that particular ring secret, but you never know.) Or hell, maybe they weren't after me at all, it really had been random luck, and they were sittin' back in the center of town marveling at the rattle-brained *sidhe* who'd just fled at the mere sight of 'em.

Whatever the case, though, they didn't have anybody waitin' between me and the way home, which left me in the clear to get my keister outta Elphame and back to my office, my desk, a *massive* glass of warm milk, and a whole lotta unanswered questions.

# CHAPTER SEVEN

You got any friggin' idea how many cemeteries there are in Chicago?

Me neither. I ain't counted. But I can tell ya it's a whole bunch, and the vampires' victims weren't concentrated enough in one place to narrow it down much.

Hell, it might not've even been a cemetery I was lookin' for. Coulda been an old church, or a massacre site, or a dozen other delightful sorta places. If I hadda search each of 'em one by one, and hope I found or picked up on somethin' at random, then the "deathly magic" Áebinn had sensed was gonna be me putting my wand to my head and offing myself to escape the tedium.

Probably best to find another approach.

I noodled over the idea of starting with Orsola. She still felt like my best suspect. But I didn't *know* it was her, and after I wasted so much time hunting Goswythe earlier in the year, I wasn't gonna let myself get fixated on another assumption. Plus, it wasn't as if I'd had any success in finding her so far, anyway. No, helpful as it'd be if I knew who I was gunning for, I hadda keep my mind open.

So, the next morning, after another round of salt and other protections—plus a big slug of cream to fortify myself—I gave Detective Keenan a ring on the blower.

The call was brief and not helpful. Three more bloody murders, just in the two days it'd taken me to visit the Otherworld and then start my search. He'n the whole damn department were scrambling, tryin' to keep a lid on everything, and he didn't have a single lead to offer me. Told me I could give the scenes an up-and-down if I wanted, but it'd have to wait until the cops were done with 'em. He'd let me know.

And once he *did* let me know, givin' 'em the once-over proved a big fat waste of time. I learned exactly squat.

All right, what next? Didn't see a lotta choices in front of me, so—much to your surprise, I'm sure—I went out trawling for the usual gang of lunkheads. *Again.* No, none of 'em had given me much to go on earlier, but I knew more, now. I wasn't just askin' over Áebinn or some nebulous "dark powers." Now we had vampires, weird magics, and these violent killings in the mix. Much better chance one of my contacts or informants had heard *something*.

And it was still preferable to pickin' random graveyards off a map.

Problem was, Franky wasn't at the first of his usual haunts. Or the second. Or the third.

He hadn't said anything about going dormy last we'd spoken. And yeah, he ain't always the easiest mug to find, but this felt hinky. I started to worry a little.

Then the bartender at one of Franky's favorite dives, a place as dark and dingy and generally sleazy now as it'd been during the height of Prohibition—maybe even more so—told me he'd been in yesterday, lookin' jittery. Hadn't stayed long, just put down a single hard drink, asked if anyone's been poking around after him, and left.

Now I was worrying more'n a little.

I knew most of Franky's hidey-holes, and I checked 'em all as fast as the L and my own two hocks would carry me. Nothin'.

People started to avoid me on the street, either 'cause of my expression or the dark emotions rolling around in my aura, heavy enough for you lot to feel even if you'd never recognize the sensation for what it was. I know I talk tough about Franky, and I've had to get rough with him a time or two, but he was one of my people. If something'd happened to him, someone would pay with a lot more'n a pound of flesh.

So where would Four-Leaf Franky go if he was in really behind the eight ball? Well, usually to me, but that hadn't happened. Where else, then?

Ah. Or *who* else?

Before long, I stood before a rickety door in a dirt-caked and piss-scented tenement, one of the poorest in the poor neighborhood of Canaryville. I rapped a knuckle on the wood, tryin' to make sure I didn't accidentally knock the damn thing in.

It felt a *lot* more solid than it looked. Even more solid than it'd been the last time I was here.

No answer, except a quick waft of what smelled like soap-suds. 'Sokay; I hadn't expected one.

"We gotta go through this every time, Lenai?" I asked through the closed door. "You know I can get in if I want. I just wanna talk. To both of you."

"Both of who, jackass?" The wood between us made her voice sound that much hoarser and scratchier than it already did. "It's just me! You think I have a gentleman caller?" She punctuated the question with a wheezing cackle, to heighten the absurdity.

"I get along with him okay, but I wouldn't call him a gentleman."

A moment of silence, then, "Go away, Oberon!"

"Open the door, or I will."

"Why can't you just leave u— me alone, you cocksucker?"

I don't want you to think I was gettin' any joy outta this. On the square, I felt like a bully. For all the profanity, I heard some real upset in her tone.

"Because it ain't about what I want, or what you want, Lenai. If I could afford to walk away and let you be, I would.

Quicker we do this, quicker I'm outta your hair."

A few harsh whispers, which I pretended I didn't hear, then the scraping of furniture—guess that's why the door felt solid—and finally the clicking of the lock.

The tiny dame glaring up at me with murder in her peepers looked to be on the younger slope of middle age, which was a problem. Lenai normally appears to be older'n dirt and worn as shoe leather. She only starts gettin' younger when she's really stressed. Angry...

Or frightened.

"Get the fuck inside if you're coming, ball-wrinkle!"

I did just that, and the first thing that hit me was the scent. Not the general miasma of the building, not even the soapy washerwoman smell that usually accompanied her, but the garlic.

Whole strings of it, draped around the apartment like bunting. I also spotted half a dozen crucifixes tacked to the wall, and one on the side of the door. An old broom leaned against the doorframe, and the end had been snapped off and sharpened.

Hmm.

I also smelled a faint trace of old, dried blood—not that I needed it. I could taste the pain radiating off the figure sprawled out on Lenai's mattress.

"Nice of you to take him in," I said, not turning back to her as she relocked everything up behind me. "Didn't you call him a 'gold-sucking clover-cock' last time he came up in conversation?"

"I'm sure she did," Franky said weakly from beneath the blankets. "She's called me a lot worse. But she meant it in the nicest way."

"Fuck I did," Lenai grumbled. "Meant every word, and whole lot more I never got around to."

I stepped a bit closer so I could examine his battered face, his swollen jaw, and the jagged lacerations across his cheeks, neck, and shoulders. "What happened, Franky?"

"He tripped!" Lenai insisted before he could answer, stomping over to the bedside. Franky said nothing.

"Tripped?" I stared, first at them, then at the garlic, the crosses, the sharpened broom. "So, you, what? Got careless and took a tumble down a flight of vampires?"

Franky muttered something unintelligible. Lenai got another five or so years younger.

"He doesn't want to get involved, Oberon," she said—pleaded, almost.

"Take a good look at him, sister." I tried to sound sympathetic, but I hadda keep pressing. "He's already involved. And those wounds? That ain't the face of someone they're finished with."

"Fuck you, jackass!" But it was aimed down at her feet, not directly at me.

Didn't seem any reason to keep arguing if she wasn't gonna fight anymore, so I turned my attention back to Franky. And his wounds. "Shouldn't those be bandaged?"

"They were when he got here," Lenai said. "Filthy, too. We were just changing them."

*Just?* He'd been here a while; the rumpled sheets, and the blood stains that'd long dried in 'em, spoke to that. I raised an eyebrow.

"Well, we might've been arguing for a spell. That might've slowed the process down."

Eyebrow stayed up.

"He won't hand over his goddamn chains!" she finally screeched.

"I'm lost."

"My gold chains," Franky said, reaching up with a fingertip as though to make sure they were still around his neck. "Daffy broad wants to melt them down to coat the bandages!"

"She…" I was gonna get dizzy if I kept twistin' around between the two of 'em this way. "Why would you do *that*?"

For the first time, her mug came over uncertain insteada irritated. "I thought… Franky's part leprechaun, right? Gold's supposed to be good for them!"

I take it back. I was gonna get dizzy regardless. "They're

sure fond of it," I agreed. "Even take some comfort in touching it. But that's it, Lenai. They don't, I dunno, feed on it or have it running through their veins or whatever whacky notion you had. Where the hell'd you come up with *that*?"

She grumbled at the floor again. Most of the words weren't clear, and the ones I could make out all started with F.

"Lenai? Dollface? Would you kindly go bring some clean bandages and some alcohol for poor ol' Franky?"

"I'm going, jackass, I'm going!" But she was starting to look older again, which was good. While she puttered around and collected what we needed, I turned once again back to Franky.

"Spill," I ordered, gently as you *can* give an order like that.

"Not a lot *to* spill, Mick." He winced, wriggled around tryin' to find a position that didn't aggravate one injury or another, then gave up. "I got word someone'd been asking around after me, so I was already nervous last night. He caught up with me couple hours before dawn."

"Vampire," I said. It wasn't a question, so he didn't bother to answer. Then, "Wait. Askin' for you, personally?"

"Name and description both."

Son of a bitch. "So he knew all about you."

"Well, not *all*. I think he expected me to be human. It threw him when this—" he waved at the worst gash on his neck "—didn't kill me. That hesitation's the only reason I got away." Maybe sayin' it out loud made it real, because he started to tremble.

"It's okay, Franky. You're safe." I looked again at the various defenses Lenai had put up. "Probably more here'n anywhere else."

"Still, if I hadn't been so close to her place, or if she hadn't let me in…"

"She'd always have let you in. Lenai's got a good heart."

"The fuck I do, grass-cock!" drifted sweetly from the kitchen.

"Somewhere," I added a lot more quietly. "Probably in a jar."

Franky laughed, then winced again.

At which point the lady of the house returned. She poured a good portion of rotgut leftover from early Prohibition down her guest's gullet, which near made him choke, and another good portion over the wounds, which near made him scream, and finally got to work with the bandages.

"Not so tight!" he wheezed as she wrapped one around his neck. "I still have to breathe!"

"If it'll keep you from yapping your damn fool head off, you'll just have to learn to do without!"

Unfortunately, I didn't really have the time to wait until he was in better shape. "Can you describe the vampire, Franky?"

"Uh, dead? I dunno, Mick, it was a damn vampire!"

"Man? Woman?"

"Still going with 'dead.' Who can tell?"

"You ain't helpin' much, here."

"Gee, I'm real sorry. Next time, I'll ask the undead for ID before they try to suck me dry like an orange."

Guess I couldn't really blame him. It *could* be kinda hard to tell, and I'm sure he had other concerns. "How tall was it? Taller than me? Taller than you?"

"I don't... Wait. Shorter. Shorter than me, anyway. I remember it reached *up* when it backhanded me." Again he gestured to a wound, this time the shiner and split skin around his left blinker. Lenai barked at him to stay still, only she took a lot more words to get the point across.

"Good man. Not quite useless after all."

Shorter'n Franky meant we weren't talkin' about Varujan. The nosferatu who'd visited me'd been a pretty big boy. Markedly taller'n me, and Franky only had me beat by an inch and change. (Here in the mortal world, anyway.)

Another vampire. Another vampire who'd deliberately tried to rub out a friend of mine.

And suddenly I wondered if the L King's death had been a coincidence. Two vampire attacks against people I knew? Not-entirely-human people I knew, to boot?

That definitely sounded like the work of a certain witch. I wasn't quite ready to scrawl Orsola Maldera's name in my own blood as absolutely positively bein' the mastermind behind this affair, but I'd definitely moved up from pencil to ink.

"Just need one more thing from you, then."

Franky gave me directions to where he'd been jumped, and I made for the door. "Take care of him, Lenai."

"Fuck no. I've just been cleaning these disgusting wounds and bandaging him and sheltering him to see the surprise on his shitty face when I let him die."

"Ain't too late to come with me, Franky. The vampire might be easier."

"Don't tempt me."

I walked out and headed for the stairs, the sound of furniture scraping and thumping back against the door in my wake.


The vampire'd gone after Franky in an alley behind one of the many elevated train stations, but I didn't go straight there. Figured I'd have a chat with the attendant inside first, see if he'd seen anything helpful. Turned out he had, but not in the way I'd expected.

"I only came on shift a couple hours ago," he explained, after first tellin' me to buzz off so he could deal with payin' commuters, and also after I'd gotten into his noggin and juggled a few of his emotions and attitudes like bowling pins. "But you ain't the first one here askin' about a carrot-top with gold chains and cheap glad rags."

"Oh?"

"Yeah. Night before last, had a real live Bureau of Investigation agent in here, gunnin' for the same guy."

Well, well. What to make of that? I could drum up reasons why a vampire mighta been after Franky, but what on Earth— either of 'em—could Áebinn want with him? Hell, I still wasn't thrilled that she knew about him, or my other contacts, at all.

Had she been lookin' for me? I had stepped Sideways for a while…

Ah, nuts. One thing at a time. I'd ask her when I saw her. Right now, time to go spend what would doubtless be several wonderfully scented minutes examining an alleyway.

Yep. Grimy bricks, trash-and-glass covered cement. A real pungent bouquet of wet newspaper, rotting food, flivver exhaust, oil from the nearby trains, spilled alcohol, and stale piss. And the charming company of bugs still willing to brave the chillier weather.

I managed to find a bit of dried blood, and I forced myself to stick my schnozzle close enough to smell that it wasn't entirely mortal. I mean, I'd figured it was Franky's, but I'd hadda make sure, see?

Now that I had, though, I wasn't sure what to do with that knowledge. It wasn't pointing me anywhere. I needed—

The lovely perfume of the alleyway vanished beneath a thick blanket of pungent rot. I spun, hand under my coat.

"Varujan." No way this was coincidence, not even for us Fae. "I don't much like bein' tailed."

"Pleasant evening, Oberon." Ignoring my complaint, the corpse stepped out into the dull yellow light of a nearby streetlamp. It didn't make him any prettier.

"It's morning. Dawn's in a couple hours."

That ugly rictus smile again. "It is dark. This is evening enough for me."

"Swell. What parta 'get the hell outta my town before I put you under it' was too tough for you to understand?"

"I understand all this. *You* do not understand that we must cooperate in this matter."

"I don't fuckin' think so. Especially since it's been a couple days, and three brand spankin' new stiffs, since we talked. You gonna try and tell me you *still* ain't fed? That none of those bodies were your doin'?"

"I will not try to tell you such things, no. But only one.

We all do as we must, Oberon."

I had the L&G in my fist before I even thought about it. "Yeah, we do. For instance, I made you a promise, and I 'must' keep it. All over you."

"I understand." But he was already fadin' away, turning into mist again. "You will wish you had my assistance tonight. Maybe after this you listen." The last was a whisper, echoing between the brick walls, and he was gone.

Dammit! I was gonna have to be quicker next time, put Varujan down before he had a chance to—*why hadn't the smell of decay vanished when he did?*

I dove for the pavement, hard, but I didn't have quite enough swift to pull it off. Something sharp and painful and *ugly*, like an infection given form, raked across a shoulder blade, sending me skidding through the grease and gods-knew-what-else, to fetch up against a broken wooden pallet. My wand went skittering, because that woulda just made it too easy, wouldn't it?

And for a second, all I could think was *Not* another *coat! Nuts to buyin' in bulk, I oughta buy* stock...

I scrambled upright, hissing in pain as something feverish raced through the wound and across my already blood-streaked back. I drew the old leaf-bladed sword and dropped into a fighting stance I hadn't assumed in centuries, but was still etched into my muscle memory like the Commandments in stone.

The vampire hissed back, unfortunately not in pain. About the width of a nickel shorter'n me, I think it *mighta* been female at one point, though between the sunken flesh and patchy hair, tattered rags and old bloodstains, I honestly couldn't say for sure. No wonder Franky'd had trouble.

"Okay, ghoul o' mine. You as chatty as your pal Varujan, or we just gonna get right to the—?"

It lunged, moaning some kinda awful, dirt-gargling rasp. Fine, then.

I met it halfway, blade spinning. Given how bad I was

already stiffening up, I'm pretty proud of landing the first clean shot. It leaped away, howling, clutching an arm with the opposite paw. A watery black soup—almost a photo negative of fresh pus—oozed from the cut.

Didn't slow for long, though. It came right back at me, put me on my heels, and it was all I could do to keep it at bay. On a good day, I'd have plenty of swift to match it, but with that gash in my back, I wasn't exactly running with a full team in harness.

Sword and jagged nails flew, and we circled around each other best as the cramped confines of the alley allowed. Every move was agony, but I ignored it. I had no choice.

I got in a few more cuts, wet the blade with more of that grotesque drainage, but nothin' near as deep or as telling as the first. Meanwhile, my arms were startin' to resemble the side of a cat's favorite sofa. Trickles of blood ran over my fingers, threatened to make my grip on the sword dangerously slick.

This vampire wasn't dumb, either. At one point I suddenly fell back, movin' to make a grab for the fallen wand. It jumped, nearly flew, over my head with a screech worse than the braking of the L, stuck briefly to the wall, and landed between me and my goal.

Fuck.

I tumbled to somethin' else, too, somethin' that didn't make me feel any better about my situation. All the little wounds on my arms? They weren't there because my arms were all the vampire could reach. Its stance, the angle of its strikes... It was trying to hurt me, not rub me out.

I hadn't a clue as to why, but it sure couldn't mean anything good.

Would I have been a goner if it'd meant to kill me? Wish I could say. Maybe I was doin' well enough to cling to this immortal coil, or maybe not. Ain't the sorta thing I enjoy not knowing, either, but there it is.

The dancing and circling and striking and defending and just generally struggling not to be shredded into *aes sidhe* confetti dragged on for… well, probably just a minute or two, but it sure seemed to be forever. And comin' from someone old as me, that's sayin' a lot.

But I knew I hadda make a move, somethin' the nosferatu didn't expect, or this wasn't gonna end well. So I fell back again, this time away from the L&G. It followed, of course, but not as quickly; it didn't figure it had any reason to rush. Until my foot came down right on the spot where I'd fallen when this whole mess started.

I made a sudden lunge, just enough to startle it and drive it back, buy me an extra second. Then I reached down to the pallet I'd smacked up against earlier and snapped off a jagged length of wood.

Its dry yellow peepers went wide as it saw what I'd done, watched as I switched hands to hold the sword in my left, the stake in my right.

I don't guess it was having fun anymore.

You can kill a vampire with a sword, sure, but only if you behead the thing and destroy the body afterward. Possible, but not easy, especially if you're too slow to get inside its guard like I was that night.

Stake through the pump, though? Not as simple as it sounds, but quicker'n easier than the alternative.

It hiss-screeched at me one last time—just hadda get the last word in, I suppose—and then, same as Varujan'd done, faded away into mist and vanished into the early morning darkness.

Leaving me a bloody, agonized lump that wasn't gonna accomplish squat hangin' around here—or anywhere else, tonight. I sheathed my sword, collected my wand, and started my long and aching journey back home.


I think the most painful part of the trip was the constant jumping at every bump and clatter, the efforts to watch every direction at once—kept tuggin' at the open wounds. I couldn't help it, though. The vampire had meant to hurt me, and it'd succeeded.

But I still didn't know why. Which meant it coulda been a setup for absolutely anything.

Which meant I hadda be wary for absolutely anything.

Staggered off the train, staggered a couple blocks to Mr. Soucek's building, staggered down the stairs. Starting to become second nature, staggering. The whole way, nobody'd so much as given me a dirty look—or any look, other'n the occasional gawker who noticed the big bloody rents in my flogger—let alone started anything. On the other hand, I'd damn near given myself a permanent crick in my neck tryin' to pull an owl act the whole way, so maybe I'da been better off if someone had just taken a poke at me.

Slowed up as I was, it took me over an hour to get home, even though the mornin' crowds hadn't really built up yet, and my back and arms weren't feeling any more pleasant when I reached my office than they'd been in the alley. If anything, the burning was gettin' even more feverish.

I'd known it was comin'. Unnatural wounds like these, they weren't gonna heal up near as quick as any mundane injury. Me expecting it didn't do jack to make it any less painful, though. I needed time and rest, and…

And judgin' by the fact that the horn started ringing off the wall the literal minute I fumbled my key into the office door, I wasn't gonna have an easy time catchin' either.

I near ignored it. Probably woulda, if I'd taken time to mull it over. Last thing I needed right now, on top of everything else, was the discomfort of puttin' that diabolical contraption to my ear. Still, I answered. I could tell you that was because I was worried it might be somethin' urgent, given how many plates I had in the air. But the fact of it is, my noodle wasn't workin' quite right, and all I could think was *I gotta shut the goddamn thing up*!

"'Lo?"

"Hello, Mick? It's Bianca."

"Yeah. Yeah, it is."

"I see." Silence, then, "Fino wanted you to know, he doesn't think Saul Fleischer's your man. He's out of town right now, and has been for weeks. New York. Something about a meeting with the Five Families."

"Good. Great. Thanks. Good." She was still on the line, though. "Anythin' else?"

"I just… Well, we haven't heard from you, and we wanted to see if you'd learned anything."

I nodded, even though I meant *no*, and even though it ain't as though she could see me anyway. "About what?"

"Um. The Unseelie? Watching our house? Their possible interest in our daughter?"

"Oh, right." I nodded again, or maybe shook my head. I dunno. I did something involving my neck. "Yes. Yeah. No."

"Mick? Are you all right?"

"I'm fine," I told the carpet. Then I wondered why I was yammering into the carpet and not the blower. Then I decided I didn't care and went to sleep.


So again, bein' entirely square with you, I hadn't handled that well.

No, I don't mean the damn phone call, though I pretty obviously didn't handle *that* too neat, either. I mean the undead Broderick I'd been handed.

Vampire wounds are a nasty business, but I coulda mitigated *some* of it. Coulda dosed myself up with luck and a touch of ambient magic, taken the edge off 'em. But I was so outta it in the alley, between the injuries and all the questions racin' around in my noggin, that I hadn't thought of it until I was on the train. The pain made it hard to concentrate—too hard for me to be near as subtle as normal. I wasn't about to perform any obvious hocus-pocus in fronta witnesses; I'd decided I

could put up with it until I'd gotten to my place. And then…
well, maybe if I hadn't been interrupted, I'da had a chance to
deal with it before my body took it outta my hands.

Point is, I'd been off my game, bad. Still was, some, when I
woke up. Which is why…

No. I'll get to it.

When I woke up, first thing I saw was a ceiling. Real
fascinatin', right? 'Cept of course that I'd been peepers-deep
in carpeting when I went night-night. And this sure wasn't the
ceiling of my office, or anywhere else I recognized. (Though, to
be fair, I dunno that I *would* recognize too many ceilings. Just
ain't my area of study.)

Place didn't feel or smell familiar, either, though I recognized
a few scents. Alcohol, milk, and the Ottatis among 'em.

*Goddamn it, they didn't!*

I turned to get a slant on the room, and sure enough, they had.

I was laid out on the sofa of a pretty swanky living room.
Handful of over-cushioned chairs and a small table stood
nearby, and all of 'em—including the cushions under me—
were pretty new. A radio, also young enough that I doubt it'd
ever belted out more'n a hundred tunes or so, huddled in the
far corner. I could feel even at this distance that it was not only
off, but unplugged, which I appreciated. A few just-starting-to-
wilt flowers here, a colorful curtain-tie there, and some newly
hung crucifixes added a touch of home.

We were in an apartment, not a house. Even if I hadn't been
able to tell that by the tiny sliver of view permitted by the
curtains and the autumn rain, I'da known just from the weight
of the walls and the general feel of the room.

The whole Ottati family was gathered around me; Adalina
paced while the others sat, Fino with a drink in his mitt, Bianca
clickin' beads of her rosary, Celia with a book unread in her lap.

"Mick!" Guess she'd seen my eyelids flutter open. Adalina
was at my side in an instant, on one knee beside the sofa, glass
of milk held out in offering.

"Better be," I said, "or we're *all* gonna be confused. Slow down, doll." I forced myself to sit up, tried to pretend that didn't make my back—my bandaged back, I realized as I felt the tugging—scream like it was being sawed in half. Only when I was up and sure that I wasn't about to topple over did I take the glass, tossing it back in a few quick swallows.

"Thanks," I told her, and then looked over her head at the others. "Fino?"

"Yeah?"

"Are you *completely* outta your head?"

"Good to see you, too."

"We talked about this! We—"

Bianca leaned forward, her beads falling silent. "We didn't know what else to do. You stopped talking, I heard you hit the floor…"

"So you drove straight to my place, where anybody coulda shadowed you back!"

"I know how to shake a fuckin' tail," Fino said. "We weren't gonna just fuckin' leave you, *capisce*? And with you not even bein' human, it ain't like we coulda just dropped you at a hospital."

I took a deep breath—to show them I was tryin' to calm down, since that don't come natural to me. "I get that. I even appreciate it. But I didn't wanna know where you were holed up!"

"You still don't. You weren't exactly alert on the way here. And yes, I've fuckin' thought about the trip back. We'll, I dunno, blindfold you or somethin'."

"I'm a detective, Fino. Even knowing you're in an apartment, what floor you're on, I could—"

"Mick, you can be a real fuckin' *stronzo*, ya know that? I ain't an idiot. I got a handful of properties all over this town, under fake names and fake businesses. Trust me, I don't wanna be found, nobody's fuckin' finding me. Not the law, not the North Side Gang. Not even you."

I figured he was underestimating me, but hell with it. I was already here, and while I was startin' to improve some, I still hurt way too bad for me to wanna argue it. So I just nodded. "All right. Fair. And thank you."

"You know, as many enemies as Goswythe made," Celia said suddenly, "you've been beaten up in two years more often than he ever was in sixteen."

I stared at her. Her tone, her expression, even her damn aura... I honestly couldn't say if she was just makin' an observation or takin' a shot at me.

And I was a little startled, to boot. I'd almost forgotten she was there. She never actually seemed to have much to say when I was around.

Her parents were lookin' about as puzzled as I felt, and Adalina's jaw was twitchin', so I said, "We all gotta have our hobbies."

She tossed me a shallow smile that couldn'ta said "I'm humoring you" more clearly if she'd tattooed it on her lips, and didn't comment any further.

"Any chance you could bring me a little more hair of the cow, sweetheart?" I asked Adalina, to keep her from blowin' her wig at her sister.

"Of course." The glass was full and in my fist almost immediately.

"So what happened, Mick?" Bianca asked, after I'd taken a quick slug. The question had been floatin' in the air since I woke up. Guess I oughta be impressed they'd been patient long as they had.

Fino was nodding in response to his wife. "I've seen you beat up, but never fuckin' wounds like that!"

"Heh. You shoulda seen me when I got shot in the head earlier this year." Then, before they could ask, I went into it. They deserved some answers—especially since I had none for 'em regarding their own problems—and I figured there was no harm in it.

What the fuck did I know, right?

So they got the story, about Áebinn and her premonitions,

about the vampires and their connection to the murders. Even told 'em that I didn't see any obvious way this could all be tied up with the Unseelie staking 'em out, or any danger to Adalina, but I couldn't swear they were unrelated, either.

It was Adalina who asked, voice small and frightened. "Who do you think is doing all this? What do they want?"

And gods help me, I answered.

I told you, I was hurtin'. I was still out of it. I had a million things I was tryin' to keep track of, to put together and get straight in my head.

That's not a justification, it's an explanation. I'm tellin' you how I could make such a fool move, but I ain't tryin' to excuse it. It can't *be* excused.

Maybe, someday, I can at least forgive myself for it, for everything it led to.

"Can't be sure," I said, "but I'm figurin' Orsola's still my best bet."

I didn't even realize what I'd just blurted out until I felt the air drain from the room, saw the expressions on all four mugs starin' down at me.

*Aw, fuck.*

"What are you sayin', Oberon?" Fino asked, barely more'n a whisper.

I opened my yap to claim I was still disoriented, that I'd misspoken, hadn't meant to say her name. Opened, and shut it again.

They weren't gonna buy it, not a one of 'em. I didn't have to taste a lick of their emotions to know it. All lyin' to 'em would accomplish was to make things worse.

I don't think I slumped down into the sofa, but I sure felt as though I should.

"I think your mama's alive, Fino. You remember I was tryin' to track down Goswythe, make sure he wasn't gonna come after Celia or any of you? The trail led me to Orsola's grave. The bones in her coffin are the *phouka*'s, not hers."

Celia gasped, a rush of mixed shock and relief, but the others scarcely noticed.

"You dug her up?" Fino carefully put his drink on the table. The golden liquid was still sloshing, his grip'd been shaking so bad.

"It wasn't her, Fino."

"But it coulda been. And you never said a word."

I gotta tell you, for a guy who ran as hot as he did, the fact he was bein' so quiet, that he hadn't thrown in a single "fuck," was a scary sign.

"I wasn't sure that—"

"When?"

Goddamn it, I'd really hoped it wouldn't occur to him to ask me that.

"Fino, you gotta understand—"

"When?"

Nothin' for it. Maybe I shoulda lied, but... "A few months back. Right around when Adalina woke up."

"Months. A few months."

Still no shouting, still no cursing. Shit, this was bad.

He pushed both hands into the armrests, leveraging himself up and outta the chair like a man twenty years older. "I trusted you. I called you *mio amico.*"

"I *am* your friend, Fino. I..."

But I was talkin' to his back, and then to nothin' at all. He vanished from the room, and a minute later the front door slammed shut.

"Celia," Bianca said, "go after your father. I don't want him leaving in this state."

The girl swallowed a scowl and ran.

"Bianca." I don't like to think how close I sounded to begging. "You *know* how he got when his mother was concerned. I hadda be sure, hadda figure out what she was up to, before—"

"I understand, Mick," she said, flat and distant. "I get why you thought you had to keep it from us."

Not "why you had to." "Why you *thought* you had to." Oof.

Celia returned shaking her head. "He's already gone, Mama. I can't find him."

Bianca nodded dully and stood. Her rosary dangled from a clenched fist, seemingly forgotten. "I'm suddenly very tired. Please stay as long as you need to recover, Mick."

"Bianca…"

"Good night."

Another disappearance, another closed door. Celia followed a moment later.

Left just me, and Adalina, still kneeling beside the sofa.

I drained the last of my glass of milk. "That went smooth. Don't you think that went smooth?"

"What's going to happen now?" She sounded miserable, poor kid.

"Look, your father'll be back once he's had time to cool off. I gotta keep diggin' into whatever the hell's going down, especially if it involves you at all, but I'll find a way to make things right. You got nothin' to worry about."

She tried to force a smile, then gave it up as a bad move and just shrugged. "I'm not sure I believe that."

"Yeah, I probably wouldn't, either. I honestly don't know, Adalina. Your, uh, peculiar nature may be a bigger deal than I thought. If the Unseelie are still interested in you—or interested again—I gotta figure they've tumbled to somethin' about you I ain't yet. And that it's something others are gonna be interested in, too, if they catch wind of it. I'll do everything I can to keep you safe, but… well, you may be lookin' over your shoulder a lot more'n we'd hoped."

Adalina squeezed her peepers shut tight, then nodded. "Thank you for telling me the truth," she said, standing. "About this, anyway."

"Wait. Whaddaya mean?"

She'd already turned away. "I always knew there were things you weren't telling me, Mick. To protect me, or so I wouldn't worry. I didn't much care for that, but I accepted it.

"But now? Now I feel like I can't trust you to tell me even when I need to know. To recognize when it's time to *stop* keeping secrets."

And with that, she was gone, too, leavin' me alone, in the dark, in the living room of a family that used to call me friend.

# CHAPTER EIGHT

I dusted outta there late the next morning.

I wasn't near a hundred percent yet, but a good night's sleep—well, a night's sleep; wasn't much good about it—had fixed up a lotta what ailed me. The rest just needed time, and a bit of luck-slinging with the L&G, which I wasn't about to do around the Ottatis. They didn't need me muckin' with their fortunes any worse'n I already had.

And I needed to get away from them, figure how I was even gonna start makin' things square. Especially with Adalina. Not trustin' me could get her into all sortsa dutch, maybe more'n I could ever yank her out of.

Woulda been easier if I was someone who deserved that trust, but whaddaya gonna do?

Yes, I left on my own, which means yes, I knew where they were layin' low. Somehow, askin' Bianca to arrange a ride for me didn't feel like the wisest course of action just then.

After hoofin' it a few blocks, so I wasn't in quite such a fancy neighborhood, I stopped in at the first clothing shop I could find that didn't look to be *completely* outta my price range. Picked out a shirt to replace the one the Ottatis had wrapped me in while I was out (it didn't fit that well), and a coat, to replace the ones the vampire'd shredded. And then a second coat because I figured I was gonna need a spare. (My sword drew some odd looks from the salesman, but I stared soulfully into his eyes and made him forget about it.) Got to the counter, found out they were still outta my price range, had a conversation with the salesman where we once again stared soulfully into each other's eyes—I was gonna have to buy him flowers at this rate—and then they weren't outta my price range anymore.

Yeah, I know. It ain't a trick I pull much, but you do what you gotta do, right? Besides, the country was still in a depression. They shouldn'ta been charging so much, anyway.

Got myself a paper—no murders in the last day, or none the newshawks had caught wind of, anyway—and made my way back to the office, just to check on everything.

Nothing to check on. No mail of importance, no scrawled notes, no clients waiting, and if anybody'd tried to reach me on the payphone, neither Mr. Soucek nor any of the other tenants had taken a message.

Not that they often did.

I went inside, did some ritual salting and sweeping, waved the Luchtaine & Goodfellow overhead a few times, and felt a tiny bit better. So now what?

Still had no leads on the vampires, and I wasn't any more eager to start diggin' around random cemeteries than I'd been yesterday. Still no leads on Orsola, either, and after gumming up everything with the Ottatis, that wasn't a topic I wanted to spend too long mulling over. Yeah, I'd have to, sooner or later, but right now I was votin' strenuously for "later."

What I *could* do, though, was do some sniffin' around to determine if I could rule out any of my *other* suspects.

Which meant I was gonna have to bump gums with someone *else* who was real sore at me, but hell, rate I was going, trying to avoid everyone I'd irritated would mean just hibernating in my office for a decade or two. So I slung my new flogger on and headed back to the L.

Since I'd gotten a late start leavin' the Ottatis, crossed town to get home, spent a long while puttering and dithering around the office, then crossed town *again*, it was already within spitting distance of evening by the time I got where I was headed. I stood soaking my Oxfords in a puddle left from last night's rain, examining a swanky-but-not-*too*-swanky redbrick house that I'd never had much interest in coming back to.

Lights were on, but I didn't see much movement, so I headed for the door. Got about halfway when it opened up and she came out to meet me, as slinky and "poured into her dress" as ever.

"Evening, Ramona."

"Mr. Oberon."

And us with no audience, this time. Yeah, this was startin' off swell.

"So, um."

"So?"

All right, direct route. "How's about you let me take a quick look through your boss's digs? Just so I can make sure he ain't summoning vampires to Chicago or otherwise playin' with dangerous necromancies? Y'know, for old times' sake."

If nothin' else, I had the pleasure of knowing, just from watching her blink, that I'd completely knocked her for a loop.

"You know," she finally said, "I genuinely can't tell if you're serious or not."

"Yeah, honestly, me neither."

She nodded, then stopped short like it was some kinda slip, and crossed her arms. "Either way, you must already know the answer to that."

"Yeah, but I'm an eternal optimist. Ramona, please. I just gotta be sure, and I can cross him off my list and not bother you again. If that means sneaking in while you and Baskin are out, you know I can pull it off."

"I wouldn't be so sure. We've improved security since you were here last, and I don't just mean the bolts on the windows."

"I'm sure you don't. Ramona…"

"Please leave now." She started back up the walk.

"They're goin' after my friends."

"What?"

"They cut Franky up somethin' bad. The L King's dead. The Unseelie've been watchin' the Ottatis, and I got no idea if it's connected or not." I shouldn't have been spilling all this to her, but it was building up inside, and—even after everything—we still had a connection. I just didn't know what kind, anymore. "I don't really figure Baskin for my guy on this, I just hafta make sure! I'm not gonna lose anyone else over this, dammit!"

"And does that include me, Mick?" she asked—not softly, exactly, but less stiff or angry than I'd heard in a while.

"I don't know." And whether I was tellin' her I didn't know if whoever this was would come after her, or that I didn't know if we were friends at all... Well, I didn't know *that*, either.

"I can't let you in to just toss the place, Mick. You know I can't. But I can assure you, it's not Daniel. He doesn't practice even the most minor rituals without me knowing, and usually assisting. He's not dabbling in anything remotely as powerful as what you're implying, or anything necromantic. He wouldn't even know where to start."

"You're sure?"

"I'm sure. I promise."

And there it was. Did I *trust* a promise made by Ramona Webb? *Could* I?

Yeah. Maybe I was still just a tiny bit dizzy over whatever it was we'd had, or I'd been manipulated into feeling we had, or... whatever. But every instinct in me was tellin' me, yes, I could believe her.

On this, at least.

Sure, *maybe* she was an even better liar than I thought, though that woulda been damn near impossible. And maybe Baskin had somehow managed to hide what he was doin' from the succubus who lived in his house and helped with his magic, but that didn't sound any more likely. For now...

"Okay. Thanks, dollface. As of now, he's off my list."

She smiled that damn smile, the one to make you think the sun's forgotten the time and is tryin' to rise again. I returned it, best I could, and started off down the block.

"Mick? Good luck. I hope you find who you're looking for. And give Franky my best."

It's a good thing she walked back into the house without waiting for a reply, 'cause I sure didn't have one to offer.


After that, there was nothin' else for it. With Fleischer off the suspect list, I couldn't think of any other locals who might be able to pull this whole thing off. So until I tumbled to a better lead, it was time to bite the bullet and start searching the cemeteries and other death-touched, vampire-friendly places.

One. By. Friggin'. One.

I roped Pete into it, when he wasn't walkin' his beat or otherwise on the job. An extra set of peepers couldn't hurt, even if he didn't really know what we were lookin' for the way I did, and his badge got us into a few private boneyards without too much hassle. (Yeah, I coulda used my own mojo for that, but his way was quicker'n easier.)

Mostly, though, if I was gonna be stumbling around blind, I wanted the company.

We didn't just start pickin' at random, though. If nothing else, we could start with the graveyards nearest to where the murders had taken place, where Franky'd been bushwacked, where those poor mugs had been terrorized by contentious fruit. Those spots weren't *too* close to each other, but we could at least poke pins in 'em on a map and then work out from the center, all methodical-like.

Didn't help. Whether with my buddy the bull or on my own, I covered a couple days' worth of cemeteries, plus the occasional mortuary, hospital, and murder scene. Found a lotta dirt, a lotta dead guys, a handful of mourners, and—on one occasion—a pack of small barghests in black dog form, feasting on a recently disinterred corpse. They ran, howlin', when they saw me comin', but their mere presence was a bad sign. A death omen.

Since we hadn't had enough of those already.

But nothin' that led me anywhere. Even the barghests, I decided after an extra close up'n-down of that particular cemetery, had been random. Drawn to whatever magics Áebinn was hunting, but no *direct* connection to it, or the vampires, or anything else.

By the third night of this nonsense, I needed a change of pace. So even though I had no cause to figure it had any connection, I decided I'd go and take a quick spin around the Field.

Yeah, yeah, I get it. You're tired of hearin' about the Field Museum. I won't linger.

I had good reason. Lots of relics and old magics pass through the place, either ending up part of an exhibit or just stored away in the basement somewhere. Occasionally, one of 'em proves to be pretty damn powerful, or attracts the wrong sort of attention. The Spear of Lugh, just for instance.

So yeah, if some big bad artifact was the source of our problems, it could well have been there. That made it worth checking.

Mostly, though, I was just bored.

Found jack that was at all relevant. But I did spend a few minutes walkin' the halls, examining whatever caught my fancy and thinking back over my last few visits.

Old artifacts and artwork, some of which made me downright homesick—by which I mean, it made me think of my Old World home, and those memories made me sick. Exhibits of these animals or that, locked in stasis: Foraging elk and grazing gazelle. Slinking tigers. Deer falling to wolves and zebras fleeing lions (all bloodlessly, of course, so it wouldn't upset the kids). The taxidermists had given one of those zebras an expression that, to me, looked a lot more exasperated than frightened.

"You'n me both, bo," I told it.

The banner I'd clung to when tussling with Herne the Hunter was gone, replaced by a new ad for a new exhibit. They were cyclin' through 'em quick right now, tryin' to catch the attention of folks who were in Chicago for the World's Fair, hoping they'd spend a day at the museum before leaving town.

All the damage from a year ago was, of course, long repaired. The display case Herne had destroyed; the glass protecting multiple exhibits that Grangullie and Raighallan had shattered—or, like with the taxidermied carcasses of the Tsavo man-eaters, just knocked loose—with the magic of the Spear... All brand-spanking new. You'd never have known I'd been here.

I think, convoluted as that smarmy little redcap's schemes had been, I was more frustrated now than I ever got on *that* case.

Screw it. This'd been a nice diversion, but that's all it was. Time to move on.

To searching more graveyards. Oh, boy.

Where was a lunatic Unseelie with a Tuatha Dé Danann relic when you needed one?


It was the next day when a few of those alternative leads I'd been hopin' for finally dropped on my head like a goddamn anvil.

I really gotta stop hopin' for things.

After a morning of yet another trip-for-biscuits to a couple more graveyards, I stopped back by my office for a visit with a newspaper and an icebox full of milk. Or that'd been the plan, anyway.

Waiting by my door—or should I say pacing by my door, stomping like she was beating the carpet into submission—was a woman who woulda looked perfectly average if she hadn't been wearing an old blouse, skirt, and shawl that were all at least two generations outta fashion.

Even with that cue, it took me a second.

"Lenai?"

"'Bout time you got back, you jackass! You think I have all day?"

I dunno if I'd ever seen her this young. Not a single wrinkle on her map. "What's wrong?"

"Wrong? What's *wrong*? We barely fended off a goddamn vampire, you lunkhead, that's what's wrong!"

Nobody else in the building was likely to hear her, even with the shouting, but... "Why don't we talk about this in my office?"

"Took you long enough to invite me in! I remember when people had manners!"

Since absolutely no good could come of the obvious retort, instead of making it, I unlocked the door and ushered her inside.

"Now," I said, after hanging my flogger, offering her a glass of milk, gettin' told off, and pouring myself one. "What happened?"

"I just *told* you what happened! How stupid are you?"

A big sip, and then, "Details, Lenai. What happened *in detail*?"

"I dunno. I guess the fucker finally tracked Franky to my place."

*Or else was after you, personally.*

"Tried the door, tried the windows, multiple times. But the garlic and the crosses and whatnot seemed to do the job. It buggered off after about an hour." In a softer grumble, she added, "I was afraid it might just decide to burn the whole fucking building down."

"Yeah, well, I think they're tryin' to stay subtle." Then, at her expression, "For vampires, anyway."

"Well, what the hell are you *doing* about it, you cock-sucker?" In her heated flailing, she backhanded the coat rack, then clutched her wrist and glared at me as if it was my fault.

"Same thing I've *been* doing! I'm workin' to dig up whoever's behind the mess, find out what the hell they're tryin' to accomplish, and stop them!"

"Do it faster!"

Another sip of milk. Nice, warm, *calming* milk.

"How's Franky?"

"He's fine! I told you, it didn't get in!"

"Ah." Then, after realizing what she'd just said, "Wait, he's still at your place? You've never let *me* stay longer'n about ten minutes."

"He's not well enough, you ass! He doesn't heal as fast as you. And if the vampire's still hunting him, it's not safe for him out there."

"I see."

"And nobody fucking asked you!"

"Uh, nope." This conversation was wrigglin' out of my grasp like a greased kitten. "Nobody did."

She ground her teeth at me—yes, *at* me—growled, "Fix it already!" and stormed out.

Well, I appreciated her letting me know. Hopefully, her defenses would hold long enough for me to, as she'd so politely requested, fix it.

Finished the milk, finished the paper—two more murders in the last three days, that they knew about—and was about to head back out, when...

Yep. The phone. Again.

When had I become so damn popular, and how could I stop it?

"Mick? It's... it's Bianca."

"Oh! Hey."

I wasn't sure what to say. I hadn't figured on hearing from the Ottatis for some time yet, and while it wasn't a bad thing, she sure coulda picked a more convenient time for whatever kinda heart to heart she had in mind.

Plus, as always, the blower... Not the best way for a drawn-out chinwag with me.

"It's swell to hear from you," I started, "but—"

"Mick, Fino's missing."

Between my own distraction and the buzzing in my noggin

from the cursed dingus, it took a second to sink in. "He *what*?"

"He's just gone!" Now I was payin' full attention, I heard the panic beneath the surface. "He never came home, and we haven't been able to find him anywhere! I thought he just needed a few hours to work it through in his head, but it's been *days*!"

Days? Never came home? "You don't mean he's been gone since I was there!"

"Yes! Yes, that's what I mean! He never came back after storming out, after you... Oh, God..."

Shit. Shit, this wasn't good.

"All right, sister, calm down. You haven't been out lookin' by yourself, have you?"

I heard her pacing, heard the rosary, even over the line. "Of course not! Archie's had the boys all over Chicago, even called in some other Syndicate men to help search! Until..."

Yeah, that wasn't a word I wanted to hear. "Until what, Bianca?"

"We got hit today." She was on the verge of tears, one foot over the edge. "Some of Fino's people, I mean. We don't know by who. Archie... Well, Archie's in charge, with Fino missing. He had to look into it, no matter how much he'd rather be trying to find..."

Made sense. But while the gangs always had little territorial disputes, personal beefs, misunderstandings, things between 'em had been more or less quiet of late. No way I was buying this as a coincidence.

"He there now?" I asked.

She didn't answer for a second; at a guess, she'd nodded, forgettin' I couldn't see. Then, "Yes. He only got the call an hour or so ago. I didn't know who else to—"

"I'll get into it. Where are they?"

She gave me an address that, after some heavy thinkin', I recognized as a narrow street runnin' behind a row of shops. One of 'em, at least, was Fino's: a hock shop that doubled as a low-rent fence and bookmaking operation.

I made some assurances to Bianca we both knew were empty, strapped on everything I needed to carry under my coat, and dashed out the door.

The clouds were hangin' real low, barely pushed away by the Chicago skyline, but it wasn't raining again yet. Might still be some halfway decent evidence, if Archie and his palookas hadn't trampled all over it.

Couple big lugs with obvious bulges in their cheap coats moved to block my way as I turned the corner behind the shops, but Archie spotted me and called 'em off with a "He's okay."

The "street" was basically an alley with pretentions and smelled of old garbage—and new blood. Couple fresh stiffs lay sprawled around the three steps to a metal door, and even from here I could sense, and sniff, that there were more inside. I stepped over, makin' sure not to drag my plates through any of the blood or the spent casings.

"Archie."

"Mick. Bianca call you?"

"Yep."

"She tell you what's happening other'n this mess? 'Bout the boss?"

"Yep." I crouched down to get a better slant on the dead guys. Ugly. Not vampire-ugly and I'd sure seen plenty worse, but ugly.

"So whaddaya think?" I asked while giving it all the up'n-down.

"What do *I* think? Ain't that why you're here?"

"Humor me, Archie."

"Humor you. Yeah." He actually sighed. "I think I got no idea who hit us, but we better figure it out before they do it again. I think we can't afford a war, but maybe we can't afford not to have one after this. Especially if whoever did this is behind Mr. Ottati disappearin', too."

"Oh, I wouldn't fret too much about war, Archie. This

wasn't a hit—not the way you mean it." I stood up, checked to make sure I hadn't dipped the hem of my flogger in anything wouldn't easily wash out. "This was staged."

"Staged? What're you talkin' about?"

I pointed, first to the roscoes the stiffs on the concrete held loose in their hands, then, after trompin' up the steps, to the ones that'd hit the floor near the bodies inside. I knew Archie wouldn't be able to smell what I had—or hadn't—so I said, "Check the clips. Not a single one of these heaters have been fired. You think every person here had exactly enough time to pull a gat but not squirt metal?

"And look here. Your boys are all facing away from the door, whether they're inside or out. Regardless of which way the shooters approached from, even if they didn't seem a threat, your people woulda at least turned to 'em, right?"

"Coulda been multiple shooters," Archie protested.

"Don't figure. Each person here was shot from a single angle. Measure the wounds if you don't believe me. Gotta figure, multiple shooters, some of the targets would be hit from more'n one direction. Plus, look at the walls. Only a few impacts, and those match up to the spatter. Not a single missed shot."

I dropped my voice low, so only Archie could possibly hear. "No, someone put your people exactly where they wanted 'em. And then the boys stood and waited their turn to get shot."

"Waited their turn to... Why the fuck would—? Oh." The snarl thrashin' around behind his mug woulda scared off a rabid Doberman. "So this was someone from your side of the tracks, not ours."

"'Fraid that's how it looks, yeah."

"Why?"

"Now that's a real fine question, Archie." I paced a few steps away to stare absently down the street. He moved to stand beside me but kept quiet.

I thought about the vampires who'd been gunning for my

friends, but chucked the notion. Yeah, technically a vampire *could* mesmerize someone into standing around to get shot, but there was no call for it here. They hadn't been shy about attacking Franky or the L King. Most of 'em weren't even capable of this sorta subtlety, and I couldn't come up with any reason why they *would*.

Besides, Fino was my pal—maybe Archie, if you stretched the definition—but I didn't know these guys from nobody. No reason to target 'em to get at me.

Not *me*...

"Archie?"

"Yeah?"

"If Fino wasn't missing, what would he be doin' right now?"

"What would he be doin'? Same thing I'm doin'. Lookin' over his people and trying to figure who'd done this to 'em."

"Even though he's supposed to be lyin' low?"

Archie scoffed. "You know the boss better'n that."

"Yeah, I do. I think that was the point. I think this whole mess was meant to lure him out."

Which coulda meant, in a strange way, it was a good thing I'd made him pull a Jack Griffin. Somehow, though, I didn't expect that logic to go over real well with the rest of the Ottatis, so maybe I'd keep the notion to myself.

"Why?" he asked.

"Dunno yet, but it's part of what I'm digging into."

Archie didn't look too satisfied with that answer. I couldn't blame him. "You think we gotta worry about more of this?"

"I hope not. Especially since nobody has the foggiest idea where he or his family are." I'd raised my voice for that last bit. Archie gave me a curious look, but the extra volume hadn't been meant for him.

If this *had* been a lure, someone might still be watching. I wanted to make it clear this wasn't a winning play.

"I'm not sure what you're gonna tell your people," I said, "but you need to wrap this up and dust."

"And what about you?"

"Me, I got a notion where to look next."


Said notion being the Ottatis' place.

No, not the apartment where they were layin' dormy, I mean the house. Ain't as though I didn't already know of at least one bunch who'd been all too interested in keeping eyes on the place. Whether they were the same ones tryin' to draw him out... well, I'd just hafta ask real politely.

They were still usin' the milk-wagon. Maybe they couldn't lay their mitts on another non-motorized vehicle that wouldn't stand out, or maybe they just didn't take me serious as they should. Still, for redcaps, they'd made an effort to be subtle: the contraption was parked two blocks away, insteada right across the street. Took me an extra, oh, almost five whole minutes to find 'em.

Driver's bench was empty this time, which seemed hinky. Even if most of them were over by the Ottatis'—I hadn't poked around too hard over there, wanted to find their bucket first—they'd want somebody playin' lookout, wouldn't they?

I moved toward the wagon, alert for hidden sentries, felt like I was bein' ranked the whole way. But nobody took a shot, jumped up outta hiding, or so much as said "Boo!" Far as I could tell, only one who saw me comin' was the horse, and he really didn't give a damn.

When I got within a pace or two, I started to get an inkling why.

The stench was hidden—somebody'd tossed an olfactory glamour over it, to avoid drawing attention and maybe to keep from panicking the horse—but this close, I could sniff through it. This wagon held a lot more'n milk, and the new cargo was goin' sour a lot quicker.

Hand on the butt of the wand, I opened the door just enough for a quick gander.

Redcaps. Dead redcaps. Five of 'em. Couldn't swear on the megaliths of Stonehenge whether the one I'd bumped into earlier was one of 'em, but I was willing to make the assumption.

Every one had been chilled with a single cut, neat as you please. Throat slit here, stabbed through the pump there. No signs of fight, but a few of 'em still wore their last living expressions, like death masks.

They'd died in fear. No, fear ain't the right word. Absolute mortal terror, the kind that paralyzes you, kills you before you're dead.

Right.

"Okay, Áebinn. C'mon out and chat."

Nothin'. Branches scraped each other with dead leaves in the wind, flivvers rumbled by in the distance, faint and grainy tunes leaked from radios and through poorly sealed windows up'n down the block.

"Look, we ain't either of us got all day. I dunno if you followed me from the shop or if you were already here, but I know you *are* here. I know you croaked those redcaps—and Fino's boys, too, which was *not* called for and I ain't happy about—and I know you're hopin' if you keep your trap shut, I'll lead you to Fino. It ain't happening. I don't even know where he is."

For another moment, still nothin'. I was certain the *bean sidhe* was responsible for the bloodshed, but I was startin' to wonder if I was wrong about her still lurking around, when…

"I'm beginning to doubt you even want this matter resolved, Oberon."

She was standin' right beside me, and she smelled of blood. Not just redcap blood, either. Mixed in with that lovely bouquet, I caught a whiff of human, too, and even a tiny trace of some kinda animal I couldn't immediately identify. Where the hell had her investigation been taking her?

I barely deigned to turn my head. "How many people you murdered today? Do you even know?"

"People?" she scoffed. "Unseelie. Redcaps."

"And Fino's men!"

"Mortals. Are we even counting those?"

I needed to keep my cool here, much as I was yearnin' to do otherwise. "This ain't like you, Áebinn." Sure, she'd never thought real highly of humans, but casual slaughter? To say nothing of the possible political ramifications with the Unseelie…

"You don't understand. You say you do—you *all* say you do—but nobody does. Nobody but me has *felt it*! The redcaps were a threat to my mission! You can't comprehend the danger we—"

Yeah, she was windin' up for a good ol'-fashioned maddened rant, and I wasn't in the mood. "What do you want here?"

I swear she almost hissed at the interruption. "The Ottatis."

"Well, yeah, I'd actually tumbled to that much. I meant why?" I already knew the redcaps were interested in Adalina, had recognized her as somethin' outta the ordinary. If Áebinn had tumbled to that, too, I wasn't sure what I was gonna—

"Because they are your… friends." She spat that last word out on the sidewalk like it was a rotten spot in a ripe plum.

My exasperation at that was actually a good thing; it helped me hide my relief. "We back to that again? You got no leads better'n 'Mick's been touched by this death whatsis so I'm gonna put the screws to all his pals like they were shelving'? Find a new tune, sister. This record ain't sellin'."

"The Ottatis, Oberon. Take me to them."

"I told you, I got no idea where Fino is."

"The others, then."

"Don't know that, either," I lied. "And even if I did, I'd sooner pitch woo to a carburetor."

"Are you trying to make an enemy of me, Oberon?"

And now, finally, I did turn completely to face her. "No, doll, you're doin' a fine job of that on your own. I'm still lookin' into this mess, and if you wanna know what I've dug up and maybe work together on stoppin' the undead, we can work somethin' out. But you're gonna leave my people outta this until we have *real evidence* one of 'em's actually involved."

I hadn't actually verbalized the threat, but it was hardly subtle.

"Or else what?" she asked, soundin' more curious than angry or worried.

She really shoulda been both. So I spelled it out.

"Or else I'm gonna arrange for you to 'sense death' a whole lot more personally, and if there's consequences for that with the Court, I'll deal with 'em."

Her not-eyes went wide; I ain't sure if she'd ever been threatened that overtly. "I could arrest you for merely *saying* that to me!"

"Try it, sister. See how far it gets either of us."

She did nothing, said nothing, just glared like she wished I would up and fall into one of those gaping pits in her mug. I nodded and walked away.

I also took a few extra and unnecessary turns on my way back to the L, just in case.

Did she just have emotional blinders on, that she couldn't see any way forward that didn't involve the people I was close to? Was her vision that I'd been "touched" by this deathly power—whatever that even meant!—really her only damn clue? And if so, was it because she *really* couldn't find others, or was her narrow-mindedness part of the obsession Queen Laurelline had warned me about?

Her killin' those goons and the redcaps, and still gunnin' for my friends, had convinced me of one thing, though. I definitely couldn't afford to keep goin' at this alone.

"Not a visit or a letter for months, and then two visits in one week? A suspicious gal might question your intentions."

We were standin' on the walkway of Dan Baskin's lawn again. If we kept meetin' here for our chinwags, I was gonna hafta ask them to put in a table and some chairs.

"Good thing you ain't at all suspicious, isn't it?"

She took a long pull off a snipe, tapped the ash off to fall in the rain-damp grass. "What do you want this time?"

No way to get there but straight through, I figured. "I need your help, Ramona."

"I already told you that—"

"No, this ain't about Baskin. I mean I need your help. You'n me, together. Like last year."

She froze in the middle of another drag; the thin trail of smoke actually stuttered, almost like Morse code. If she were mortal, I think we'd have seen one hell of a choking fit.

"And why the hell would I want to do that?"

"Look, if I'd brought my hat, it'd be in my hands. You want me to beg? I'll—"

"You lied to me! Used me as bait!"

"Well, fuckin' fiddle-de-dee! And how's that any different than the fakeloo you were runnin' on me when we first met?"

"That was before we really knew each other!" It was a weak excuse, and she knew I knew it.

"And it worked, didn't it? Got a rival demon off your trail, for good!"

"I can't trust you, Mick!"

And I couldn't trust her, either. Never could. That's where this argument was leadin' us, where it'd taken us a half-dozen times before we'd mostly stopped speaking. Round and round and round we go.

Except this time, that's not what came outta my trap.

"So what? You *never did*!"

You'da thought I'd slapped her. She honest-to-God fell back a step. The butt tumbled from her fingers to land with a spray of sparks on the wet lawn.

And immediately after, her peepers lit up, as if a bulb had clicked on in her head.

"You really believe that." She didn't sound angry, anymore.

It was a tone of wonder, of genuine revelation.

She'd known I didn't trust her. Hell, for her, once anyone knew what she was, that was pretty well assumed. But I guess it never even crossed her mind I might figure the reverse. Thing about succubi; I guess they're such experts at lies, they ain't always so good with truths.

I wanted to follow that up, more'n anything. But I'd come for a reason. "It won't just be me you're helpin', sweetheart. If this works out, we'll be given a whole nest of murdering vampires the bum's rush from your boss's jurisdiction, too."

Did that last argument sway her? Would she have given me the brush-off otherwise? Or was it her excuse to say the "yes" she'd already wanted to say?

I got no idea, and it never seemed to be the right time to ask.

"All right, Mick. What precisely is it you need?"

# CHAPTER NINE

Lookin' hale and hearty, Four-Leaf Franky sauntered along with the evening pedestrian tides. He ankled his way down Halsted, smug as a cat in the cream. His gold shone, freshly polished, and even his glad rags looked as though they'd briefly shared a room with an ironing board.

He exuded the kinda cheerful makes you wanna haul off and take a poke at someone. Waved at anyone who so much as glanced his way, shook hands with anyone who looked like anyone he mighta recognized. This was a man in love with the world, and he was gonna talk your ear off about every bit of it until you really, really didn't.

If he passed a bar, he put something back; passed a club, he cut a rug for at least a tune or two; passed a bookie, laid a few bucks on whatever there was to lay bucks on. The cloudy nighttime skies above, and the cloudy glowers all around, slid off him like condensation on a frosty beer glass.

By the time he finally reached his more usual haunts, his steps—jaunty as ever—had started to wobble. Much as he'd been pounding down, any full-blood human woulda been completely over the edge with the rams. Probably wouldn't have been able to form a sentence or stagger more'n a few paces. Franky, of course, *wasn't* fully human, but he was still showin' the early signs of begin' well and truly lit.

His story was startin' to shift some, too. Now, when he explained why he'd vanished a while, he hadn't been sick; now he'd gotten into a real nasty scuffle, one that put him down for days, "but you shoulda seen how bad the other Joes looked." That got him sympathy, sure, but also his fair share of rolling eyes and ginks hiding their disbelieving scoffs in their cups. Anyone who knew him, anyone who'd heard of him, knew Four-Leaf Franky wasn't exactly rugged.

And when he got to his few *real* close buddies—the ones who, like him, weren't strictly speaking mortal, or at least were wise to the unnatural—his tale got wilder still. "Attacked by a vampire," he told everyone in a position to believe a word of it. "Tried to tear my throat out, but not me! Four-Leaf Franky's not so easy to kill! Shook him off like a pesky puppy, sure as I'm standing here!"

Anyone didn't know better, it might almost seem as though Franky *wanted* the damned undead to hear he was out and about. As though he was *darin'* them to have another go at him.

Considering that the vampire who'd slashed him up the first time had been gunnin' for him personally, had even tracked down Lenai's bunk to try again, it ain't so surprising that it took him up on that dare.

It happened in another alley. Of course it did; this is Chicago, and none of the non-residential streets are ever completely empty, even after midnight. If you don't have an office or storefront but want privacy to conduct some business—or tear the head off some cocky half-leprechaun and drink him like a milkshake—an alley's really your only option.

Sickly gray arms, desiccated and draped in tattered scraps, shot out of that alleyway as Franky sauntered by. They yanked him away from the light in less than a blink, hurling him back over fallen garbage cans, and the empty body of a real unfortunate bum, to crash into the far wall. Dust shook from the bricks and the old fire escape above rattled and creaked at the impact.

The thing wearing some poor slob's corpse twisted to face its prey, blood- and dirt-stained maw gaping to show broken, jagged fangs.

And its prey picked himself up, dusted himself off, and faced the vampire in turn.

Only it stopped being a "him."

"I suppose I should thank you." The last of her clothes and flesh rippled as Ramona shed every trace of Franky and assumed her true form. And I don't mean her usual gorgeous tomato disguise, I mean her *true* form: skin crimson as boiling blood, twisted horns, black and pitted talons, membranous wings that stretched and creaked, pressed up against both sides of the alley as they unfurled. The scents of the potent hooch and thick sweat of the bar next door, of the pedestrians and flivvers of the streets beyond, smothered beneath a choking cloud of sulfur.

"We were afraid this might take days," she continued, and her voice was thick, now, syrupy sweet and poisonous as hemlock. "Playing the buffoon for so long might've just about driven me around the bend."

The vampire had fallen back, jaw hanging slack. It snarled something that mighta been a question, if anyone coulda understood a word of it.

"Sorry, what was that?" Ramona asked. "I didn't quite catch it. Why don't you try a little closer?"

Four sets of clawed fingers flexed, two throats growled sounds no human coulda reproduced, and two monsters— the risen dead and the so-called demon—threw themselves at each other.

Ramona snagged the vampire's wrists in her own fists. Half-unfurled wings brought her leap up short; in defiance of momentum, she stopped and twisted, yanking her opponent outta the air and slamming it hard into the building beside her. It rebounded off the wall, leavin' a cobweb of cracks in the brick, and right back into her waiting mitts. This time she struck claws first, rippin' handfuls of flesh and muscle from the vampire's chest.

I hoped, ears achin' from the creature's agonized shriek, that she remembered we needed to take this thing alive.

Uh, so to speak. Not-dead, anyway.

I guess I needn't have worried, though. Even as it screamed, the vampire clamped its hands on her arms and hauled itself forward, sacrificing even more tissue to her hellish talons—like a boar impaling itself on a hunter's spear to get at the fool who'd dared attack it. Its own jagged nails made a grab for Ramona's face.

Her left wing curled in, shielding her and knocking the creature away, but not before the nosferatu raked those nails down, and through, the thin leathery skin. Torn membrane fluttered, a grotesque pennant, and while Ramona kept the pain from showin' in her expression, the whole wing drooped, twitching and flopping.

The vampire picked itself up, dug a small ribbon of wing from under a nail with its teeth and sucked it down like a strand of spaghetti. For a long moment, the opponents locked stares. If this'd been the Old West, I'da half-expected to see a tumbleweed roll on by between 'em.

Instead, it just started to rain again. And I decided the vampire was hurt bad enough for part two of our little ambush.

First, the wand. I drew, aimed, and fired. No finesse, just as much power as I could channel through the dingus. I sucked away as much luck from the vampire as I could in the half-second I had, weakening his magics and giving myself a boost for what was to come.

Then—speakin' of cowboys and all—I started whirlin' what I'd held in my other hand over my head like a lasso, and tossed it. Even through the rain, and even though the dead gink saw me comin', the extra fortune I'd snagged was enough. It spun down from the roof, where I'd been watchin' the whole shindig, and settled around the vampire neat and tidy as you please.

"It" bein' a string—an extra-long string—of garlic cloves, tied in a loop.

Our target crouched, snarling, twisting in search of a way out. The loop wouldn't hold it long; thing could pretty easily turn into a bat or into mist, or, hell, maybe even just leap high enough over it that it could cross the boundary. It was hurt, though, confused and surprised, and that probably bought us a few seconds.

Still woulda been nice if it'd been hurt worse, though.

I jumped down, coat flarin' around me, and landed with a splash beside Ramona. Plan was to close in, hit it hard at once, her woundin' it bad while I drained away the rest of its powers and its luck. We'd figured on that givin' us enough time to put the screws to it, get ourselves a few answers.

Mighta worked, too, if somethin' hadn't gummed it all up. Same thing that gums up near everything else.

Humans.

Yeah, *you* mugs.

Maybe they'd heard the commotion, the vampire's screech, even over the sounds of the city? I dunno. But a couple passersby appeared in the mouth of the alley, starin' until I thought their whole heads might just pop.

I wasn't too worried about what they'd witnessed. Between the weather and the poor lighting, I doubt they could make out more of me'n Ramona than general shapes. As for the vampire, well, they'd eventually convince themselves they'd just seen a real skinny, filthy fellow—maybe a sickly vagrant. You're all pretty skilled at self-deception.

Except it saw them, too. Saw, and made eye-contact.

Even through the creature's dead, rarely used, dirt-and-clotted-blood-choked throat, its next words were crystal clear.

"Kill them."

The poor saps charged, the hems of his flogger and her skirt sweepin' up wet trash and mud. They weren't swift, they weren't strong—I doubt either of 'em had lifted anything heavier'n a spoonful of cereal, or fought anything more rugged than a head cold, in years—but it didn't matter. Their faces were hollow masks, and if we'd let 'em, they'da done exactly what their undead master ordered.

We didn't. Ramona'n I knocked 'em down with as little violence as we could, and once that was done, it was duck soup for me to get into their heads and put everything right. But it cost us those extra few seconds we needed. Even as I dropped the gink comin' at me with a quick poke to the gut, the vampire shrank, sprouting wings. I couldn't do much but watch as an ugly, piebald bat took to the sky, fading into the night and the clouds.

"Ramona!"

She turned so that the alley wouldn't constrain her wings, spread 'em wide—and staggered, wincing. The glare she turned my way wasn't actually aimed at me, I knew, but at the wounded membrane. Still, I felt the heat along its edges.

"I can't. Not for another few minutes, at least. I… I'm sorry, Mick."

"*Fuck!*"

All this for nothin'. No leads, no way to track the fleeing—

"Now maybe you think is good time to accept my help, yes?"

Varujan. Outta nowhere, again.

"What'd I tell you about followin' me?" But I didn't wait for a response to that; I had far more immediate things to be steamed about. "You were watching. You coulda stopped it from gettin' away!"

"Maybe, yes, but why? We do not work together. Unless you say otherwise?"

I really wanted to hit him. Or better yet, let Ramona hit him. How long had he been shadowin' me, waiting for his opportunity? Hell, for all I knew, maybe he'd even sent this poor dumb couple into the alley, hopin' this would happen.

I didn't like this. I trusted it even less. But you tell me what choice I had, 'cause I sure didn't see one.

"Mick," Ramona began, "what's going—?"

No time. Never any time. Shit.

"All right, Varujan. You run that bastard down and we got a deal."

"You are sure of this? I would not wish for misunderstanding."

"*Go*, damn you!"

Again that horrible, crooked, rictus grin, and he was gone, a second bat flapping wildly and swiftly out of sight.

Shit.

Ramona stepped up beside me while I watched him disappear. When I finally uncricked my neck and looked her way, she was wearin' her usual human—remarkable for a human, but human—form.

"How's the wing?" I asked.

"What wing?"

"I mean, don't it still hurt? Uh, somewhere?"

"Why would it? It's gone."

I decided not to press.

"So, Mick. Those details you told me you were skimping on, when you spun this whole story out for me?"

"Yeah?"

"Time to stop skimping."

"Yeah."

We drifted into the bar next door, not because either of us was lookin' to dip our bills—me especially, since it ain't as if this kinda joint was gonna offer milk, warm or otherwise—but because it felt more natural, and sure *looked* more natural to anyone ankling by, than jawing the rest of the night in an alleyway in the rain. The aroma of cheap fried foods was actually stronger'n the hooch, which seemed weird, since the alcohol had been the dominant smell outside. Maybe it just carried further.

Whole place stared our way soon as we stepped through the door, and it wasn't 'cause we were strangers.

"Hey, doll? Maybe damp it down a little, huh?"

"Right. Sorry."

The supernatural attraction she exuded dwindled to a dull spark. Lotta the folks turned away and went back to what they'd been doin'. More'n a few didn't.

Ain't like she *needed* anything supernatural. Way she looked, way those mugs still looked at her, the *natural* attraction was more'n enough.

I felt good about only sufferin' the tiniest twinge of jealousy.

We found ourselves a small table near the back, did a little mental nudging to "convince" the staff we had every right to be there even if we weren't buyin'. And I told her all of it, every little event and detail that'd brought me—us—here, at the midnight hour.

Well, not *every* detail. I didn't spill much about Adalina. I mean, Ramona already knew a little about her, was wise to her bein' something special. And yeah, we were gettin' along famously, a real nifty change from the last months, but c'mon.

Uh, this is also where I interrupt myself to remind you that I ain't a bunny. Me'n Ramona, we had a lot of lies and betrayals and broken trust between us. I was still drawn to her, yeah. Not sure anyone with a pulse, human or Fae, coulda said different. But I wasn't lookin' to get, y'know, involved.

Havin' her back in my life, though, havin' her as a bona fide friend after all that'd gone down, as complicated as my life in Chicago seemed to be gettin' over the past couple years? That woulda been just dandy. And if that went smooth enough for long enough, *then* maybe.

Not now. But maybe.

"So what—?" she started, then zipped her lips when a waiter or runner or whatever approached the table, askin' if we wanted anything "else" and offerin' us a bowl of peanuts. I told him to scram.

"What," she said again, pullin' a deck of Old Golds outta God-knows-where, "do you suppose he wants with you?"

I waited until she struck a match and lit her snipe before

answerin'. "Believe me, I've been noodling on that a lot. He *says* he just wants my help diggin' up the source of whatever summons called him here. Can't blame him for wantin' the dope on that, especially if he's gotten wise that this magic, whatever it is, affects the spirits that *become* vampires. Nobody's done that before, that I ever heard. So it could be he's bein' completely square with me."

"But you don't buy it." I swear the smoke wove a braid between her lips and each word. Can't pretend she wasn't absolutely fascinating, whatever my intentions movin' forward were.

"Eh, let's say I'm renting. I got nothin' but my suspicious nature—and the fact that he's a walking corpse full of dark magic and a predator's soul—to suggest he *ain't* tellin' the truth. But I'm sure as hell not gonna take him at his word, or let my guard down."

"Good. I'm glad you're still being careful about who you trust."

I couldn't for the life of me tell you if she honestly didn't see the irony in what she'd just said to me, or was puttin' on a fine show of innocence.

"It's too bad," I said, and yes, it was a deliberate change of topic, "that Franky couldn't see your performance. I think he'da been impressed."

She chuckled around the cigarette. "Especially since there's never going to be an encore."

"You hated the role that bad?"

"It hardly matters how *I* liked it," she corrected me. "I think if she caught me spending any more time even *thinking* of Frankie, Lenai would actually try to kill me."

"Lenai?" If I was one of you, I'da been blinking enough to cause a draft. "Why?"

Ramona stared for a moment, and then broke out into peals of genuine laughter. It was a joyful, hypnotic sound. Half the bar turned to watch, and a lot of 'em lingered more'n they needed to (or than their companions were happy with).

"Oh, Mick," she finally said, dabbing at one blinker with a napkin. "You may not be human, and you're a wonderful detective, but you're still such a *man*."

"Wait. Wait, slow down. Franky? *Lenai?* Are you pullin' my leg? There's no way she—"

The rest was gonna hafta wait. A low murmur spread like a spilled drink from the crowd nearest the door as a peculiar, ankle-height mist wafted in from outside. In and, soon as I pushed my chair back and stood, back out again.

Well, guess it was preferable to him strolling in and letting everybody catch an eyeful of walking stiff. For one of the nosferatu, Varujan was downright subtle.

Wasn't sure I cared for that.

I dusted, Ramona on my heels, pushin' through a whole collection of conversations about the peculiar weather, chilly concrete, the unusual winds of the Windy City.

Best to let 'em go right on thinking that.

The two of us followed him back into the alley. A stray cat who'd moseyed in after the garbage hissed us his irritation, and then decided to hunt up dinner elsewhere. Once we were well back from the street, Varujan resumed his normal—ha—form.

"I prefer the mist," I said.

"We—" was it me, or did the dead guy seem a teensy bit embarrassed? "—might have problem."

"That ain't what I like to hear from *anyone*, bo. From a vampire least of all. Don't tell me you lost him!"

If this murdering undead bastard wasn't even good for tailing one of his own...

Or had he even tried? Maybe he'd *let* the other one go. Maybe they were pullin' some sorta con job of their own. I—

"I did not lose him," Varujan snarled. Then, in a more natural tone, or as close as he could ever get, he added, "Exactly."

"Aw, for the luvva... How did you not lose him exactly, then?"

"He did escape me," the vampire admitted. "But his destination is close to where this happened. It must be. It is only way I... can lose him, if he drops into nearby building before I can tell which."

Okay, that actually made sense. And even if he *had* seen which building, Varujan might not've been able to follow. If these other vampires were workin' with a human warlock... Well, he'd been able to enter my office because it *is* an office, and maybe because I ain't human. I'm not real sure how that works. But a mortal's place? Invite only.

"All right. Where was this?"

"Is on or near 114th. Near lake."

That'd be Lake Calumet, then. And 114th...

"That's still a lot of doors to knock on," Ramona grumbled.

"I may have another option," I said.

This wasn't gonna be fun for a whole *lotta* reasons, and it might not pay off at all. Depended on whether my suspect was who I thought she was.

I left the succubus and the vampire in the alley, dug a nickel from my pocket, and went in search of another one of your goddamn torture devices.

Took a few rings before anyone picked up. Since it was well after midnight, that was hardly surprising.

"'Lo?"

"Evening, Bianca. It's Mick."

"Mick." She was instantly awake, alert. I heard hope in her voice, if maybe less affection than I once had. "Have you found him?"

"Not yet. I need some information from you. I'm sorry to be callin' at this hour, but it's important."

"This damn well better be part of your search for Fino!"

"It's connected," I hedged.

Probably. Maybe. Possibly in multiple ways.

She sighed, and I heard her scrabblin' for pencil and paper. "All right. What do you need?"

"Those properties Fino mentioned? The ones that ain't in his name, can't be traced back to him?"

"Yeah?"

"He got any in or near Pullman?"

She told me she'd hafta make some calls and I should get back to her. I let her go, so she could wake up people who'd be a lot less thrilled to hear from her this late than she'd been to hear from me. But when I dialed back in thirty minutes, she had what I needed.

A house, older'n a lot smaller than the one they lived in. Hadn't been used in years, so far as she knew. Wasn't even sure what Fino'd meant to use it for.

Just at the edge of Pullman proper. South of 114th. I knew where to go.

And I knew who to expect to find waiting.

It's funny. I don't remember much about the house itself.

I can tell you where it was. I know it wasn't big, wasn't ostentatious, just pretty nice. But anything else, anything specific? Color, shape, how many floors, how many windows? Just a blur.

Maybe it's 'cause I had so much else on my mind, so much else to deal with. Maybe it was a side effect of the wards I'd suspected—and then learned for sure—were there.

But after everything that happened at that house, how it's the exact spot, the exact minute, that so much started to go wrong... you'd think I'd remember.

There were three of us walkin' abreast down the street toward that house, a couple hours after midnight. Me. Ramona Webb. And Pete Staten.

I'd been real hesitant about involving Pete any further. Even if he didn't wind up in a wooden kimono over it, this whole shindig could land him in serious hot water. I wasn't too eager to risk that. Plus, last time he'd dealt with a succubus, he'd been enslaved and nearly killed. It hadn't been Ramona, or even her fault—well, not mostly—but I still didn't feel great askin' this of him.

But I needed someone I could trust absolutely, and that someone hadda be human. Given who I figured we were up against, there was a decent chance of wards or other magics that could take me'n Ramona both outta the fight. Not for long, probably, but not long was still *too* long.

So I'd sucked it up and asked him, and it says somethin' about Pete's loyalty—or maybe just his sanity—that he didn't balk.

Varujan? He was around somewhere, a bat or a patch of mist, the gore-mouthed bastard. But he'd announced, right around Kensington Station, that runnin' down his fellow vampire for us was as much as he was willin' to contribute. Sure, if this turned out to actually be the source of his "summons," he'd happily jump back in, but until and unless we learned that for certain, "Is not my fight."

Fucker.

We were maybe a couple blocks away, soaked to the skin, when Pete stumbled over a curb, picked himself up, and kept walkin' like nothing happened. He wasn't watching where he was goin'; he was watching Ramona.

Come to think, my focus was startin' to wander some, too.

"You're doin' it again."

"What?"

"That thing. With the emotions and the, uh, blood flow."

She stopped, ran a hand over her skirt to smooth out the wrinkles and brush off some of the rain that'd gotten in under her coat, which didn't exactly help the problem any. "You do understand that it comes naturally, right?"

"Still need you to do somethin' about it, doll. Makes it hard enough for *me* to concentrate, let alone a certain someone else who's had his conk fiddled with enough for one lifetime."

"I don't hear Pete complaining."

"Me, neither," Pete insisted dreamily.

"Ramona, please."

"Oh, fine."

I felt the emotional pressure ease up. Pete started blinking.

"Tell me, Mick," she said, "were you *ever* any fun?"

"Me? I'm fun!"

"Yeah, that's our Mick," Pete said. "More fun than a barrel of junkies."

I got his version of "cherubic innocent face" in trade for my glower. Not his best look.

"I'm plenty fun, when it's the right occasion! I'm chock fulla laughs!"

"Oh?" Ramona smirked. "Is *that* what you're full of?"

Pete snickered.

"Can we *please* get back to huntin' vampires now?" I almost begged.

Her rain-soaked hair flopped around her neck as she shook her head. "You see? There's the problem. If that's your idea of fun…"

"More than this conversation, anyway."

We went on, the both of 'em chuckling.

Lookin' back, I'm glad they had that chance to laugh.

The rain stopped right as we reached the house, a curtain parting on the next act. It still dripped from bare branches and a hundred eaves, the puddles sloshed with every step, and the wind occasionally rustled like the pages of a program, but otherwise the audience fell silent.

"Still wish we'd waited until dawn," Pete muttered, hand on his heater.

I couldn't really blame him, but we'd decided it was better to do this while Varujan *could* still chip in, if he deigned to bother, and while we wouldn't have to deal with a street full of witnesses.

Then again, a sudden screech from above as the shorter vampire appeared above the rooftops, bat-like membrane stretched under its arms, kinda felt like an additional argument for the "wait for daylight" contingent.

"Ramona? Can you—?"

"Eggs in the coffee." Her voice twisted, her body changed, and with a sharp *whoomp* of air she lurched from the ground and soared upward to meet the creature, her own great wings no longer cramped and confined by alley walls.

"Holy Christ," Pete whispered.

"This from the guy who turns into a wolf at the full moon."

"Go climb your thumb."

He stayed where he was, which was part of the plan. He'd come in squirtin' lead if he had to, but until then we didn't need a bull barging into a private house uninvited.

Me? I sauntered up, poked the lock with the L&G until it didn't have even a shred of luck remaining and completely fell apart inside, and pushed it open.

A worm of mild nausea coiled itself through my guts. Yep, warded. Surprisingly *light* wards, though—they weren't much fun, but I could push through 'em easy enough. Either she'd lost her touch, was supremely overconfident, or she had a reason for holdin' back.

I really didn't care for that last option. I tossed my wand to my left hand, drew my bronze-bladed sword with the right, and crept inside.

The door opened into a long hallway, closed doors to both sides, and lit by a single bulb, old and yellow and dim. For a human in off the street, place woulda been only a couple steps better'n pitch black.

Me, I could see okay. Well enough to know that the hall took a sharp right after this array of doors. Since I didn't hear anything through the thin wood, I decided on movin' ahead for now. I'd backtrack and start poking my schnozzle into the rooms if I didn't find anything.

No way Pete could see me from outside, even before I took that corner. I wondered how long he'd stand there, nervous and fretting, before he decided to play cavalry.

So I took that corner—and there, in another short hallway as poorly lit as the first, I saw him.

"Fino!" He started toward me, and I lowered the wand and the blade both, though not by a lot. "What the hell are *you* doing here?"

He didn't say a word. Just kept coming.

"Fino?"

Step. By slow. Methodical. Step. No changes. No swaying. His arms didn't swing. It was almost a lurch, like a brat just learning to walk, except he never came near to losing his balance.

"Talk to me, pal." But it was said entirely outta denial, outta my need to be wrong. Because I already knew full well there was nobody in there to talk to.

He stopped a couple paces away, and I could see it now. His eyes, already goin' milky, had rolled all the way to the left and stuck there. His jaw hung open, but also a little bit left. That musta been the side he'd landed on, and lain on for a good while, after...

After he'd died.

"Aw, goddamn it, Fino..."

"*You will not blaspheme here, creature!*"

The wards flared, high and hot, and everything was agony. *Familiar* agony.

I recognized it even as it hammered me to the filthy carpet, as my gut roiled and every nerve screamed. If I hadn't expected her, if she hadn't announced herself with that bitter, furious, self-righteous screech, I still woulda known who was behind 'em.

Quivering on my hands'n knees, refusing to take that last tiny sprawl to lie flat, I watched her drift into the feeble light, the axles of the old wheelchair squeaking like the ghosts of a thousand rats.

Orsola Maldera.

# CHAPTER TEN

She shoulda been dead.

Whatever witchcraft had saved her wretched life from Fino's Chicago typewriter that day, almost two years ago, in the unholy ruins of a holy place, it hadn't come anywhere close to protecting her completely. She hunched in the chair, curled against it. Her head lay heavily to one side on a neck too shriveled and damaged to hold it upright. One arm hung limp, resting on the arm of the wheelchair. The other she held folded tight against a chest that, even obscured by layers of heavy blouse, showed concave pits where it had been shattered by flyin' lead. Her legs were hidden under a thick quilt, but I couldn't imagine they were in any better shape. A couple gallons of stale Le Jade tried and failed to cover the stench of unwashed flesh and piss-stained cushions.

Her jaw sat just a touch crooked. Spittle flecked her parchment chin, dangled in strings from one corner of cracked lips.

Doubt I sounded near as rugged, or even steady, as I wished I had, but I still managed to grunt out, "You've looked better, Orsola."

She cast a withering sneer down at me as I quivered on the floor near her feet. "You have not."

Ain't sure what I woulda said next, done next, if Fino—or

what'd been Fino—hadn't stepped back into view, movin' past momma and tromping off into the darkness on some errand or other.

"Your own fucking son…" I think it came out a hiss.

"Yes."

"He has a family, you—"

"*And he was mine!*" Spit flew, and the witch spent a moment choking before she could continue.

"He did this to me," she went on, hoarse and near inaudible. "If it was deliberate, his soul burns now, as it should! If it was not, if you forced him or tricked him into it… then he is safe with Christ, beyond your reach, demon!"

"I see you're just sane as ever."

Woulda been so easy to let her disappear behind the pain, but I struggled to speak same as I struggled to gather my strength and push through the wards. I hadda get her to spill as much as I could, however much torture came with waiting for those answers.

Plus, the longer I kept her jawin', the better the odds Ramona or Pete'd come bustin' in before she did somethin' I'd hafta react to, no matter how bad off I was.

"So you—what?—summoned…" The hallway swam. These were even stronger'n the wards she'd had on the house, way back when. I wondered how long it'd taken her, in her condition, to inscribe 'em. "Summoned a flock of vampires to Chicago to take your revenge? So much for all your protests about God and black magic and—"

"Do not *dare* accuse me of such foulness!" Again she choked, and for a minute it was just the two of us sufferin' together. There's probably a moral in there. Neither of us gave a hoot.

"I am devout," she croaked, when her throat worked again. *Devoutly nuts.*

Problem was, I believed her. And that was a problem because it meant, after alla this, I still had no notion of what was actually goin' down in my city, who the bad guy I was gunnin' for actually *was*.

Well, the other bad guy. It ain't as if Orsola didn't still qualify, with honors.

I wonder, if she'd had a chance to think on it, if she'da lied to me. If she'da realized the advantages of givin' me a bum steer. But she was so incensed at the idea that anyone might think she'd resort to such profane magics—yeah, I know—that I never doubted every word she said was square.

"I did not bring these abominations here, creature. I merely sensed their arrival and... borrowed one of them before its summoner could leash it. It serves me, now."

"You just happened to have the mojo to command a vampiric spirit? Somethin' I didn't even know was possible until a few days ago? Right. Pull the other one, sister."

I didn't really doubt her, like I just said. I was proddin'. And it worked.

"It was similar enough to what I already studied to wreak my revenge on you! It didn't prove difficult to adapt."

Oh, great. So what *had* she been studying, exactly?

"So that's why it was attackin' my pals? To draw me out?"

She spat. "I know where to find you when I wish to. It attacked those foolish enough to stand by you for the same reason I cursed you with misfortune. To make you suffer, before the end!" Wasn't just spit, now. A bubble of snot popped in her left nostril and hung, wobbling.

Charming.

"Too bad for you," I groaned, almost standin' and then collapsing again, "it ain't gonna be around long enough to do me or mine any more hurt."

"Oh, yes, your demon harlot." Again she spat. "Let her destroy it." She smiled, showin' a jagged yellow landscape not any more attractive than Varujan's kisser. "It will be back."

"That's not how... What'd you do?"

"Do? I fed it, Oberon! Not blood, but hate, sacred and pure! I shared with it my own loathing for you, bonded it to you as I did my righteous hex! Let it die. It will find a new form and come for you, again and again! It, like my hate, is eternal!"

Son of a barghest...

Somethin' else occurred to me right about then, somethin' I'da wondered about minutes ago if I wasn't half-blinded by pain, wasn't puttin' every bit of strength I had into focusing through it and learning everything I could from the whacky broad.

Mainly, that she hadn't tried to rub me out, or do anythin' to me, while I was caught in her wards. That she seemed as eager to talk as I was to *keep* her talkin'.

That I wasn't the only one stallin'.

And I realized that for all her bravado and contempt, all the power she had—and maybe even the extra power I'd given her, in my head—she was just a badly injured little old lady in a wheelchair. Her wards, the ones that'd taken God-knows-how-long, were all she had; even if her mind was up to tossin' around magics the way she used to, her body wasn't.

She hadn't been ready for me to find her.

Pretty sure I screamed out loud, not with pain—though there was plenty of it—but sheer effort. I squeezed the L&G until I thought my fingers'd snap, forced myself to concentrate. Shards of glass tore my thoughts to shreds, jabbed at the inside of my head, but slowly, *real* slowly, a trickle of fortune began to seep from the magic of the glyphs, through the wand, and into me.

Drop by drop, the witch's protections got weaker, and I got stronger.

And she saw it. For everything else that went wrong that day, I'll treasure the look on her mug when she felt the magics start to shift as much as I treasure any of the trophies and knickknacks in my special drawer.

If I'd had the time, just a few more minutes, I'da had her.

But I guess she'd shouted (mentally, not aloud), and same as he'd done nearly his whole life, her boy Fino came running.

I heard a crash and a shatter—found out later he'd been packin' her most important supplies in the back of his V-16

Caddy while she'n I had our little chinwag; she'd been preparing to vamoose since I'd first barged in—and then he appeared at a quick shuffle. Her chair was already driftin' back, seemingly on its own, but slow. Soon as he had his dead mitts on the handlebars, though, he spun it around and they were gone.

I wanted to follow so bad it almost drowned me, a need so deep and thick it had weight, it had taste. Even against the pain and the pressure of the wards, I crawled forward a yard or so without even realizing I'd done it. And again, if I'd had time...

But the pain wasn't subsiding fast enough, and even if I coulda climbed to my feet I'da gotten maybe two steps before I fell a third time. And already I heard, felt, the engine cranking from a garage that might as well've been leagues away.

"The favored luxury transportation of dead men and mangled witches." Didn't figure Cadillac'd be running with that particular ad campaign any time soon. I hoped the stiff who'd been Fino Ottati, or whatever craft kept him up and about, could handle the Chicago streets without killin' anyone else.

Cursin' every bit of the way, furiously hot over lettin' Orsola slip away and at the notion of startin' the hunt for her all over again, I shuffled my keister around and crawled back the other direction.

I was upright again by the time I got to the front door. Between the constant flow of luck and mojo from the glyphs to me, they'd gotten weak enough that I could work through 'em without losin' a step. (If I'd only had more swift!) But it wasn't until I cracked that door open that I heard the shouting.

Ramona shouting. Shouting for me.

And between and around those calls, a hideous snarling, a predatory howl, piercing the night louder'n any siren. Folks were gonna be wakin' up, snapping on lights and lookin' out their windows any minute, if they hadn't already, and I did *not* want any of 'em gettin' a slant on what I knew was out there, even if I was utterly stumped as to *how*.

Y'see, no vampire ever made *that* particular sound. But I

knew what did, no matter how impossible. I'd heard it too many times after my best pal had vanished into the depths of the woods of Elphame.

A few hours before dawn, on a night when the moon was just a clipped crescent of fingernail high above the rain, and the layers of oil-soaked cotton clouds, Pete had *changed*.

A few tatters of shirt and trousers flapped from a pelt of gray hair—and no, I don't guess I meant "fur." The stuff was almost more like what you'd find on a silverback gorilla than any wolf you ever saw. It was long, knotted, ugly... Almost diseased. Open sores wept in a couple of mangy bald spots. Streaks of watery goo matted the hair down in random splotches across his body, and even from here I could smell the sour tang of pus.

He'da been close to nine feet tall if he'd stood up straight, but the hunch and bulge of his shoulders brought his head down closer to seven. His snout, his arms, his legs... All long, twisted, as if some mad sculptor had taken a clay model of a man and stretched 'em out. But the claws and the fangs, slick with blood that dripped steadily from the gums and the nailbeds, those looked straight and sturdy.

No simple animal. Nothin' natural. Nothin' *clean*. "Werewolf," you lot call it.

Ain't near that pretty.

But I'd seen him change before, and this was worse'n normal. An already corrupted process had been corrupted worse.

Ramona swooped over his head, just outta reach of those horrible, impossible arms. I dunno if she held back because she didn't wanna risk hurting my pal, or just because she had no idea how to close in and bring her own talons to bear without Pete rippin' her in two. Either way, I appreciated it, but she was runnin' low on options.

"Mick! For heaven's sake, do something!"

Even in the middle of everything, I couldn't help but chuckle at her, of all people, usin' that expression.

But what the hell *to* do? He hadda be stopped, sure, before he hurt anyone or anyone saw him. As it was, somebody'd run an old Model A coupe into a tree a half-block down and left it there, door hangin' wide, engine exhaling steam up into the bare branches above. I wondered what the poor driver'd thought he'd seen loomin' in his headlights, or how the cops were gonna react to his wild tale.

Since a lotta folks didn't wait for the dawn to be up and about their day, though, it wouldn't be long before we had a whole lot more'n just a single late-night driver to worry about.

Werewolf, werewolf. How'd you fight a werewolf? Silver, of course, but I didn't exactly make a habit of carryin' any on me, and besides, I wasn't lookin' to *kill* Pete! Wolfsbane, which woulda been great if, again, I actually had any on me.

And that was assumin' the standard rules applied, if whatever'd caused this off-schedule transformation hadn't…

Wait.

"Where's the vampire?" I shouted, sheathing my sword and closin' with wand aimed.

"The vam—?" She spun, spiraling upward as a sudden leap nearly snagged her. "It's dead!" she shouted back, and while she didn't say it, her tone told me I was a twit for even worrying about that now. "I was just coming down to tell Pete we should go look for you when—"

Pete roared, so I couldn't hear the rest, but it ain't as though I didn't get what she meant.

Right. "We've gotta hold him!"

"*Hold* him? Are you nuts?"

I fired the L&G, not at him, but at her, sending a large dose of what I'd drained from the witch's protections to mix with her own aura. Even from the ground, I saw her peepers go wide with the influx of power.

"On my mark!" I yelled, and then I turned the wand on my best friend.

The agony I'd suffered inside the house, the sickening torment of the wards, was still fresh; in fact, I was still feelin' a good bit of it. I squeezed off a small burst of mojo, enough for just a quick sting of bad luck.

Pete's attentions had been fixed on the succubus overhead, a predator's instinct recognizing her as a threat, but now he whipped his snout around, fixed me with a murderous glare. And now I had his attention, he recognized me.

No, *it* recognized me. 'Cause the hunter, the mind I was dealin' with now, wasn't Pete—werewolf, human, or otherwise.

"C'mon, you bastard!"

Gods, he was fast! A sudden lope and he was almost on me. But between us lockin' eyes, and the boost from the L&G, it was enough.

I bundled up every scrap of the pain I felt, or *had* felt in the last few minutes, and shoved it through the wand and into his noggin.

Pete flopped to the street with an ear-splitting scream, twisted and clawed hands clasped to the sides of his skull. He thrashed, kicked, and I swear he started diggin' at his own hide, maybe tryin' to tunnel down to the pain and let it out.

"Ramona, now!"

She hit the concrete beside him and lunged. Between one step and the next her wings vanished and her whole body swelled, her shape changing to layer muscle on top of muscle. She slammed into the writhing werewolf with a grunt, snagging him in a pretty impressive wrestler's hold, but even with the extra strength and the magics I'd sent her way, she wasn't gonna be able to keep it up for long. Already she was strainin' and struggling with every toss and turn; soon as Pete—or what was wearin' Pete—got over the pain enough to really fight back, she'd be behind the eight-ball, bad.

So I hadda do this quick.

"Get the hell outta my friend!"

If anyone'd been watching, I probably looked to be conducting a symphony. I wove every bit of my own magic, magnified through the wand, through the werewolf—body, aura, and soul. Or souls. I pulled whole ropes of luck and strength away, turned 'em to my own purposes, and fed 'em right back in.

Tryin' to pass it all to Pete while draining it from the thing *inside* Pete. And if that sounds easy or simple, you're a twit.

I dunno which exact part of the process we broke. Maybe we gave Pete, or the natural cycle of the werewolf, enough get-up-and-go to reassert themselves. Or maybe we gave the spirit enough of a shellacking it couldn't maintain the forced transformation, or it hurt too much, or...

Nuts. Whaddaya want from me? It worked.

The werewolf trailed off in mid-growl, whole body goin' slack as a dropped yoyo. A single wet, nasty sound rang like a shot through the neighborhood as flesh twisted and bone cracked, all at once. Hair dangled and fell in two or three massive clumps, turnin' brittle and cracking away into dust before it even hit the ground.

And just that quick, he was Pete again, naked as a jaybird, starin' up at us with an expression first empty as a mannequin's, and then as horrified as I've ever seen on a man.

"We've gotta get inside," I said. "Off the street."

Still wearin' her own impossibly bulging body, Ramona picked him up and cradled him like a puppy. "Where to?"

Dammit. "Orsola's digs. Only option."

"Wards?"

"I did some work on 'em. It won't be any fun, but we can tolerate 'em long enough to find the glyphs and deal with 'em proper."

She grimaced, but made for the door. Me, I scooped up Pete's broken belt—and the heater attached to it; he didn't need to lose his department-issue piece, on top of everything—and followed.

I'd been right. The wards *weren't* fun. But they packed nowhere near the punch they had when they'd first clobbered me, and I managed to locate most of the chalk-and-iron-filing glyphs—under carpets, on the backside of furniture—and break the lines.

Now I'd had a chance to give the whole place a good up'n down, it was clear Orsola'd been here a while. Months, at least. And she'd been busy. I found all sorts of scrawled notes and incantations scattered around what'd been some kinda study or library. Some in Italian, some in English, all spindly and spidery and damn near incomprehensible. I thought a couple pages might prove useful, the ones where she was obviously talkin' about the vampire spirits, how they'd been summoned, how to steal control of one of 'em. No such luck, though. Lotta ramblin' about grave dirt and corrupted funerary rights, new moons and intercessionary spirits, sacrifices and heart's blood, but nothin' too intelligible. I crumpled 'em up and stuck 'em in a coat pocket.

She'd also had help, gettin' around, cleanin' herself up... No idea who her assistant mighta been, prior to Fino (goddamn it, Fino), but we got lucky in at least one respect: The guy'd left some clothes, sloppily folded in a dust-covered old bureau.

He'd been bigger'n Pete, who now looked like he was wearin' an older brother's hand-me-downs, but it beat sittin' around—or tryin' to get home—with Little Pete swinging free.

Right now, he was hunched in a chair, its upholstery cracked and yellowed with age, mitts clasped around a cup of tea that'd gone cool without him takin' so much as a sip. No idea where Varujan had scrammed off to, and at the moment, I didn't much care. Me'n Ramona—who was once more back to lookin' just supernaturally gorgeous insteada full-on supernatural—stood across the room, jawin' softly.

We didn't whisper, exactly, and it ain't as if we were tryin' to keep anything from Pete. It just... didn't feel right talkin' about this in front of him out loud, like it was nothin' big.

Plus, I was keepin' half an ear on the real faint sounds from outside. People were up and about, now that the bulls had come to investigate whatever crazy story they'd been told and were examinin' the crashed Ford. No doubt they were catchin' all sorts of hinky reports from folks who'd seen bits of pieces of what went down, witnessed from between heavy curtains on a night-darkened street. They'd nod, and try not to scoff out loud at the nice hardworking citizens with their ridiculous imaginations, and then they'd go back to the clubhouse and guffaw and slap their knees about it. But one or two, who'd seen a few things, been around the block a couple times, would laugh just a little nervously, and wonder if just *maybe* the stories weren't *quite* as goofy as they sounded.

They wouldn't say anything about it to their fellow elephant ears, or to anyone else. But they'd wonder.

"Mick? You still in there?"

"Huh? Sorry, doll. Got distracted."

"You don't say?" She took a puff of her cigarette, cast about for something to use as an ashtray, and then—maybe remembering whose place this had been—shrugged and let the ash fall to the floor.

"Got a lot on my mind."

"Yeah. What I said was, I've never heard of a vampire surviving beyond the destruction of its body before. Are you sure?"

"Well, I can't be *completely* positive, but yeah, pretty well sure. I think when you killed it, its spirit was drawn to the predator lurkin' inside Pete, and it tried to move in insteada goin' in search of another convenient stiff. Didn't work out too well, and I don't think it woulda lasted long even if we hadn't driven it out, since Pete was still in there, but... obviously it clung on for a bit."

"I don't know much about the spirits that inhabit vampires," she admitted. "Never really even thought about it until today, and I'd never heard of any sort of non-human or non-corpse vampire until your... um, watermelon." She shook her head, setting her hair to waving like a soft tide.

"Not many *do* know much about 'em. I mean, they're not

even really individual spirits, per se, just fragments of spiritual… I dunno, energy? Essence? They got no personality, no individual existence. Maybe they ain't just the source of vampires, but other undead or death-related Fae, too. I got no idea. Normally, when a vampire dies, the essence is just… absorbed back into that whole. Like pourin' a bucket of water back into the ocean.

"But after what Orsola did to this one, or says she did? I dunno. Maybe it really does hang together, keeps its identity, its memories—or at least enough of the personality she gave it to be a real pain in the rear."

We both froze at a knock on the front door. Wasn't the first time, either. The bulls were canvasing for witnesses to the crash and the fight—or whatever it was—that'd happened out in the street. We kept quiet, waited for 'em to assume either nobody was up or nobody was home, and to move on. Hopefully, it was the last time they'd bother.

"Do you believe her?" Ramona asked, even more quietly, after we'd given it a few minutes. "Do you think this thing's just going to keep coming for you, over and over, life after life, forever?"

"I've been noodling on that." I had, too; it'd been in the back of my mind, picking and nagging at me, since the minute the witch had threatened me with it. "I'm just guessin' here, you understand, but given the nature of these things? No, I don't think she coulda transformed it that completely. I figure, sooner or later, her magic—and the beef with me—are gonna fade. It's gonna dissipate, go back to bein' just a shred of potential, mixed in with the others.

"But I got no notion of *when*. Whether it's just a matter of time, or a matter of how many incarnations it goes through, or what? So yeah, it's gonna keep on gunnin' for me for a while before I'm rid of it."

"Or it gets rid of you," she whispered, taking another long drag.

"Anything's possible, sweetheart, but that ain't the current plan."

She reached out, squeezed my arm. It was nice, especially after the last few months.

Didn't seem to be much to say to that, so I scooted across the room to stand beside the old chair. "How about you, pal? How're you doin'?"

He swirled the tea, which we'd taken from Orsola's kitchen, seemed to be fascinated by the spin and dance of the leaves. Wasn't sure he'd even heard me, at first.

Then, "How long's it been, Mick? About two and half years?"

"Uh." We'd known each other longer'n that, though we hadn't drunk outta the same bottle that whole time, so I didn't figure that's what he meant. Which left...

Since he got bit.

"Yeah, that sounds about right. Give or take."

"You know what I been most afraid of, every second since then? What's given me fuckin' nightmares at least three times a month, no matter how much I tried to get used to this, how many full moons you took me Sideways?"

I could take a pretty solid guess. "Pete, you—"

"That, one full moon, somehow, you wouldn't be around. Or I'd get caught up in somethin' and not be able to make it. Or a dozen other things. That I'd lose control." He finally looked up, and his eyes shone wet in the weak lamplight. "That I'd hurt someone, kill someone. That the monster in me would—"

"Pete, you didn't hurt anyone." I crouched next to the chair. Didn't feel right makin' him look up at me. "Things coulda gone real sour out there, sure. No denying it. But they didn't. We—you—got through it."

"And what about next time?"

"Ain't gonna be a next time, pal. That vampire, spirit, whatever you wanna call it, it's moved on to somethin' else. It knows it can't hold onto you now. And there ain't any others like it. You're all aces."

"But now I know, don't you see? Now I know it's *possible*.

That even when it's not a full moon, I can't be absolutely sure I'm safe, that the people around me are safe. Okay, so maybe that damn spirit won't grab me again, but what if something else does? You didn't know this was possible until today, Mick. So you can't know what *else* might be able to... to change me." He had the full waterworks goin' now. It was hard to look at; Pete wouldn'ta wanted to be seen this way.

I tried to reassure him, tried to tell him that the odds against him runnin' into anything *else* in his life that could do this— could do what I'd thought, after thousands of years, was impossible—were so high I wasn't sure numbers even went that far.

Maybe... Maybe I got into his head, some, too. I didn't do much, wouldn't do that to him. Just enough to calm his emotions, let him get hold of himself.

I wish I could say I did that solely for his sake. *Mostly* it was. But we hadda get back to it, hadda keep workin' on the case. People *were* gonna die, not by the claws of a werewolf but the fangs of vampires, and Dagda-knew-what other magics, if we didn't run this down.

And just a little bit, if I'm being square, because it ate at me seein' him so broken.

Judgin' by the blank stare Ramona was pointin' my way, she knew what I'd just done. I couldn't tell if she approved or not, and she obviously wasn't gonna spill her feelings on it either way.

"All right," I said, once Pete seemed steady again. "If you two are jake with it, I'm gonna ask you to head back to my joint and wait for me there."

"Can do," Pete said, with almost no quaver.

"That's fine by me," Ramona said, "but why? Where are you going?"

*Last place in the world I wanna go, dollface.*

"I gotta go talk to some friends," I answered. The words almost wouldn't come. I hadda force 'em through my throat by main force. "I got..." I looked around, and I had a sudden image, a sudden *urge* to burn the whole fucking house to the ground. As if doin' that could change one iota of what'd happened here. What I'd discovered here.

Damn you, Orsola.

"I got somethin' I hafta tell them."

# CHAPTER ELEVEN

It was just comin' up on first light, a couple early hints of pink blushing beyond the waters of Lake Calumet, when I reached the Ottati apartment.

Yeah, after all the chiding I'd given 'em about me knowin' where they were bunked, all the worries about someone bein' shadowed back there, maybe it was a bad idea. But what was I gonna do, pick up the blower and call? Some things… Some things people deserve to hear face to face.

No matter how much you don't wanna tell it that way.

Oh, I took steps, sure. Doubled back more'n a few times, wound myself in a tight cocoon of extra luck, checked every reflection and every shadow in the street lights. No way anyone, mortal or Fae, was on my tail.

All that effort gave me an excuse not to think about what was comin', too. But now I was inside the building, knuckles raised to rap on their door, all I could do was think. About what'd gone down.

About what came next.

Was a time I was just like most of the others of my kind. When mortal lives meant squat to me, and I could play with 'em—or end 'em—without the idea of remorse ever crossin' my mind, let alone actually feelin' even a sliver of it.

That was a me I'd worked hard to kill, or at least bury. A me from long, long ago. A me who mighta had some affection for a human as a pet, or something to lust after, but who woulda been appalled, even offended, at the idea of callin' one of you "friend."

I know a lotta you personally, now. I got a lotta contacts and connections, a lotta allies.

Not so many friends.

Now, one fewer. And I guessed maybe Fino wasn't the last I was gonna lose today.

I knocked, because what else could I do?

A few latches clicked and the door swung open. Even this early, Bianca was dressed, though she wasn't exactly dolled up to go anywhere. I doubted if she'd gone back to bed after our phone call.

Soon as she saw me, her fist clenched around her rosary, her lips parted in a short hitch of breath. Maybe she didn't already know what I hadda say, but she knew somethin' was wrong.

No call for me to just show up this way otherwise. Not alone.

"Can I, uh… Can I come in, Bianca?"

She stepped aside, silent. She shut the door softly, didn't wanna disturb the neighbors, but it was still the loudest thing I'd heard in years.

I found myself standin' by the table, beside the sofa I'd slept on a few nights and centuries ago. Don't remember walkin' over there.

"What is it, Mick?"

Strong woman, and make no mistake. I think most woulda been screamin' for answers or sobbin' already. Bianca Ottati? Her voice barely quivered.

I'da near sold my soul not to be in that room.

"Bianca, he… Fino found Orsola first."

"He…?" Click-click-click went the rosary, and I swear each bead shook the room like fallin' boulders. "Don't tell me he's thrown in with her again? Not after what she did to us!"

She didn't wanna believe that, except her body, her aura,

screamed at me that she *did*. Because it was still the better option.

"I don't think she ever even gave him the chance." I was reachin' both hands out, beseeching for I dunno what. "She…"

"No."

"I'm so sorry, Bianca."

"No!"

She bit her lip like she was tryin' to catch the shout before it escaped. Tears streamed down cheeks gone white as her teeth, and her whole body shook with the effort of keepin' quiet, keepin' control.

For an endless minute, she cried in silence.

Then the rosary slipped from her fingers. Beads clattered as it thumped into the carpet, and that… that was one step too far.

It wasn't exactly a scream, wasn't exactly a sob. It was short, sharp, wracked her body with a single violent shudder, and was gone just as quick.

But it was enough. Celia and Adalina about tumbled through one of the doorways to stand side by side, staring at us across the living room. Both of 'em wore frilly nightgowns that, though more than modest enough, they probably wouldn'ta wanted me to see if the circumstances…

Well, yeah. Circumstances.

No bunnies, either of the Ottati girls. They saw me there, with the sun barely up. Saw their mother, one of the strongest dames either of 'em ever met, tear-streaked and steady as a single snowflake in a flurry. And they knew.

Adalina's mouth opened, once, twice.

When she finally forced the word through, it wasn't even a whisper. "Daddy?"

Bianca tried, she really did. "Darling, I…"

She couldn't do it. It caught in her throat, whatever she'd meant to say, and all she could do was choke. Adalina fell to her bony knees, hard enough to shake the floor, arms wrapped around her stomach, rocking violently as she sobbed.

And Celia…

Celia knelt, gently holding her sister by the shoulders, bringing the rocking to a slow halt. But her eyes, shining and rippling with tears she wouldn't yet shed, never left mine.

"You were supposed to be better. You were supposed to be better than Goswythe."

"What?"

*Don't.*

"Daddy... It was his mother, wasn't it? He knew where to look, and you didn't."

"I... Yeah. I'm afraid so."

*Don't do it. Please.*

But she did.

It wasn't as if I hadn't already thought it a thousand times. If she'd said nothin', I coulda dealt with it in my own time. If she'd screamed it, shrieked it, sobbed it, I coulda closed myself off against the emotional ing-bing and protected myself from the words in the process.

But she just crouched there, glarin', completely in control, and her words bored into me like an iron drill bit.

"If you'd told us she was still alive at the start, if you'd *trusted* us like you always wanted us to trust *you*, you could've found her together. He could've led you right to her, and he wouldn't have had to face her alone.

"He wouldn't be gone."

What could I possibly say to that? What could I do?

Nothin'. Not one damn thing.

Maybe I'da just kept right on standin' there like a stump, doin' nothing at all. But I guess the grief—not to mention the fear she'd been livin' with for days, that the Unseelie were gunnin' for her—had been building up in Adalina faster'n her sobs could let it out. It erupted.

She wailed, long and loud, a cry of undiluted anguish. It filled the room, drowned the mind. On and on, wavering, falling, rising in ways no human throat coulda produced. Breathless and seemingly endless, it continued long after any mortal, or even most Fae, woulda been forced to break off and gasp for air.

And still it wouldn't stop.

Celia and Bianca both stared my way, now, not just in grief but in fear, lookin' to me to do something. I took one step, tryin' to figure what I *could* do...

The light bulb flickered, sizzled, and bust with a sharp pop, leavin' the glow of morning between the curtains as our only illumination. Cracks spider-webbed across the window with a sharp, almost tinkling sound, and the ceiling fan above us slowly spun backwards. The faucet in the kitchen—no, the whole sink—started to shake, like some dragon roared and crawled through the pipes toward us.

Oh, this was familiar, sure. Way too familiar, of late. Only it wasn't me doin' it.

Took another step toward the girl, tryin' to figure some way of talkin' her down without gumming things up even worse... And then things got weird.

Knobs twisted on their own and the faucet began to run, fillin' the sink faster'n the drain could swallow it up—but this wasn't the usual city juice. Even from across the apartment, I could smell rotting kelp, the crisp tang of saltwater.

The cracks in the window? They started *changin' shape*, some closin' back up and fading away, others writhing like reeds in the wind, but leavin' the glass completely intact after they passed.

And the light...

The shattered bulb started to glow again, but it was a dull crimson hue, the kind you see at the edge of firelight. Nothin' at all stood between that source and the far wall, but shadows streaked the paint, skipping and stuttering like bad film at first, but growin' smoother with every heartbeat. Almost-human forms swam across that wall with frog-like strokes and serpentine undulations. Others rose to meet 'em, with dull shapes that mighta been swords or clubs in their hands. But all of it was blurred, smeared, so that anyone coulda thought they'd imagined it all, that they saw only blotted shades in the dancing light.

*What in two worlds* are *you, Adalina?*

Wasn't until the murky seawater started to overflow the sink and spatter across the linoleum, until the cracks started to tentatively, questioningly, reach *out of the window* like a curious goddamn jellyfish that I tore my attention away from the question. I all but sprinted the last couple steps and dropped to my knees in front of her.

"Adalina." I took her hands. She tried to pull away, but without any real strength. "Adalina, sweetheart, you gotta simmer down. Get a hold of yourself."

Nothin'. She kept wailing, things kept moving.

"It'll be all right, it'll…"

No. That wasn't gonna cut it. Even if she wasn't so far gone, when did hearin' that kinda hooey *ever* really comfort the grieving?

I could get into her mind, *make* her stop—but gods, I didn't wanna to do that. It woulda been one violation too far.

"Adalina!" Celia and Bianca both jumped at the shout, but they weren't the ones needed to hear me. "You nix the tantrum *now. You're gonna hurt your momma and your sister!*"

The keening stopped so sharp, you'da thought I'd cut her throat. The red glow faded. The water stopped flowin'. And she caught me with those wide, bloodshot blinkers and wouldn't let go.

"I'm sorry, doll. I know that was cruel. You got more right to cry than anyone. I only… I hadda get you to hear me."

She hiccupped, nodded, and bent her head to watch the floor.

Bianca, trembling, staggered over to pull the curtains, let more of the light inside, and then knelt to wrap her arms around both her daughters. They turned, wet faces pressed tight to her shoulders, her chest, and all three of 'em shook.

I moved away, and found myself almost steppin' on the

fallen rosary. I picked it up, studied it a minute, and then went back to hand it to Bianca.

The look she laid on me when she took it wasn't exactly one of gratitude.

I stayed a few more minutes, just enough to be certain Adalina's fit had truly passed. We were gonna hafta look into that, have some words, but... Later.

Later.

Then I left; it seemed the best thing for everyone. The door shut behind me, and nobody'd said a word.

And even after all that? I *still* hadn't spilled everything. I still hadn't told 'em Fino wasn't just dead, but was shamblin' around, animated by dear momma's damn magics. That even as a stiff, he couldn't escape her.

Probably not for long—it ain't easy to keep a dead body up and about, to say nothin' of presentable—but still. Should I have told them? Was it a kindness to keep my trap shut, or was I repeating the same mistakes I'd just made?

I dunno. Didn't then, still don't. But I walked away without going back, and if you wanna judge me for that, you go right ahead.

It ain't as if I haven't.


After a longer opportunity than I wanted to ruminate on everything that'd just happened, and the usual discomfort of crossin' Chicago on the L, my mood hadn't much improved by the time I got back to the office. I about kicked the door in, and near drew my sword—or at least spat some ungentle words I wouldn't have been able to take back—when I saw Ramona'n Pete waiting for me.

It'd utterly slipped my mind that they'd even be there, honestly.

I threw my coat at the rack, stormed to my chair, and landed like I was tryin' to punish it.

Ramona had been reclining in the other chair, though she half-rose when I barged in. Pete'd taken the liberty of pulling down the Murphy, and had been catchin' some doss until my grand entrance. Now they both watched me—though he was blinkin' so much, it was hard to be sure—I guess waiting for me to proclaim our next step.

Right. 'Cause I was battin' a fuckin' thousand so far.

"What?" I demanded.

"Um." Pete knuckled at his face, cleared his throat. "We expecting Varujan?"

"He's sleeping somewhere dark," Ramona said. "With at least a small sack of the earth of his homeland, if I recall correctly?"

"Yeah," I said grudgingly. "Somethin' like that. Not a big fan of sunlight, the nosferatu. It's just us."

Pete nodded, his chin vanishing into the collar of the shirt that really was too big for him. "So what now?"

"*How the fuck do I know?*"

The both of 'em actually jumped a little. I squeezed my peepers shut a spell.

"Sorry." I got up, hauled open the icebox and took out the carton of good cream I'd been saving for a special occasion.

Nothin' special today, but it sure as shootin' was an occasion.

"Didn't go well, Mick?" Pete ventured.

Good thing I'd already thrown back a slug, because if my kisser hadn't been full, I'da said somethin' nasty. By the time I *could* talk, the sympathy in Pete's tone had smoothed over the fool question.

Besides, he'd gone through his own hell this morning, too.

"I'd rather spend a week wrapped up in that damned broad's worst wards than ever have to relive a half-hour like that."

"I'm sorry, bud."

"Me, too, Mick," Ramona said.

Was she? I knew she could be upset, be hurt—emotionally, I mean—but did a succubus really understand grief? Or guilt?

Well, whether she fully understood or not, she sounded like she meant it. I forced a shallow smile for her.

I took a few more gulps, offered some milk to Pete—he took it, since I didn't have any coffee—and waited for Ramona to poke through her purse and decide if she wanted a gasper. She didn't.

"Sorry," I told them again. "But I got no idea what's next. Orsola didn't just kill my friend, she killed the trail. She was my best suspect."

"Are we sure she still isn't?" Ramona asked. "You've explained your thinking, and it's solid, but still, are you *that* certain you can believe what she told you?"

I couldn't help it. I laughed, sharp and bitter. "Sweetheart, I ain't certain of much. Right now, I trust my judgment about as far as I'd trust a hungry redcap with a baby. But everything I got, reason and instinct, says Orsola ain't our guy. She's got a heap to answer for, and you better damn well believe she will. But not summoning the vampires, not whatever's been tickling Áebinn's nose."

They had their doubts; I saw it in their mugs, tasted it in the air. But they went along with it.

Unfortunately, that left them about as stumped as it did me.

"The Unseelie?" Ramona asked, shifting in her seat. I'da thought she was nervous, but if she was, I'm pretty sure it was for me, how I was gonna respond, not for the investigation or the thought of the Court. "You said they were stalking the Ottatis."

And yeah, I had more'n a small urge to shout, or change the topic, when they came back up, but... "Could be. I still haven't tumbled what they were even after, whether it was Adalina, or somethin' to do with me, or what else. And calling a pack of vampires down on Chicago? That ain't anything I'd put past 'em."

Pete, who'd scooted back on the mattress so he could lean against the wall, said, "But you don't buy it."

Well, he *had* known me a while. "No, I don't. They *would*

do it, but I don't think they *can*. They wouldn't know how, anymore'n the rest of us."

Ramona half-frowned in a pretty moue that instantly snagged Pete's attention. He knew what she was, and she was tampin' the sultry way down—not just in her behavior, but the general waves of emotion succubi were always puttin' off—but it waxed and waned with her concentration. And no matter how wary Pete mighta been, or the fact that he'd seen her in some far less dishy forms, he was only human.

"A lot of the Unseelie," she said, totally missing Pete's longing puppyish gaze, "have one foot in the grave already. Or deal with spirits of destruction and darkness far more often than most other Fae."

I allowed how that was true, yeah.

"So just because *you've* never heard of any magics that affect the spirits of the nosferatu before they find a corpse to pin on, or even because Laurelline hasn't, I don't think that means you should write off the possibility that *they* have."

I looked at Pete, who had his cop face back on, whether he was really feelin' it or not, then back.

"All right. That ain't a bad point. Thing is, though… Redcaps and trolls and all those guys are pretty hot-tempered and impulsive, but Queen Mob and the other high pillows? They ain't dumb. If they were gonna spring a surprise like this on us, I'm pretty sure they'd want to hold off until they could really hit the Seelie hard. This? Unless you count gettin' Áebinn all wound up, they haven't even *inconvenienced* the Court. All they're doin' is causing some mayhem in the mortal half of Chicago."

"Isn't that all they appeared to be doing a year ago, with the Spear of Lugh?" she asked, just a bit smugly.

Dammit.

"You really figure they'd expose their new vampire party trick just to pull the same kinda swindle they ran on us last year?"

"I'm not saying it's probable, Mick. I'm saying it's possible."

"Fine." I started to take another drink, realized I'd finished the cream, and near stood up from the chair just so I could kick my own keister. I'd gotten distracted, chugged the rest while we were jawin'. Top shelf stuff, and I didn't even remember tasting it.

I glared at the bottle, snapped, "Fine!" again, and put it aside by the typewriter. "The Unseelie stay on the list, not that we got any good way to investigate 'em.

"But I still guess a mortal's more likely. Ramona, you're completely sure it ain't—"

"I'm sure."

Her tone said, *Don't argue,* so I didn't. Pete wisely kept his trap shut.

I went through the roster, same as I'd done when this whole shindig kicked off, and it wasn't any more helpful this time around.

Once, centuries ago, I saw a *cu sidhe* get rip-roaring lit—this was in the Otherworld, so findin' stuff for Fae to get drunk on ain't a problem—and spend an hour chasin' her own tail like a common hound, only even clumsier. Trippin' over her paws, fallin' flat on her snout, even tumbling ass over ears a couple times. When we talked the next day, she admitted to me that part of the reason she'd been havin' so much trouble tryin' to catch her tail was that'd she'd been seein' three of 'em, and they weren't even waggin' in unison.

I was startin' to feel like I imagine she must have.

"Um."

Me'n Ramona both craned our heads to look Pete's way.

"I'm not the expert in the room where Fae or vampires or any of that's concerned," he said. "And I'm just a beat cop, not a detective. And, uh..." He hesitated, shot me an apologetic smile. "And I know you're usually able to fit the puzzle together around the missing pieces, and *then* go find 'em."

"But?"

"But maybe we don't worry right now about who the best

suspect is. Maybe we just go back over the evidence and see where it leads us."

"Oh, look at the *evidence*! Damn, I'm such a bunny! Why didn't I ever do that?"

He scowled at me. I don't blame him.

"I've *been* over it all, Pete. It led me to right where we're sittin'."

"That *was* a few days back," Ramona chided. "There have been a few more murders, if nothing else. And we weren't here to look at it with you."

So, without any better ideas, I hauled out the copies of the police reports, the map where I'd marked off the sites of the murders, the autopsy reports on the victims. All of it. The three of us bent our conks over it all and got to readin'.

Sadly, after a few hours at it, we still had bupkis. I hadn't stumbled over anything I'd missed the first time, and they hadn't spotted any new details or been struck by any new inspiration.

We added the newest bloody deaths to the map, but if it held a hidden picture, the damn thing wasn't comin' into any better focus. Same as before, other'n a few outliers, most of 'em were clustered in one chunk of Chicago—but because of how quick and how far vampires can travel in their hunts, it was a large enough chunk that it was basically unsearchable.

Pete seemed particularly glum. I guess he'd hoped his suggestion mighta broken the whole thing open. "I'm sorry, Mick."

"Me, too." Ramona stubbed out a butt in a small saucer I'd given her to use as an ashtray. "Maybe if we knew more about how the magic had been cast in the first place, I might come up with something, or at least have some idea which of the boss's grimoires to consult. But without knowing what we're looking for, I'm afraid I—"

I straightened up from the desk. "Hold up."

I chewed on her question. I looked at the pile of records and reports. I studied the map. I removed a crumpled mass of paper from my pocket and laid it out beside that map.

And damn if they hadn't been right. It was because of Pete's suggestion to go back over it all, and because of Ramona's comment, that it came to me.

Not an answer. Barely even a lead. But at least it was a direction.

"Get your coats, folks. We've got a trip to take."

Pete grinned and sidled over to the stand. He started with Ramona's coat, not his own, and held it for her. Her smile nearly bowled him over, and she'd barely given him half strength.

"Where to?" she asked as she slipped an arm through a sleeve.

"Only the nicest places for you, doll," I told her. "We're headin' to the morgue."


The morgue attendants somehow managed to look both overwhelmed with work and yet bored to tears, and they weren't real keen on seeing me again.

"We're already showed you everythin' there is to see. There ain't no more."

"The new stiffs don't got anythin' on 'em the old ones didn't."

"We got too much on our plates to be wastin' time like this."

But I had my authorizations, and we had Ramona's smile, and we had Pete's badge. (Also, I suppose I oughta mention we stopped by his digs so he could put on clothes that actually fit, so he didn't look like he'd shrunk in the wash.)

Plus, of course, I coulda *made* the ginks change their minds if I needed to, but we hadn't come to that. Yet.

Point is, despite the grousing and delays, they hauled open a disturbingly large number of refrigerated drawers and dumped a stack of reports on an empty steel table so we could examine to our heart's content.

Too bad for them I didn't actually need anything from these bodies. I was just reestablishing my bona fides as an investigator on the case and otherwise double-checking before

I got to the real meat—so to speak—of our visit.

I gave 'em a casual slant, then wandered over to the leaning tower of paperwork, tapped it to get their attention, and then plunked my marked-up map down on top if it all.

"Swell. Now I wanna see all the stabbings and other sharp-force deaths brought in from this chunk of the city—I circled it here so you don't gotta go tryin' to figure out addresses—in the two weeks *before* this string of bloody killings started."

Well, you woulda thought I'd just demanded they yank the fillings from their own pearly whites to hand 'em over.

"You got any idea how many reports we'd have to go through?"

"Most of those bodies ain't even here anymore!"

"Does it look like we're just sittin' around? We're workin' here!"

"Besides, you ain't even authorized to see those! The department's only given you access to the one case!"

I wanna state it clearly, on the record, that I *did* try to be reasonable. I explained that this was part of the same investigation into the same case. I pointed out that diggin' through reports was part of their job. I told 'em that "most of the bodies" bein' gone meant a few were still here, waitin' to be claimed. I even offered 'em a bit of folding green as incentive, though I only had a few bucks to give.

Only after alla that flopped did I catch their gaze, one by one, and play kick the can with their emotions until the resentment and suspicion and laziness had all landed way down the road and I found a clear path to more cooperative moods.

Took a while, even after that. I mean, they weren't wrong that it meant searchin' through a lot of paperwork, seeing which murders had the right cause of death and fell within the zone, checkin' evidence labels, wheeling the bodies out from cold storage (since, as older cases, they weren't takin' up space in the drawers). After loitering for an hour or two, though, we had our prizes.

Seven stiffs, a few dozen boxes of evidence, and another tower of folders, some with a single form, others stuffed thick to bursting.

I sent the attendants back to their other duties, leaving me, Pete, and Ramona gathered at the far end of the cold, tiled room.

By this time, both of 'em had completely run outta patience.

"Okay, Mick," Ramona demanded. "You've got your bodies. Would you *please* tell us what the hell we're supposed to be looking for?"

Pete added, more'n a touch grumpily, "Yeah, that. But without the 'please.'"

"We're startin' with two assumptions," I said, wandering back and forth between the tables of corpses. "One, the vampires' current lair is the same spot they were summoned to in the first place, or at least pretty near. And two, that this was also the lair, or at least the workspace, of whoever summoned 'em. He'd want to know the area, have time to set up the ritual, et cetera."

Two nods. They were on board so far.

"So if those're both accurate, it makes sense that the sacrifices, the murders used to invoke the spirit-summoning ritual, would also come from that same area."

"An area that encompasses a sizable portion of the city," Ramona protested, "and that you said, more than once, was too large to reasonably search."

"Yeah. Until you'n Pete made me stop and think, and I realized I might know what I was lookin' for.

"Orsola's notes," I explained. "It occurred to me, what if she wasn't bein' metaphorical? When she wrote about 'heart's blood,' what if she meant it literally? So, *that's* what we're lookin' for in our sacrificial victims, lady and gentlemen."

I'd told Laurelline even I wasn't good enough to separate a handful of sacrifices from all Chicago's murders. But a handful of sacrifices from a smaller subset of Chicago's murders, when I had a pretty good sense of what those murders'd look like, sounded a lot more doable.

Which ain't remotely the same thing as "easy."

There was a *lot* to go through. Gettin' plugged is certainly more common, but stabbin' ain't exactly unheard of in the Second City. We spent hours in that chilly morgue, being bumped and glowered at by assistants and coroners whose space we'd annexed, suckin' up foul mixtures of chemicals and cleansers and rot, tryin' to pinpoint those tiny details that just might, if we listened real intently, whisper to us that, yeah, *this* was the one.

We read reports until the letters stopped makin' sense, looked over boxes and bags of evidence, examined bodies that'd long been washed of almost everything that coulda been useful.

By the time we were done, we were all of us irritable, frustrated, ready to blow our lids at the slightest inconvenience. I wasn't sure if I wanted to put my companions on one of these steel slabs, or just say nuts to it all and let 'em lay me on one.

But we'd found it.

One of the stiffs we still had—and four others, based on the written reports—stood out to me. They'd been shivved straight through the pump, all five.

They weren't the only stabbin' victims we looked at, by a long shot. Not even the only ones stabbed in the heart. But it ain't as easy as you might figure to croak somebody with a single thrust, not if they're movin' or aware that you're comin'. And if you *do* manage to make a sneak of it, get 'em when they're none the wiser and drop 'em in one stab, it's almost always gonna be from the back.

These five? Dropped by a single, neat thrust, from the front.

One or two? I coulda bought that as coincidence, maybe wouldn't have been convinced I was on the right track or that I'd interpreted Orsola's chicken scratch right. But five, in the same week, week and a half?

Yeah. We had our sacrifices.

So I dove right back into it, examining that one body and

those four reports closer'n you'd ever wanna get. Read over every word, every note, every number. Opened bags I wasn't supposed to open. (Because let's be square: If anyone caught this bastard, it was gonna be us, in which case "proper procedure" and "chain of custody" wasn't gonna matter squat. I *did* juggle a few memories, though. Didn't need it gettin' back to the department that I was the one who'd ruined the evidence; not if I ever wanted another job with the city.)

I even, accompanied by a lotta disgusted gasps or snorts from Pete and a few of the attendants, took my time to actually *sniff* the entire corpse, inch by inch. Always possible the wash left somethin' behind I could pick up, even if you lot couldn't.

And, in fact, on a couple fingers of the left hand, it had.

Mud, under the nails. Just a tiny few flecks left behind after the wash, preserved by the cold of the freezer.

More mud, in the evidence. Taken offa two other stiffs who'd been stabbed. Wasn't any collected or recorded from the last couple, but even if it hadn't been there—or if the examiners just missed it—three outta five was good enough for me to call a clue.

Not that the stuff *was* a clue, in and of itself. Mud? In a rainy month? Big deal, right?

It had a… tang to it, though. I'd caught just the smallest whiff of somethin' more'n dirt and water.

I cleared my head, shouted for quiet, leaned in so close I damn near shoved those two fingers up my nostrils. Soft, gentle breaths. Sniff, don't snort. Let it come…

Yeah.

Stuff had blood mixed in with it. And not just human; you'd expect human blood on shivved dead guys, wouldn't you? No, this was animal.

So why… Oh. Well, hell, of course.

Had a quick flashback to the displays I'd wandered past at the museum, the frozen and almost serene hunts as predators chased, leapt at, brought down prey. The real thing wasn't near so peaceful, was it? Maybe it woulda never occurred to me without those Field exhibits fresh in my conk, but... all this time I'd been contemplating places of *human* suffering, fear, death, when nobody'd ever said all of it hadda be human, had they?

The Union Stockyards were practically their own small town of pens, offices, and more meat-on-the-hoof than you could count, sittin' smack in the middle of south Chicago.

And between the damn near biblical floods of bloodshed in the slaughterhouses and processing centers, and the suffering of the poor dumb beasts in conditions that woulda made even a goblin flinch, the place *absolutely* had the symbolism, the resonance with predation and horror and death, for the vampire-spirit rituals.

Sure enough, the stockyards, as well as parts of the Packingtown neighborhood where most of its workers lived, fell within the rough circle on my map.

Pete'n Ramona musta seen somethin' in my expression, some hint that I'd finally tumbled to it. The both of 'em stood rapt, waitin' for me to spill. I straightened up from the table, grinnin' big enough to break my mug wide open, ready to do just that.

But I didn't. I froze, and I think my smile mighta cracked a tile on the floor, it fell so hard. 'Cause right then I remembered somethin' else.

I remembered when—and on whom—I'd recently smelled the faint whiff of animal blood.

Every theory I had, my entire picture of the investigation, flipped over in my head, and a ways lower down, my gut was doin' the same. I snatched the map off the table, crumpled it into a pocket, and made tracks for the door and the nearest L station, my bewildered and ever-more worried friends at my heels.

# CHAPTER TWELVE

In case you've never seen it, I ain't kiddin' about the size of the Union Stockyards. They stretch for block after block. Well over three hundred acres, all told, with more'n two thousand separate livestock pens—*plus* all the offices, abattoirs, packin' plants, loading docks, storehouses, equipment sheds, granaries and feed stores... It's a community unto itself. A community built entirely on pain and fear and death.

The earth, the pathways leadin' in every direction beyond the massive main gate, was sludge. Mud and rainwater and the runoff of blood and piss and shit. The stench was enough to choke even a *dullahan* who'd left his noggin behind in Elphame; I actually hadda use a little hocus-pocus on myself, sort of an olfactory illusion that it wasn't so bad, to manage it. I wasn't sure Pete was gonna be able to stick with us, but even though I'd never seen a human go quite that shade of green, he waved us on every time I asked him if he needed to drop back.

Didn't seem to bother Ramona one iota, though. I guess, considerin' where she's from, she'd smelled worse in her time.

The scent wasn't the worst of it, though. The air felt... sticky. Like all the blood and sweat and the rest of it just sorta loitered around, a spectral miasma haunting the stockyards insteada any actual ghosts. I felt slimy, kinda uncomfortably warm, even though the evening was cool, drizzly, and breezy.

The place had once been swampland, before people built over it and turned it into what it was. And I think maybe it was usin' what humanity had done to it to remind everyone of that fact.

You'd think, in alla that, it woulda been a trip for biscuits tryin' to find our bad guy's hidin' place, the vampires' actual lair. Turned out it was the simplest part of the whole mess.

They wouldn't wanna be discovered, see? The stockyards were never entirely empty, and the last thing the undead needed, if they'n their new boss were tryin' to lie dormy, was to have workers stumbling over them in the middle of their daytime nap.

So all I hadda do was find one of those workers—as I said, there were plenty to choose from, even after sunset—and get into his noggin a little. Find out which office or building they'd been recently ordered to stay away from, or had been taken over by a new manager who wanted to be left alone, or what have you.

And that brought us here. A small wooden structure in one corner of the yards, basically a combined office and storage shed and not much else. It was locked up tight—with, I couldn't help notice, a swanky new lock—but that didn't prove much trouble.

Didn't look like much on first slant, just a small, dim cave of an office. One hangin' light bulb, a crummy fan, a desk facin' a window closed off by a cheap but heavy curtain, and a door leadin' into the other half of the building.

We weren't here for just a quick slant, though.

The occult runes and glyphs were carved into the floor of the next room, the supply room, hidden beneath some burlap sacks and a barrel of rakes and hoes. I'd never seen that precise combination of symbols before, but then, I already knew this wasn't any magic I was familiar with. Old blood, dried and flaking, was embedded in the lines.

Human blood, by the smell of it.

What interested me even more'n the glyphs, though, was the collection of papers and notes and files in the bottom drawer of the desk. (It'd also been locked. I was done bein' subtle, and fixed that with a sharp tug.)

Copy of Pete's personnel file from the clubhouse. Some hand-scrawled notes describin' Four-Leaf Franky, Lenai, some of the others. Even a page on Baskin and Ramona.

But those? Those were just a few scribbles, reminders and places to jot down random thoughts. The bulk of the material? That was on the Ottatis.

And lemme tell you, it was pretty damn comprehensive. Names, not just of the family, but everyone in Fino's crew, the priest and staff of Orsola's old church, Bianca's friends, Celia's teachers, Adalina's teachers up to the point they'd stopped sending her to school. A column for known allies, a column for known enemies. Addresses, not just of the Ottatis themselves but most of Fino's covers and storefronts, legit or otherwise.

If the cops'd had half of this stuff, they'da sent Fino up the river long ago.

Only two things stood out as missing, really. First, anything much to do with Adalina for the past couple years. That made sense, since she'd been unable to pass for human during that time, and unconscious for most of it.

And second, I found nothin' about Fino's hidden properties. Also made sense, since the whole point of those was that they were under false names and *couldn't* be tracked back to him.

But it was more'n enough to tell me this whole thing was all about the Ottatis. It'd *always* been about the Ottatis.

Part of me already figured why, too, though I wasn't ready to listen to that part. Woulda meant makin' some connections and acceptin' some truths I wouldn't have cared for much.

Opened my yap to say somethin' to the others, start workin' out our next steps, when the shadows in the doorway thickened with fog and he appeared again.

"Oberon. Webb." Dunno if his failure to greet Pete was

a deliberate slight, or just 'cause he wasn't accustomed to thinkin' of humans as anythin' more'n lunch.

"Varujan."

"Is good you are here." He stepped—I almost woulda said "slunk"—into the office, shoulders forward, sniffin' around like some decomposing bloodhound. "This is source of call, yes? I feel it here. Very strong."

I jabbed a thumb over my shoulder. "Next room."

He drifted that way, stuck his head through but didn't go in. I traded a quick glance with Ramona'n Pete, otherwise kept my peepers fixed on the vampire.

"Yes. I see." Then he was back. "Others are here, too. I sense them."

"Swell. Take us to 'em."

If he'd been an actual stiff, bits of lips and nose woulda fallen off when he shook his head. (I mean, leavin' aside the fact that if he'd been an actual stiff, it woulda been weird for him to be shakin' his head at all.) "Is not so easy, I fear, Oberon. Sensing other nosferatu is not… precise. I know they are near, but no more. Especially with so much blood seeped into mud and walls and the air." He affected a deep sigh. "I think we have no choice but to search whole stockyards."

Uh-huh. And the fact that'd take all night—or longer—was just our own bad luck, right?

Horsefeathers.

"Help me out with somethin' first, Varujan, if you don't mind."

"Of course."

"You can't have been followin' us this time. We went to the morgue in daylight, and came here straight after. So how'd you find us?"

The sudden tilt of his noggin was even more dog-like than the earlier sniffin'.

"The summons is strong here. I told you this before."

"Yeah, except you also told me you couldn't pinpoint it

from across Chicago. That's why you needed my help to find it. So unless you expect me to buy that you just *happened* to be waltzing by the stockyards close enough to feel it tug at you, right at the exact moment on the exact evening we found the place—and just to save you the time, no, I *ain't* buyin' that—it means you were either lyin' before, or you're lyin' now."

Varujan was movin' as I spoke to him. Not quick, nothin' obviously hostile, just sorta idly shufflin' to one side. By the time he stopped, he had a real good angle on me'n Ramona both—the two threats—just right so neither of us could try'n bushwhack him from behind.

Wise. Not subtle, but wise.

It also meant he *couldn't* keep a line on Pete. Why should he, anyway? Wasn't as if the mortal was any kinda danger, least not compared to the succubus and the *aes sidhe* with his trusty wand.

I dropped my right hand down at my side, started movin' my fingers and hoped my pal tumbled to what I was sayin'— and that the vampire didn't.

"I admit," Varujan said, "I followed you. As bat, as mist. We are allies, but I know you do not trust me, so I do not know I can trust you."

*Closed my hand into a fist, then straightened my pointer finger and brought my thumb down on it, like a hammer.*

"Strike two, bo. Sun wasn't quite down yet when we left my office."

*Reached up, scratched my noggin with that finger, let it fall again.*

"Been a long time since you hadda actually put one over on anyone, hasn't it? You usually just grab 'em or mesmerize 'em. Afraid you ain't a good liar, Varujan."

Guess he accepted that the jig was up. "So it appears." He wasn't in a hurry to start anythin'. After all, he could just turn to mist if Ramona or I made a move toward him, right?

*Clenched my fist again, then three fingers straight out.*

Varujan glanced at my mitt, but still didn't seem worried. Why should he be?

"And since you *are* a lousy liar," I continued, "I gotta figure you were tellin' me the truth when we first met. You really *didn't* know what the summons was, who was behind it, where it came from. Since it was aimed at baby vampire spirits, not big-boy undead, you really were stumped. So what changed?"

You ever seen a corpse shrug? Even talkin' about the walking dead, it's weird. "I am in Chicago long enough that I know the call better. I feel it more. I followed summons, flew over city until it grew strong. The occultist offers to teach me these magics, if I spy on you, report on progress."

*Two fingers out now.*

"Yeah, I just bet the ability to conjure up and influence a whole clutch of brand new vampires would be valuable to you. Tell me, did Áebinn ever let you in on exactly what it is she's tryin' to pull?"

*That* threw him. I didn't even have to sense it in his aura—what little of one he had—I could see it plastered all over his mug. I wasn't supposed to know that.

But I had, since the morgue. Since I remembered the smell of animal blood on her, when we'd jawed outside the Ottatis' place.

I just hadn't the foggiest idea as to *why*.

*One finger.*

"What does she want?" I demanded again, when Varujan said nothin'. "Why is she gunnin' for the Ottatis?"

"Mick," Ramona said softly. "You know why."

Yeah, goddammit, I did. Adalina. I hadda stop pretendin' it hadn't always been about Adalina.

Even if that meant that what Áebinn had sensed…

*Oh, fuck me.*

I'd gone back to their apartment, to tell 'em about Fino. I'd been so careful, takin' false turns, checkin' for a shadow every block.

But I'd done it *before dawn*. And not even I woulda spotted a single bat, flitting and fluttering high overhead, watching and snickering with every detour…

He couldn't have reported back then. Too close to dawn; sky was already turning pink at the horizon when I knocked on their door.

But tonight, before she'd sent him here—maybe because we'd tripped some psychic alarm, maybe just on a regular check to see if she'd been found out—yeah, they'da had plenty time to chat.

I knew why Varujan was stallin' us, and I knew I couldn't afford to let it go on.

My fist clenched. *Zero.*

The vampire went taut, bracin' himself. I mean, it was a pretty obvious signal, right? He was ready for either of us, me or Ramona, whichever one came at him first.

In the tight confines of the dimly lit office, the bark of Pete's .38 was a short, sharp peal of thunder.

A chunk of Varujan's face just went away, sprayin' the floor and the wall between me'n Ramona—and both of us leapt aside with plenty of swift, lemme tell ya!—with a thick, clotted ooze that was too filthy and too glistening to be called black. Gobbets of decayed flesh slapped against the wood, wigglin' like worms at the impact, and a yellow, tacky film that mighta once upon a time been vitreous fluid wobbled offa my coat sleeve.

You can't rub a vampire out with a bullet, of course, no matter how good a shot. But there also ain't too many critters out there, nosferatu included, can just shrug off a slug through the skull. Varujan staggered forward, toppled to his knees, hands thrashin' blindly out in front.

I honestly dunno how long it mighta taken for him to recover from that kinda blow. Seconds? Days? Somewhere between?

Didn't matter, I guess, 'cause we weren't inclined to give him either.

Ramona lunged in, hard and fast, fingers sproutin' those pitted black talons. She opened him up and scooped him out, the flesh and organs between the hip and ribs on his right side transformed into a massive handful of quivering rot. The nosferatu's shriek was a damn railroad spike through the ears, set the cows to lowing in the nearest pen.

I dipped down and caught him by the collar as he crumpled to the floor, hauled him upright with my left hand, L&G held not as a wand but as a stake in my right. I was already gatherin' ambient luck from the room, ripping it from the vampire, more'n enough to make up for the blunted tip.

The scream faded out and Varujan… chuckled.

"The other… hunts you." It was awful watchin' his lips move beneath that twisted wreck of a mug, seein' that putrid meat-rimmed hollow of shattered bone wobble along with the words. "Was easy to… find and coax him… to follow…"

I mighta demanded more from him, then, but even in his broken condition he lashed out, tryin' to grab my arm while I was puzzlin' over what he'd said. Except I hadn't let myself get too distracted, and what he got for his effort was the Luchtaine and Goodfellow, punched into his chest and through his sour, rotted heart.

No dramatic death throes, no burstin' into flame or crumblin' to dust. Varujan just sagged, limp as fresh-boiled spaghetti, and slowly bits of putrefaction sloughed off as the state of his carcass caught up to him. I let the body drop, backin' away from the sudden miasma. It hit the floor with a damp splat.

"Shit." I grabbed a handful of paper off the desk, crumpled it up and used it to wipe the gore from my wand. Whole point of takin' Varujan by surprise was so I wouldn't *need* to get caught up in some prolonged scuffle. I hadda get to the Ottatis, to Adalina, before Áebinn did, and she already had a solid head start. But…

"If the bastard's tellin' the truth…" I began.

"We can take another vampire, Mick," Ramona assured me.

I couldn't help but glance Pete's way, remembering the events of the morning. "That's assuming," I reminded them, "that it *is* just another vampire. But that spirit—"

Then the cows weren't lowing any longer. Then they screamed.

And not just the cows. Hogs squealed, sheep wailed. Across the length and breadth of the Union Stockyards, the beasts gave voice to a terror beyond primal. Hooves launched geysers of mud to rain down in torrents. Several gates and even a wall or two collapsed as tons upon tons of animal flesh hurled themselves against the barriers, desperate to flee what now walked among them. Buried in the tumult, the voices of a few of the nighttime workers cried out in confused panic, wonderin' what had set the livestock off, wonderin' what the hell they could do about it if the entire yard turned into one big stampede.

They were happier that way. Not knowin'.

My hackles were already risin', Ramona had dropped into a crouch, tryin' to watch every direction at once, and Pete'd gone from green to off-white as old milk, both hands clenched tight on his heater to keep 'em from shaking.

Outside the tiny office building, which sorta felt as though it were made of paper right now insteada wood, somethin' roared.

Or maybe, more accurately, it didn't.

We felt it, all of us. Like a gazelle on the savanna when the pride comes near, everything in us shook. Limbs went taut, ready to leap, to run, to do whatever it took to get away, to race toward the tiny flicker of hope for survival. Hearts pounded. Those of us who could sweat were drenched in it. Time slowed, every little sound magnified a dozen times over, every flicker of motion the end of the world.

But we hadn't actually *heard* a thing, beyond the livestock, as frightened as we were. We sensed that hunter's howl, but it had made no sound.

With the single exception of Sealgaire, who'd been a part of the goddamn Wild Hunt itself, I hadn't felt anything even comparable to this in centuries.

Pete fired a round into the shadows, spooked by a flicker of nothin' at all. Ramona'n I both jumped, whirling to glare at him. His rictus grin was the best apology he could muster.

The next movement we saw wasn't nothin'.

It slunk past the doorway on silent paws, barely even a shape in the heavy shadows, the growling end of that phantom roar trailing in its wake. Even with my senses, I barely saw it: a glassy glimmer, a creeping form, a twitching tail.

And I knew. Even in that split second before the wooden doorframe splintered and scattered across the room like so much confetti, before it was in the office with us in all its impossibility, I knew.

I knew what it was.

I knew why my thoughts—thoughts that had developed and grown for a thousand years in the British Isles and Europe before comin' to the New World, thoughts that shoulda run to wolves or bears when envisioning predators—had gone to the lions of the African grasslands.

The wall exploded inward and it crouched in our midst, head raised in a fearsome snarl even though the maw was sewn shut, even though it was nothin' but a wooden frame and fabric stuffing, wrapped in a pelt that died near thirty-five years ago, halfway across the globe.

It roared again, that silent roar—not to us, but to its partner. *Here are they are! I found them! Come and feast!* And from somewhere beyond the yard, the other answered.

Phantoms from Africa, by way of the Chicago Field Museum.

The Ghost—so the locals had named them—and the Darkness.

The Tsavo Man-Eaters.

It prowled back and forth before the door, or the hole in the wall that had held the door. It was in no hurry, and why should it be? It could afford to be patient. The other would be here in moments.

"Why is there a goddamn *lion* in the middle of Chicago?" Pete was clearly as put out as he was frightened; he'd had more'n enough surprises for the day. Ramona shook her head, in denial or confusion or just exasperation I couldn't tell.

He wasn't about to wait for me to answer, though. Pete put three rounds into the dead thing's side, sending up clouds of dust, and it didn't so much as break stride.

Me, I was tryin' to shove the spiritual terror washin' over me from this stalking monstrosity, tryin' to think faster'n I ever had.

How was this even possible? Between the two of 'em, the man-eaters had killed anywhere from thirty-some-odd to a hundred-and-thirty-some-odd people, so okay, that was enough violence to draw the vampire spirit. But so what? It shouldn't be able to possess these; they weren't alive, weren't even *corpses*. Preserved and taxidermied pelts over manmade forms, these were no more "bodies" than a statue in a mink stole, so how…?

Oh. Oh, of course.

For a split second, I wasn't in the office in the Union Stockyards anymore. I was back in the museum, a year or so ago. Runnin', divin', dodgin', doin' whatever I could to keep from gettin' croaked by the sheer magical power being fired my way.

Fired at me by the traitorous *sidhe*, Raighallan, usin' the goddamn Spear of Lugh.

Again I saw the burst, saw the glass of the display window shadow. Saw the Ghost and the Darkness bathed with gods only know precisely what magic. And saw it not do a damn thing to 'em.

At least, not a damn thing I could detect at the time. But it'd seeped in, hadn't it? Seeped and infused the friggin' things, priming them. And so they'd waited, and maybe nothin' would've ever come of it, if it hadn't been for one fucking witch who shoulda been dead and one vampire spirit she'd twisted to her own ends.

The world sped back up, and I was back in the yards, and I

had no more time to think or to wonder.

More than a pounce, it just took to the air, crossin' the tiny expanse of workspace faster'n a pixie's wingflap. Hell, it barely *had* to cross the space; it coulda covered more'n half the distance with a stretch. Damn, but it looked a whole lot bigger out here than it ever had in the museum.

I rolled aside, expending the last of the luck I'd drained from the twice-late Varujan, and even that barely did the trick. The creature missed by two fingers of whiskey.

It hit the far wall, shattering the wood yet again, twisting to come back at me before it even touched the floor. Ramona moved to tackle it, talons on both hands extended. I think, even feeling the primordial dread in the back of her head, she underestimated the thing. I mean, it had no claws, no fangs, not even a mouth to hold 'em. What harm could it actually do?

Plenty, it turned out.

It twisted, a tawny blur of movement I couldn't even follow, and swatted her outta the air. Fabric and flesh tore, I *heard* 'em tear, even over her agonized scream. No, this taxidermy monstrosity might not have claws, but it used to, when it lived. It remembered.

And between the lingering magic of the Spear and the predator's fury of the spirit, that was enough.

Thick, ragged gouges marred Ramona's chest. Blood pumped, hot and fast, but not enough to quite hide the pink tissue and glistening rib within. She clutched herself with both mitts, rolling, struggling to stand, to shift.

Slow, way too slow, the edges of the wounds crept together, knitted shut, even as the rest of her body changed around 'em. Again her skin went red, her form ropey with muscle. Horns and wings sprouted, hoving the desk over onto one narrow end where it tottered and swayed.

"Outside!" I shouted, already movin'. I threw myself at the empty space where the doorway had been, and Pete dived for the curtained window.

Didn't see what happened to Ramona at first. The thing that'd once been a lion was on my heels, roaring its silent roar, snapping at me with phantom jaws that I knew damn well would feel all too real, more than real, if I let 'em catch me. Even at that thought, they slammed shut, yankin' me to a halt by my coat.

I didn't even try to tug it loose, just folded my arms back and slipped out of it, leavin' the flogger behind. The beast savaged it, just for a sec—when I glanced back, it looked like it hung by absolutely nothin' from the lion's chin, but huge holes appeared with every shake—and then it was after me again.

The pen across from me burst as a small herd of cattle stampeded away from the threat they sensed but couldn't even comprehend, the wooden fencing not near a match for so many tons of panicked beef. A couple of the smaller cows didn't make it through, crushed against the barrier and then beneath the hooves of the rest.

I staggered, slipped, slid through the mud, tryin' to focus through the wand, to scoop as much sheer luck from anything and everything around me, to wind it around myself as a shield against the impossibility tryin' to tear me apart. Hell, I mighta been responsible for a few of those dead cattle, misfortune running them down because I'd drawn all the good luck from 'em.

I'd say I was sorry, but under the circumstances...

Another ghostly roar nearly split my noggin, and it pounced again.

I spun midstep, lettin' myself tumble backwards. Mud sprayed up and around me as I landed, coatin' me with filth, almost choking me with the scent of animal effluvia that soaked the entire stockyard. The lion-shaped horror sailed through where I'd stood, over me, and I stabbed up with the L&G as it passed.

No sense tryin' for pain; with a false body I didn't know if the friggin' thing even *felt* pain. Instead I dragged the wand through its aura, not just draining luck from it, but deliberately twisting and corrupting what remained.

Stitches burst, wood cracked, rents and worn holes ripped through a pelt suddenly subjected to every bad day, every possible misfortune, every process of age that the museum's preservative chemicals had kept at bay.

The creature landed, staggered, howled, and turned. Whole torrents of dust poured from the open "wounds," and the skin hung off it in tatters like a bad shawl.

It stared through empty glass spheres, not too different from marbles, that had served as artificial eyes. Seemed to me at first that they glowed, but no, it was... somethin' else that made 'em gleam. Something weirder.

There was no light within 'em to push away the dusk and the gloom. No, it was the darkness itself that wouldn't quite come near those orbs. Like, I dunno, a bubble or surface tension in a glass of inky water. They weren't alight, just less dark.

Best I can describe, anyway.

It started back toward me and I scrambled upright, feedin' on the new luck, keepin' my own essence fat and flush to avoid slipping again in the sludge. Tossin' the wand to my left mitt, I drew my sword with my right. It leapt and I spun, some weird combination of matador and ballerina, and the lunge didn't even come close, but neither did the slash I aimed at its side.

Another landing, more sprayin' mud. It turned again, and I tensed...

The roof of the rapidly disintegrating office building blew apart as Ramona shot into the sky, wings spread wide, the full succubus in all her diabolical glory. She hovered in the night, silhouetted against the autumn clouds, and her eyes *definitely* glowed.

No, they *burned*.

"You want to try that again, you naughty kitty?"

It roared in fury, and Ramona dove.

But not without a quick glance my way first. I jerked her a sharp nod.

The lion-thing tensed, belly nearly dragging, ready to spring and meet the plummeting demon halfway. Which meant, for just a second, it'd forgotten about me in favor of the more immediate threat.

With all the speed an old *aes sidhe* could muster, augmented by the reservoir of magic practically flooding from the L&G, I sprinted forward, hauled back my arm, and...

Well, ain't any other way to put it. I shivved that lion in the keister with my wand.

Wasn't much of a wound, considering it had no flesh or organs to puncture. But I released a blast of misfortune, ripping through not just the wood and fabric but the mojo holding the thing together.

It staggered to its knees, and then lashed out with a backward kick more mule than lion. Shirt, skin, and tissue tore at the touch of those ghostly claws, and I probably cried out as I crumpled around a gutful of burning pain and slick blood. Without the extra luck woven through my aura, I'da been clutching at my bowels as they slipped and slid between my fingers.

*How fucking strong* was *this thing?*

Even more worn and ragged, lookin' as though even the gentle nighttime breeze oughta tear it apart, it still got its hind legs under it and surged upward to meet Ramona's plunge. For endless heartbeats they spun in place, just a couple yards above the ground, claws and fangs and talons digging and swiping.

Finally, with a real unladylike grunt, she got both hands around it and hurled it away from her, desperate for room to breathe and recover. For all the power infusing the thing, it was still a taxidermy model, didn't weigh near as much as the real McCoy. Propelled by her unnatural might, it sailed clear over a nearby supply shack to crash through the roof of a distant pen.

I'd say Ramona landed beside me, but it was really more of a crash. She hit the mud with her knees, huddled around her own wounds much as I was. Neither of us had the breath for words, but a lot passed between us in that moment.

Pete popped up next to us from wherever he'd been hidin', helped Ramona to stand—ladies first, right?—and then me.

He got as far as, "What do—?" before more animal screams, dozens of terrified cattle, drowned out whatever he'd meant to say. More wood shattered and they stampeded our way, bustin' outta the pen that was no longer safe.

A few collapsed as they fled, foaming at the mouth, breath hitching once, twice, before they died, overwhelmed by supernatural terror. The rest ran faster'n you've ever seen a cow go, and from right behind 'em came that empty howl.

I shoved Pete at Ramona, who—wincing around the tug on her injuries—wrapped an arm around him and took to the air. Me, I sheathed the sword, clung tight to the wand, waited for the first of the bovine tidal wave to come closer, closer...

And then I hurled myself across its back, bruising my ribs hard on its spine, wrappin' my own free arm around its neck. Crazed beast was so damn terrified, I don't think it even knew I was there.

Cow ain't the fastest animal in the world, but they're quicker'n you'd think, and this one was goin' all out. It certainly had more swift than *I* had in my current condition, anyway. Wouldn't be enough, not near enough, to keep the vampiric man-eater from catching me up, but it'd take just that much longer to gain.

Gaining it was, though. We tore through the stockyards, makin' random turns by whatever logic or instinct a terrified cow follows, and the lion loped after us. Other cattle peeled away as it passed, fleeing down this path or between those buildings, the miniature herd parting before it like it was goddamn Moses at the Red Sea. I felt bellowing breath beneath me, the sweat soakin' through the coarse hair, and wondered how long Bessy had left in her.

I twisted around, even though it meant loosening my grip, and started firing.

With every hoofbeat, pain shot through my chest; with every hoofbeat, I blasted a small flesh wound into the lion's essence. If magic or luck were visible, it woulda left a bloody trail behind it, just another wounded animal. And even as it closed the distance, as I felt those jaws I couldn't see gape wide, I thought...

Just maybe...

It had finally, *finally* started slowing. Its long strides grew ragged, a bit clumsy.

Was just us, now. The Tsavo man-eater, me, and my cow. The rest of the cattle had vanished deeper into the yard. Again I shot it, and again, and now it was definitely staggered, but still too fast, and I readied myself to roll free before it could leap...

Ramona landed on it like a bomb, wings curled in, body crouched so her talons struck before her feet. Pelt tore, wood snapped. Hell, wood damn near disintegrated. The thing collapsed under her, near burying itself in the mud, skidding far enough to build up a knee-high wall of muck before it finally dragged to a halt.

I tumbled from the racing cow, losing my balance between the momentum and the pain in my stomach. I crawled a pace to a fencepost, hauled myself up, and staggered over. I probably resembled some sorta golem more'n any living thing, a creature made entirely of dirt and mud.

Ramona was also standin' by the time I got there. I sucked in a breath, drew my sword, and drove it through the lion's wooden skull.

"Pretty sure it was already dead," she breathed. The red skin of her true form was pale, almost pink, with exhaustion and pain.

"Me, too, doll. Now I'm extra sure."

Again, Pete appeared from wherever she'd set him down. He looked... dazed. Not all there. Guess I could understand that.

"Isn't there still another one?" In his state, it sounded more curious than frightened.

"Is there?" Ramona asked me. "Two bodies but a single

spirit, right? Any chance that killing one…?"

"It's possible, but I ain't counting on it." Though gods help us, 'cause I had no idea how we could tangle with a second of these things and possibly surv—

Time slowed.

I saw, clear as the noonday sun, the horror wash over Ramona's face at somethin' just over my shoulder.

I felt that shoulder throb and bruise beneath her hand as she shoved me aside, lunging to intercept what she'd seen comin'.

Saving my life.

I heard her shout "Mick!" as she started to move.

My name was the last word Ramona Webb spoke before she died.

# CHAPTER THIRTEEN

In the instant between Ramona's shove, and the feel of my body drifting through the air before splashin' down yet one more time in the muck, it started to rain again, slow but heavy.

The first drop spread across my neck, hard enough it almost hurt.

I hit the ground, slid a few feet. Mud sloshed up under my collar and across my back in a wet slap.

The second of the vampire-possessed Tsavo man-eaters sprang from the top of a nearby building, the leonine figurehead of a ship splittin' the newly falling rain.

Ramona rose to meet it, wings spread, toes never quite leavin' the earth.

My jaw dropped open, I think to shout somethin', but I couldn't even begin to tell you what it mighta been.

Her hands came up, talons spread. She wasn't aimin' to claw it open—though I'm sure she wouldn't complain much if she took a chunk outta the thing—but to catch it. To repeat her earlier trick, toss it away, buy us all a couple seconds to regroup, to react.

And it worked again, for the most part. As before, the thing sailed up and over, propelled by inhuman strength, to vanish over a neighboring rooftop and go sprawling in another of the now empty pens.

But this time it took a piece of Ramona with it.

In the moment she'd grabbed it, it'd grabbed at her, too. Phantom jaws clamped tight, phantom teeth ripping through muscle and bone.

I was at her side before her scream ended in a choking gurgle, dropped to my knees and caught her before she hit the mud.

There wasn't one fucking thing I could do.

She wasn't gone yet, but it was a difference of seconds. Her clavicle and shoulder were just *missing* from the neck onward. The muscles, the joint, the rest of the bones; her forearm hung from her body by a strand of underarm flesh, and nothin' more. Blood didn't even pump from the ghastly wound, it just *fell*.

We can endure a lot, us Fae. If it doesn't croak us outright, we can usually recover, given time. But not this. Not something this bad.

"Ramona? Ramona, sweetheart, c'mon." It was stupid, I knew it was stupid, and I couldn't help sayin' it anyway. "Hang in there. I'll... We'll do *something*. We..."

She shuddered. Her lips moved, but she had no breath to speak, and I couldn't see clear enough to even try to make it out.

And I don't even know if I was cryin', or if it was just the rain.

"No. Ramona, no, please. Not now. We still... We still got months to catch up on, see? When we weren't talkin', when we... Ramona, *please*!"

Her eyes, glistening with rainwater—and not with anything else, not anymore—fluttered shut.

I held her, curled around her. My shirt, already soaked, plastered itself to my chest with her blood. It was hotter'n human, hotter'n mine.

She still wasn't quite gone, but only barely. And only for a few heartbeats more.

I mighta poured every last bit of magic into her, every last iota of luck I could pull from the world around me and damn the consequences. It woulda made jack in the way of difference, wouldn'ta kept her here a minute longer let alone saved her, but I mighta done it anyway. Except...

"Mick?"

Pete's hand fell on my shoulder. The sorrow, the sympathy pourin' offa him damn near burned, but so did the fear. "Mick, it's coming back."

So it was. I spotted the darkened shape through the downpour, slinking low from around the wrecked office.

It was comin', and it would kill us.

I mean, what else could happen? We'd barely been able to take down the first, and that was when there were two of us—I guess three, but Pete didn't really count in this situation—startin' off on all cylinders. Now I was gutted, literally and emotionally, and Ramona... Well, she wasn't gonna be able to help us anymore.

Was she?

The wind picked up, makin' the raindrops dance like it carried a tune only they could hear. Far off, the sky spoke a single peal of thunder.

And maybe *it* whispered somethin' only *I* could hear, 'cause I knew what to do. What I *hadda* do.

No matter what it cost me.

"Ramona, I'm so sorry."

I couldn't save her. She was gonna die, no matter what. And as guilty as I felt, my stomach knotting up in pain had nothin' to do with my wound, I knew she'da understood. So I apologized, but I didn't ask her forgiveness.

Ignoring the growing fear, my sense that the lion-thing grew closer with every second, I focused on the L&G...

And drained every last bit of magic, every last bit of luck, from my dying friend. She shuddered one final time, struggled through the bloody foam that choked her throat for one last breath, and went still.

I'd like to think I saved her some pain there, at the end. Or at least that there was enough of her left to understand and approve of the choice I made. But I guess I'll never really know.

I carefully laid her down, and I remember the barest second of insane worry. *Her hair… She's gonna be steamed I let her get so much mud in her hair…*

The power surging through my wand was enormous. Not the most it'd ever held, certainly, but a helluva lot more'n usual. The mojo within any of the Fae, the strength of our essence, ain't anything to sneeze at. There's magic in…

In sacrifice.

And honestly, I ain't entirely certain the power was all hers. I was on the edge of losing control again, my usual barriers and focus splintered by pain, fear, rage. Grief.

Most of the lights on this side of the stockyards had already been shattered or knocked over in the chaos, but I had no doubt the bulbs would be detonating all around me like grenades if they hadn't.

I stood and turned, Pete at my side, to face the second man-eater. We stared, all of us locked in hatred and fury, eye to glass to eye, through the watery curtain.

Maybe I coulda shot it, then and there. Maybe the fortune and the magic I'd taken from Ramona, combined with my own explosive emotions, coulda torn it apart, shredding the occult essence holding it together in a single blast.

But maybe it couldn't. What if it was fast enough that I missed? Or what if the spirit and the lingering magic of the Spear were strong enough to withstand that blast? I didn't know, and I couldn't afford to waste my shot on hope.

No, I had a different plan in mind. A different target.

Like I said, I genuinely believed that Ramona woulda understood, woulda forgiven me if she could.

I hoped—I prayed, though I couldn't say to who—that someday, Pete might forgive me, too.

I reached out to rest my hand on his shoulder, as he had mine. "I'm really sorry."

He tore his gaze from the lion's to meet mine. "What? Mick, what're you—?"

Every last bit of luck I could muster, that I'd drained from the first man-eater, that I'd taken from Ramona, flowed through the L&G. Icepicks stabbed into my temples as I struggled to weave random chance into magic, to make the near-impossible into fact.

Twenty-four hours ago, I had no idea it could even happen. Now I hadda *make* it happen, no matter how stacked the odds against it.

And thanks to Ramona, to the extra boost her essence had given me, I pulled it off.

To this day, part of me wishes I hadn't.

The lion loped forward, roaring that silent roar.

And Pete loosed a howl to match it as, in total disregard for the absence of the full moon, he changed.

Swelling muscles, lengthening bones, and thick though patchy fur tore his flogger, his shirt, his trousers to flapping ribbons. Leather burst, leavin' shoes and belt behind; when I dropped to one knee, mostly outta exhaustion, I made a point of scooping up his piece once again.

The unnatural predator's sour musk, a putrid combination of wolf and pestilence, washed away the other scents of the yard. The lowing beasts and screaming pigs on the far side of the pens, pressed together into a solid wall by their panic, grew even more frantic. I wouldn'ta thought it possible.

Its maw gaped down at me, danglin' pendulums of spittle so thick it refused to break up in the rain, and for a second I figured I'd made the last mistake of my life, that I didn't need to worry about the taxidermy vampire.

But that even more unnatural thing still loped our way, and the werewolf decided not to take my noggin as a midnight snack. Maybe, as I'd expected when I concocted this mad plan, it recognized the greater threat—or maybe a small piece of Pete was still awake in there somewhere, tuggin' what strings and levers he could.

Whatever the reason, it turned from me, and the age-old

battle of cat versus dog flared up again in fronta me on a grotesque, uncanny scale.

Claws and fangs; blood and splinters and dust; deafening howls and psychic roars. They rampaged across the yard, tearing pieces from each other, crashin' through fences and walls without the slightest pause. They stomped deep into the mud, leaving depressions, damn near tiny craters, that swiftly filled and became puddles.

Werewolf jaws snagged a chunk of shoulder, ripping pelt and fragmenting wood. Phantom claws opened up canine hide, and though the weapon wasn't silver, wouldn't kill or even maim, its spiritual power kept the wound from knitting itself shut near as rapidly as it should've.

No technique, no intelligence. After the first few blows, not even much in the way of cunning. This was a battle of sheer ferocity, of ripping and slashing and chewing until one or the other simply fell apart.

And if it sounds as if I was hangin' back, letting Pete do all the work and take all the punishment… Well, for a minute, yeah, I was. I still struggled to catch my own breath, to give my gut a chance to start its own healing—which was takin' longer'n it should for the same reason as the wolf's. I was beat, off balance, and it wasn't gonna do Pete or me any favors if I jumped back in before I was up to it.

Slowly, though, I caught my second wind. Or third, or ninth, or whatever the hell I was up to. The rain on my mug stopped feelin' like small gunshots and started to wake me up some. I still wasn't in any shape to run up and start swingin' a sword; that was a good way to get myself cut down, and just as probably by Pete as by the man-eater.

So I stayed kneeling, braced my elbow on my knee, sighted down the L&G as if it had a scope, and waited.

They thrashed this way and that so damn fast, but they were both of 'em big targets. It wasn't too long until they turned just so, until they stood perpendicular to me, the lion's whole length exposed.

*Bang.*

It staggered hard, screeching in silence as a huge rope of pure luck unwound from its aura and vanished into the wand. Glass orbs blazing with that non-light, it spun my way, ready to pounce, and Pete tore into it, taking half its face and what woulda been, if it still had bones, its skull.

Back to him, taking a swipe with a paw that drove the werewolf back a step... And I shot it again.

And again.

Claw. Wand. Wand. Fangs.

And finally, with one last scream—one that I actually *did* hear, not the howl of a beast but the furious wail of the fading spirit—it fell.

Which still left me with one deeply angry, disturbingly hairy, seven-foot-tall problem.

On the one hand, I had a plan for that, too.

On the other, it was based on, at best, an educated guess. A solid assumption, but not one I'd had any chance to test.

The first dollop of power I'd taken from the man-eater I'd absorbed myself, lettin' it go to work on the injuries. The rest I'd saved, holding it in an invisible swirling maelstrom around the L&G, around me.

Pete took one growlin' pace toward me and I let it loose.

Y'see, what I'd done with him—to him—was near impossible. More'n that, it was unnatural.

Yeah, yeah, the whole werewolf thing's unnatural, but what I'd done here was abnormal even for that. I'd broken the rules that bound him, interrupted and influenced the way of things. So it should prove a lot easier, and require a whole lot less magic, to turn him back.

*Should*. In theory. If I was wrong...

Turns out that, on occasion, I actually know what I'm barbering about. Pete fell to all fours, already halfway human by the time the mud splattered, and I'd rarely been so glad to have a theory proved right.

Unfortunately, that still left… what hadda come next.

"Pete?" I'd carefully ankled my way across the pathway to join him. "Pete, you okay?"

"You bastard." It came out a choked whisper, smothered by a constricted throat, drowned in tears and raindrops. "You fucking bastard."

"Pete, I didn't have any—"

"My worst goddamn nightmare. Biggest fear of my whole entire life. I told you that *today*, Mick. Fucking today!"

"There was nobody here to hurt!" I knew I was comin' off defensive, and there was jack I could do about it. "I knew that! I knew you couldn't—"

He was on his feet, fists clenched in the thread-laced mud that'd been my collar. "Do you think that matters? Can you even begin to understand why it *doesn't*?" He fell back, staggered and leaned against a fencepost. "Jesus Christ. I can see it now. I knew all this time you weren't human, but I didn't *know*."

"Whaddaya want from me?" I realized I was wavin' his gun around, tossed it to the ground over by the nearest building where it wouldn't get lost in the muck. "There was nothin' else I could do! Would you rather have been dismembered? Rather *I'd* been dismembered?"

If I'd had mortal ears, I'd never have heard his answer. "Maybe not. But it wasn't your choice to make for me." He started to shiver; standin' stark naked in the autumn rain'll do that, I suppose.

"Um. There's probably some spare clothes, or at least someone's flogger, in one of the offices…" I began.

"I'll figure it out. I don't need your help."

"Goddamn it, Pete! I'd just lost Ramona! I wasn't gonna watch you die, too!" Or me, either, but that probably went without sayin'.

And I think, maybe, his posture softened a little at that, at the reminder of what I musta been feelin' in that moment.

But only a little.

"Go. You ain't done. I'll take care of Ramona, and we'll… deal with the rest later."

He was right. There was already every chance I was too late, that Áebinn had long since reached the Ottatis. Adalina.

Still, my feet didn't wanna take that first step. "Pete…"

"Go, damn you, while this might all still mean something!"

I went.

I *was* too late. Just not the way I expected.

Even though it'd faded back to a light sprinkle, the rain washed the worst of the mud off me by the time I got to the station, which is probably the only reason nobody called the bulls on me. Still, I got plenty of hinky glances, and what few people were in the car when I boarded the L pretty quickly moved on to a different one. Stained with filth and coverin' a suspicious parcel—my sword, though they weren't wise to that—wrapped in the ragged remains of my coat, I couldn't much blame 'em.

Actually, I was grateful. The fewer distractions, the better. I spent the whole trip concentratin' hard, hangin' on to the very edge of control. If I'd slacked, even a little, I'm pretty sure more'n the train's lights woulda gone kablooey.

But y'know, I welcomed it. Focusing on not blowin' my wig kept me from havin' to think. Or havin' to feel. About what I might find when I got where I was goin'.

About what I'd left behind.

I discovered the first stiff outside the Ottatis' apartment building—smelled it well before I spotted it  cradled in the branches of a nearby tree. I guessed it'd been hurled through a window, and I didn't hafta guess which one. It was already badly putrefied, and the constant soakin' just made it worse.

*Vampire.*

A new one, probably one of the spirits Áebinn had summoned. She hadn't come alone, then; she'd brought undead reinforcements. What weak hope I still had guttered, a candle without much wax left.

Couple people moved to stop me once I got inside the building, since I clearly had no business in a place even half as keen as this one. I made 'em forget me.

The Ottatis' door was ajar, just an inch or so. L&G in my left hand, my blade—still wrapped in what'd once been a coat, but I could shake that loose easy enough—in my right, I nudged the door with a toe and stepped in.

Lights were out, but the illumination slinking in from the hall was enough for me to work with. Enough for me to tell the place was a shambles. About a million feet'd already tracked mud and water all over, enough so that even in bright daylight, my own contribution woulda gone unnoticed. The sofa I'd slept on and the table beside it were both overturned, and several of the cushions were spread all over the living room.

So were a handful of bodies, also way too rotten to have been anything but nosferatu. All dead.

I mean *really* dead, not "walkin'-around-nibbling-necks" dead.

Quick glance to the side told me the kitchen wasn't much better off. The refrigerator door had been torn off and somethin' had slammed into it, spilling a couple banquets'-worth of food over the floor. The faucet was running: tap water, this time, not salt, though a faint tang in the air suggested that might not've been the case a while ago.

I crept through, headin' for the bedrooms. Again, one of the doors was ajar, and again I nudged it…

Áebinn sat on the bed, leaning back against the headboard, knees folded up to her chest. Even from here, I could see nasty gashes on her arm, her side, and one cheek. She looked up as I entered, a peculiar expression beneath those gaping sockets, but at first I hardly even saw her.

Bianca and Celia lay sprawled on the carpet in the corner, still dressed in their nightgowns.

I dunno what Áebinn saw in my reaction, but she shook her head, though she winced at the motion. "They live, Oberon. I gave them only a fraction of my scream, to keep them out of my way. They'll hurt when they awaken, and likely have bad dreams for weeks, but they'll be fine."

"Don't mean that you will," and it almost scared *me* how calm and steady I sounded. "Adalina?"

"Gone." And then, again, at the clouds that musta been gathering on my mug, "I don't mean dead, I mean gone. I believe she even left a note. I thought I heard the scribbling of pen on paper."

"And you think that's gonna save you, *bean sidhe*? You came here meaning to kill her. Your goddamn scheme *did* kill two…" I stopped when I heard one of the darkened bulbs pop, realized my sword and wand both shook. "I've never had a lotta real friends. Sure as hell not recently. Now two of 'em are dead, and I may have lost more than that. All because of *you*.

"Tell me why the fuck I don't kill you right now."

"Because," she said, and I only now realized how bitter her tone tasted, "you'd be wasting your time. I'll be quite dead enough shortly."

Wasn't quite a splash of icy water, but the resentment and the cold truth in her words calmed me a little. "You look like shit," I conceded, "but I've seen plenty of us recover from worse wounds than those." She was Fae, after all. As I said, usually, if it doesn't croak us outright, or at least within minutes, it ain't gonna.

"But I know what it was that wounded me." She shifted, tryin' to get comfortable against the pillows. "I suppose I ought to be grateful. She could have given me worse than death. I have minutes. Maybe, if I'm truly fortunate, a few hours."

"My heart frickin' bleeds for you."

"I'm sure it does."

I leaned my sword against the wall, knelt to examine Bianca and Celia just to make sure. Yeah, they were breathin'.

So I stood and leaned *me* against the wall. "All right. How come this place ain't swarming with cops, or at least worried bystanders? Doesn't much look like this all went down quiet."

"Nobody noticed. Not one soul. I think because she didn't want them to."

I didn't hafta ask who *she* was. "You wanna tell me what this was all about?"

"And why should I?"

My grin was *mean*. "You got somethin' else to do?"

Then, when all I got was an eyeless glare, "You cost me a lot, Áebinn. You owe me answers, at the very least. We never much cared for each other…"

Even in her pain, she laughed at *that* understatement.

"But you always had your own kinda honor."

I didn't add that I could still make the last of her time *real* unpleasant. That wasn't anywhere I wanted to go—but I would if she made me.

She didn't.

"What have you already figured out?" she asked.

"What's that, professional curiosity?"

"Something like that."

I'd gone completely still again. It's second nature to me to keep up your mannerisms—the fidgeting, the gesturing, all that—but right now, I wasn't feelin' too human.

"This was all about Adalina. You were huntin' for her. This thing with the vampires, sensing a 'great and deathly power,' that was a con."

"No, not… exactly." Was her breath comin' shorter? I couldn't tell.

"Then what was it, exactly?"

"I *did* sense something awful, something of deadly danger to us arising in Chicago. But it was months ago."

Aw, shit. "When Adalina woke up."

"Yes, though I didn't know that at the time. I knew only, at first, that it was here. Then, gradually, more detail came to me. Its connection to you, for instance. And then, finally, I recognized it for what it was."

Her voice quivered. Áebinn was *afraid*.

"So what the hell is—?"

But the *bean sidhe* didn't hear me, was lookin' past me as she spoke. Now that she'd started, she wasn't gonna stop.

"I knew I couldn't report to the Court what I'd sensed. What if they wanted to keep her alive, try to use her for their own purposes? As if such a thing could be kept on a leash! I couldn't let them play political games, not with *this*. I couldn't risk the Unseelie catching word of it, either. I had to do this on my own, had to make *certain* she was destroyed. I could trust nobody, not even Sien Bheara or Laurelline, with the truth.

"But they already knew I was investigating *something*. I had to give them a threat, something big enough that they would permit me to follow up on it in either world. Something I could put *you* onto, so I could work you for information and keep you out of my way. And I had to have a 'villain' I could eventually provide to the Court. The vampire spirits did just that. It gave you, and them, a 'deathly power' to pursue, and it gave me minions I could control, who had no allegiance or even connection to anyone else. If only it hadn't attracted a true vampire as well…"

"Stole that part of the plan from Grangullie and Raighallan, did you?" I demanded, determined to get a question in.

She jumped, as though she'd forgotten I was even there. Then, "It worked for them."

"It *almost* worked for them. Which seems to be right about as well as it worked for you."

"So it would appear."

"You had me going," I confessed. "I was so sure I was lookin' for a human suspect… How'd you pull it off?" That was the real question I'd been workin' toward. "Controlling vampires—newborn weak ones, anyway—that's magic I've heard of. But the spirits? Nobody else even knew that kinda magic was *possible*, and you're no necromancer."

"Not formally, no. But you know what I am. I have a great familiarity with, and instinct for, the ebb and flow of death. As for vampires, I've studied them for over a century. I'm quite possibly the greatest living expert on them." She laughed once, even more bitterly. "For a little while longer, anyway."

"Studied…?"

"My bloodline, Oberon." She meant the family line she'd been attached to, whose deaths she'd first connected with, as all *bean sidhe* did. "The last of them were slain by vampires. I've loathed them ever since."

Well, how do you like that?

"All right. You were after Adalina, couldn't let anyone else know, called up a bunch of bloodsuckers to 'investigate' and to help you out. Fine. But why involve me at all if… Oh."

"Oh, indeed."

She hadn't known. She was gunnin' for somethin' powerful that'd just appeared or just arisen in Chicago, even knew *what* it was, but she'd had no notion as to *who*. Maybe she finally tumbled it after I took Adalina to the Otherworld a few times. Maybe she asked around her own contacts and finally discovered exactly when the Ottati girl—whom she woulda known was a changeling—had woken up from her year-long snooze. But however she learned it, it'd taken time.

"And right after you finally sussed it out," I said, "I moved the whole family. 'Cause of the Unseelie. And all your research was useless, because you couldn't *find* 'em anymore. That's why you stopped me'n Pete—" I tried not to flinch speakin' his name "—on the street that day, givin' me the third degree about everyone I knew."

"Gods damned Unseelie," she growled, which I took for confirmation. "They really do ruin everything, don't they?"

"And you buy that they just coincidentally turned up right then?"

She tried to shrug and groaned at the pain. "Perhaps they, too, had finally learned the girl was awake. They tried to take her once before, did they not?"

"Or perhaps they wondered what the hell the Seelie Court's chief investigator was up to pokin' around 'the girl' and her family. *You* led them to her!"

"I doubt it. But it hardly matters now. Oberon, listen to me! You must find her!"

"I'm planning on it. I—"

"And you must destroy her!"

Hadda really struggle with myself not to cut her down then and there. "Of the two of us, I think you've forgotten which one *ain't you*. You're nuts, sister. I got no intention of—"

"You *must*!" She leaned toward me, almost lunged, far as her slump allowed. Her torso actually aimed itself at me from between her knees in a sharp bend not many humans coulda pulled off. Fear poured from her aura in a slow eruption, layers of the stuff flowin' over the sides of the bed and fillin' the room until I could barely breathe. "And before she comes into her full strength! I've no idea what you think you can accomplish, Oberon. What play you're making, or what revenge you seek against the Seelie Court for wronging you, but I know you're no fool! You must know you cannot control this, the calamity you're courting! You—"

"*For the gods' sake, what're you* talking *about?*"

Áebinn froze, her kisser hangin' loose. Someone pounded on the neighboring wall, shoutin' at us to keep it down, didn't we know what time it was, people were tryin' to sleep here!

"You don't know." She straightened up, stiff as the headboard she leaned against. "No scheme, no plans, you truly don't... All the time you've spent with her, how could you *not know?*"

And I gotta tell you, I wondered that myself. I'd *been* wonderin', since Adalina woke up, that naggin' little yammer in the back of my mind, reminding me over'n over that I was missin' something. Something big.

"I dunno," I said. "How's about you spill already, and then we can suss it out."

"Mick…" Jesus, had she *ever* called me Mick before? "Adalina, she…"

Áebinn gasped once, lightly, as if she'd just remembered someone's birthday or held a burnin' match a second too long. "I guess," she whispered, "I'm not 'truly fortunate' today."

Just like that, she died.

The empty sockets in her skull, those pools of darkness deeper'n they had any right to be, grew. Wider and wider, overlapping, expanding, consuming Áebinn's face, her entire skull. Then they fell, working downward, neck, shoulders, chest, and onward.

Then there was nothin' left, nothin' but a few splotches of inky fluid staining the quilts and the last fading echoes of a distant keening.

Can't say I was real sorry, but frustrated? That I'll confess.

And more'n a little suspicious. Yes, she was already dying. Yes, she'd said she probably only had minutes. But that *exact* moment? Right before she was gonna put me wise to Adalina's great mystery?

I dunno. That confused and innocent little girl'd gone toe-to-toe with a *bean sidhe* and a handful of vampires, and she'd mopped the floor with 'em. And she'd made sure the neighbors either didn't hear, or at least didn't notice, a thing. That, plus all the power Áebinn felt when she kicked off this whole disaster?

Made me wonder, anyway.

I went into the next room—Celia's and Adalina's—and collected some clean pillows and blankets. Figured I'd make the two ladies comfortable as possible for when they woke up. Then I went and scoured the place for Adalina's supposed note.

I actually found a couple, tacked to a cabinet in the kitchen, stapled there by a butter knife embedded in the wood. One for her family, which I didn't read, and one for me. It…

Look, a lot of it was personal. I ain't repeating it for you. But I'll give you the gist.

She was scared, had been even before tonight's events. The

violent dreams had only gotten nastier—and worse, she finally admitted what she hadn't, or couldn't, that day we spoke in my office: She'd started to enjoy the violence, look forward to the nightmares, the bloodier the better.

Now that she knew what she was capable of, she couldn't stay. Couldn't risk puttin' what was left of her family at risk.

And she hadn't come to me because… She couldn't trust me anymore. She assured me she knew I'd meant well, but after keepin' Orsola a secret, she just didn't believe I'd always be willin' to tell her what she felt she needed, was entitled, to know.

That hurt. In part because I knew damn well she wasn't wrong.

She told me not to try to find her. That she'd just run again if I did. And to tell her momma and her sister she loved them.

I carefully worked the knife from the cabinet, folded the note and slid it into a mud-stiffened pocket. Then I went back and planted myself on the bed, opposite where Áebinn had sat.

And I waited.

Bianca and Celia Ottati were gonna wake up sooner or later. They were gonna have a lot of questions. They deserved answers, even more'n I did. I wanted to be here to provide the ones I could.

Especially since I didn't know if they'd ever welcome seein' me again after tonight.

Or, for that matter, how much I'd even be around, after tonight.

# CHAPTER FOURTEEN

You might recall me mentioning that I'd had a hunch I was gonna need a good amount of dough soon, yeah? That's why I'd taken the job from the department, the one that led me to the rabid watermelon and... other stuff.

Turns out I was right. Those instincts usually are. Problem was, I really hadn't made much. So what little I had, was gonna hafta cut it.

Took me a spell to arrange everything, and the city didn't stand still during that time.

The murders stopped, of course, but since nobody'd been sent up river for 'em, the news rags continued to have a field day. Was the killer still out there? Would he strike again? Was anyone safe? Be sure to buy the next issue to keep up with the latest!

The Field Museum closed down a few exhibits for "renovation." When they reopened 'em after a couple days, there stood the Tsavo Man-Eaters, lookin' as artificially ferocious as ever. Fakes, almost certainly. Ain't as if the place was gonna admit to the loss of a famous exhibit, especially not after the break-ins last year.

But hell, what do I know? Maybe they somehow got their hands on the real pelts, stitched 'em back up and stuck 'em on new frames. I don't see how, but weirder things happen in this town. Maybe if I got real curious someday, I'd go take a good, close slant at 'em and see if I could tell.

Right now, though, I didn't figure I'd ever wanna see 'em again.

Fino Ottati's funeral—well, memorial, since they had no body—was a big, elaborate affair. Catholic ceremony as thrown by the rich and the criminal; ornate and maudlin vyin' for supremacy. Probably a good fifteen, twenty percent of the Windy City mobsters were present, which made for a lot more guns than you find in your average cathedral or cemetery. Suppose things coulda gone bad, but if any of Fino's rivals showed, they didn't pick any fights.

I wasn't invited, and dunno if I woulda gone if I had been.

Assistant State's Attorney Daniel Baskin also held a funeral, a much smaller and more private affair, for his "administrative assistant," Ramona Webb, who the police had reported as the latest—and so far last—victim of the murderer hunting Chicago's streets. I dunno exactly what Baskin told 'em, or how he handled the arrangements, or even what invocations he mighta dug up, but there was nothin' in any of the reports about the body havin' wings or horns.

I wasn't invited, and I *absolutely* wouldn't have gone if I had been.

My grief, more'n anything else about me, is my own.

I hadn't traded a single word with Bianca or Celia Ottati after that night. I didn't know if I ever would.

Pete woulda been happier, I think, if I coulda said the same about him. But he's a standup guy, Pete Staten. He wasn't gonna let his beef with me hurt anyone else, and the full moon rolled around again on its usual schedule, without concern for his feelings or mine. He let me take him Sideways, and he let me bring him home again. But that was all. He never spoke about what'd happened, what I'd done. And it didn't take tasting his emotions in the air to recognize that he wouldn't welcome it if I brought it up, either.

Made a brief stop myself, while I was in Elphame, and I didn't even hafta shout or get anyone (or myself) in dutch to do it.

Servant showed me around to that same secret entrance, dumped me in the same sitting room, offered me a glass of the same, or at least similar, beverages. I think I waited for maybe two hours before Her Royal Majesty and Police Chief Laurelline showed up.

"I have a dozen appointments after this, Oberon," she announced, breezin' into the room on a gust of arrogant diligence. "So whatever you've got to report, make it snappy."

"Áebinn's dead."

It ain't much fun when the full weight and attention of somethin' as old as I am suddenly falls over you like a thousand pounds of burlap. Never once lookin' away, she backed to the door, called somethin' about canceling her next guest, and then dropped hard into the seat across from me.

"If this is your idea of a prank…" she began. Not that she believed it for an instant.

"You know me better'n that. I ain't *that* big of a louse."

"No. No, you're not." She reached for a drink of her own. "What happened?"

All right, this was gonna take some doin'. Even for me, it's tough to mislead another Fae, at least one this ancient and powerful. I hadda pick every word like it had poisoned thorns.

"We identified the source of the magics she'd been sensin'. The call that was attractin' the vampires. It won't be a problem any longer, but I'm afraid Áebinn… didn't make it through the final dust-up."

Well, technically, not a word of that was false, right?

"The necromancer was some mortal," I continued, not wantin' to make her ask, to make this part of the recital stand out in any way. "Came across some old magics and extrapolated the rest. He's gone, and the secret of manipulating the vampire spirits lost with him."

And there it was. The one genuine fib in all the prevarication and half-truths. I'd rather've just left it out, but she was gonna ask who was behind the whole thing, and I hadda give her somethin', see?

I sat, concentratin' and tryin' not to *look* like I was concentratin', while she watched me around her nectar-filled glass.

"You're not telling me everything, Oberon," she said finally. Shit. "Ain't I?"

"Do not take me for a fool. And do not make an enemy of me. What are you trying to hide from me?"

Okay, so she'd picked up on the deception, but not the detail. I could still handle this.

If every. Single. Word. Came out right.

"Look, Laur—your Majesty. Áebinn got even more obsessed toward the end there. Whatever it was about this case, she fell into it, head-first. She made some bad mistakes, and to be square with you, she got herself killed because of 'em. Word of her behavior gets out, it's gonna reflect badly on the Court at best, maybe cause you some legal problems or spark some vendettas over her past investigations. It ain't gonna do you, me, or anyone else any good for me to spill the details."

Again, all fact. One way or another.

"And if I ordered you to 'spill the details'? Would you defy me?"

I kept my trap shut, and willed her to taste the truth of what I'd said.

"Very well. Thank you for your assistance, and your… discretion. I clearly have arrangements and announcements to make. Someone will show you out."

Took a lot, but I kept my relief in check—didn't need anyone tasting it spillin' off me and askin' fool questions—until I got back to my office.

Anyway, that was one full moon with Pete taken care of. I wouldn't be here for the next, though, maybe not for quite a few of 'em. A thick stack of what little money I had went to Franky, along with a key to my joint. He understood what was at stake if he didn't keep to the schedule, use my nook to get Pete to Elphame every month. He didn't come out and say he'd probably use my office as a place to bunk while he was at it, but it was understood.

Had myself a tearful farewell—his waterworks, not mine—with Mr. Soucek, too. Told him Franky and Pete were okay, that he shouldn't worry if he saw 'em using the office. He asked me when I was comin' back. I said I wasn't sure.

He didn't ask me *if* I was comin' back. I'da told him the same if he had.

I mean, I *meant* to. But it all depended, didn't it?

So finally, when I was sure Adalina hadn't left me any trail I could follow, and when all the arrangements were made, I packed up a few outfits, my wand, my sword, and my one remaining flogger.

A bag of salt, and a few other charms, so I could continue holdin' the effects of Orsola's damn hex at bay.

And one more little dingus, too.

Stuck a sign on my office door. Said we were temporarily closed for business, gave the address of a few other PIs I knew to be halfway decent, as detectives and as people. And then I left.

Normally the amount of kale I had left wouldn't have been enough to buy me a berth.

But most people don't have the, uh, hagglin' skills that I do.

So I half-bought, half-mesmerized my way into a ticket on the American Line, Trans-Atlantic travel with all the luxuries you could want. I don't remember which particular ship, but then again, I didn't *see* much of the ship.

I mean, the engines, the pumps, the radio... And while the ship itself and most of the machines are steel, there's a fair share of raw iron, too. I spent a few days sick in my cabin, talkin' to absolutely nobody except the servers when they brought me the milk I ordered.

Part of me actually welcomed the discomfort. I was gonna have a long trip to dwell on all that'd happened, and I wanted to postpone that long as I could.

I don't like losing. And, end of the day, I sorta had. Adalina was gone. People I'd cared about had died or turned their backs. Orsola'd gotten away, gods damn her. I hadda live with all that. So yeah, even if it was 'cause my head'n my guts were on fire, I welcomed an excuse to put off thinkin' on it for a few days.

Woulda been faster to fly, but it woulda hurt a whole lot more. More to the point, I still wasn't sure why I'd been havin' more "episodes" recently, and the last thing I wanted was to lose control and start gummin' up the works a couple miles in the air, savvy?

Then...

Look, there was a lotta travel. Ship. Trains. Coaches. And a mess of walking.

Most of it was here, on your side, not in Elphame. I mighta found parts of the journey easier if I'd stepped Sideways first, but I got history with the Courts of the Old World. Hundred times what I got here. And I did *not* wanna get dragged back into any of it, or let 'em learn I was visiting.

I was here to see exactly one person, and the rest could go jump.

As it was, I barely made it. I was flat broke by the time I crossed the border into the Soviet Union. Hadn't the slightest idea how I was gonna get home, but I'd worry about it later.

And no, gettin' into Russian territory ain't the easiest thing, even for me. But this ain't that story. I got in; that'll do.

I walked more. Hopped another train here, begged a ride on a cart there, but mostly, for days and days, I walked.

The ground got higher, the air thinner and a whole lot colder, the quaint little villages more'n more sporadic. Temperature doesn't bother me much, not in your world, but I was still wishin' I had heavier clothes.

The snow fell lightly during the day, heavier at night.

Trudging through it, breaking trail when it was up to my calves, sometimes my knees, started to wear even me out. But I went on, 'cause I sure as hell had no choice anymore.

I told you this story would end in the snow. Specifically the snow of northern Ukraine, near the borders with Russia and Belarus.

The snow, and the woods.

I coulda used magic, drawn on the ambient luck to increase my chances, so I wasn't just stumbling blindly through the general vicinity hopin' to get lucky. I never bothered. I wasn't sure it'd work, not in this place.

And I wasn't sure the effort, or the manipulation of these particular tides of fortune, would be appreciated.

This doesn't happen to me, ever, but I lost track of how long I wandered those dark forests. Weeks, I'm sure. In the dark shadows of the bare branches, reaching out to scratch my soul when I wasn't lookin', and beneath the cloud-shrouded stars and moon, which seemed a lot closer here than they ever did in Chicago, I wandered. It seemed that I never heard a single bird, or the howl of even one wolf. I thought I had, more'n once, off in the distance. But every time I stopped to listen, it had only ever been the wind.

I was cold. I was tired.

I was also scared, which was how I figured I was close to the right place.

I hadn't wanted to come here. I near talked myself out of it a couple dozen times. And I wasn't sure which idea scared me worse, that I wouldn't find what I was lookin' for, or that I would.

And then, one day, I did.

Did I finally stumble on it? Or did it finally decide to let me in? In this place, either was just as probable.

Cold and wonderin' if it was possible for the *aes sidhe* to shiver—I'd never done it, but I felt I oughta—I pushed through a barrier of bare, crackling branches, and I saw it. I was above, on the slope of a shallow knoll. Stretched out below was a round clearing, free of trees, and mostly free of snow. That grass was mostly brown and dormant, but a few patches of color—green, mostly, but a few reddish blossoms here'n there—broke the monotony.

At the far side of the clearing stood the hut.

It was an old thing, sporadically patched with newer timber, its thatched roof round and peculiarly pointed. A tin chimney stuck up on one end, exhaling small puffs of smoke...

*Like Ramona's Old Golds,* my brain wanted to say. I whipped and kicked the thought until it ran away to hide.

The door stood open, but from here, thanks to the angle and the lighting, I couldn't see much inside.

I *could* see what was right *outside*, though. What looked at first to be a massive cauldron was actually a giant mortar, smelted of black iron. So was the pestle that rested within. I knew I was gonna have to make a pretty broad circle around *those* instruments of torture.

And so I did. I staggered my way down the slope and into the clearing, which—despite the lack of snow—wasn't any warmer than the woods'd been. Kept my distance from the iron and got a slant at the door, but other'n the woodburning stove and the pots, pans, horns, and herbs that hung at various levels from the ceiling inside, the place didn't seem to hold much.

Took one more step, made as though I was gonna enter... and the hut moved.

It shifted first, leaning sideways as if to topple over, then straightened again—now five feet off the ground. Then ten, fifteen, more, as it rose to its full height atop a giant pair of scaled, flaking chicken's feet.

Once it was entirely upright, it took two scrabbling paces back from me, nearly plunging into the trees.

"All right, take it easy," I said. Yes, to the hut. "I ain't comin' in."

Then, calling out a *lot* louder, "You're here, ain'tcha? I've come a long ways to see you, and I'd hate to have wasted the trip. Plus, your house ain't too happy to see me. I'd rather not be left alone with it. I got no idea what kinda small talk it prefers."

First hint I had that me'n the house *weren't* alone was the sound of sweeping. She appeared from the forest off to my right, whiskin' the last bit of snow outta the clearing with a broom taller and thicker than my coat rack back home.

A broom made of a sorta silvery white wood.

"Hardly fair for you to expect an old woman to break her routine," she said, watchin' the snow as it sprayed from the end of the broom and vanished into the shadows. Her voice was the cracked breath of a sickly crone, yet it carried across the clearing, and I'm sure well beyond. As far as she wanted it to be heard, probably. She spoke in Russian, but even if I hadn't spent a while travelin' through Soviet territories, it woulda only taken me a minute to pick it up.

"Especially," she continued, "when you visit unannounced. It is your fortune to even find me home."

"Yeah. Yeah, I suppose it is. Good afternoon, Little Grandmother."

"A good afternoon to you, Mick Oberon," said Baba Yaga.

Her mug was a mass of wrinkles and crags, deep enough to sheathe a dagger, bony enough to hammer a nail. Her schnoz was a long, twisted thing, like a carrot wrapped in leather, and her stringy hair the color of iron. Her teeth and her nails *were* iron, and if you wanna know how any creature related to the Fae could survive that way, could develop that way without goin' mad and dying, well, you'n me both. It was hardly the biggest mystery surrounding the witch that even I thought of as ancient, let alone the only one.

Oh, she also stood close to four feet taller'n I did. Probably coulda outwrestled a troll with one arm tied behind her back. Not that the dumbest, meanest, craziest troll would even try.

"So, little *aes sidhe*." She took a few impossibly long strides to the mortar, laid the pestle across the rim, and sat on it as if it were the most stable and comfortable chair. The broom she allowed to drop to the ground beside her. "What brings you so very many leagues to my stoop?"

I started to speak, but she abruptly raised a finger. "A moment. I said, *to my stoop*!"

The hut dipped downward, as though chagrined, shuffled up behind her, and settled back where it'd been, so the mortar—and now Baba Yaga herself—were once more seated right by the door.

"Better. Now, continue, please."

"Well, the short version is, someone's been muckin' around with my memory."

It was the only conclusion I'd been able to come to. So many things I'd missed with Adalina that I felt I oughta recall, the various "episodes" when I found myself confused or noodlin' too hard on certain topics, my moment of confusion when I'd apparently forgotten my precise relationship with my namesake.

"Has someone indeed? Remember this happening, do you?" She snorted and chortled at her own joke, and I waited for her to finish.

"Even if this is so," she said eventually, "why come to me?"

"Because," I said, takin' the bull by the horns, "I think you did it to me."

"Do you." Not really a question. She wasn't smilin' anymore. Not steamed, not yet—and gods, I never wanted her to be!—but not smilin'. "This is a severe accusation, Mick Oberon. There are others who have such power."

"A few. Not many, though. Besides, there's this."

From my pocket, I drew the chunk of wood I'd found in my office hide-hole. White birch. Just like Baba Yaga's broom.

I tossed it her way. She didn't bother to catch it, just examined it as it lay in the mostly dead grass at her feet.

"Nobody coulda put that where I found it," I said. "Nobody but me. But it didn't make any sense to me until I realized my memory had holes in it. I musta known somethin' was gonna happen, because I left myself a trail of breadcrumbs, Little Grandmother.

"And look," I added quick. *Don't make her mad, don't make her mad.* "I ain't here to accuse you. I'm tellin' you the facts as I know 'em before I ask for your help."

"Ah. You wish me to undo what has been done to you."

"Yeah. Yeah, if you would."

"Again, there are others who could do this."

"Again, not many. And those who could? They got their own agendas. They're all tied to the Seelie or Unseelie Courts, one way or another. You're... a free agent."

Again she cackled. "Free agent. Yes. Yes, this is a good term. I am a free agent." Then, outta nowhere, "You know a hex lies upon you, yes?"

"I... Yes. Cast by a mortal witch, a powerful one. I been tryin' to counter it, but—"

She waved a few gnarled, hairy knuckles my way and I felt a hundred pounds lighter. "It is gone."

Damn. Just like that. "*Spasiba*, Little Grandmother."

"*Pozhaluysta*. But do not be so free with your gratitude. With your other matter, I cannot help you."

I don't remember decidin' to sit, but I found myself cross-legged in the grass. Gods dammit, if this was beyond Baba Yaga herself...

"You're sure? The magic's that strong?"

"It is not the magic, Mick Oberon."

It took a minute to sink in, and then I clenched my mitts around two handfuls of grass and frozen soil to keep from shoutin'. "You mean you *won't* help me."

"If I were to have hidden pieces of your past from you," she said, idly scratchin' a wart the size of a sugar cube on one cheek, "it would have been for reasons of only the greatest import. Reasons that are unlikely to have changed."

"Shit. *Shit!*"

She raised an eyebrow, said nothin'.

I rose and turned to go. It was rude, but anythin' I coulda made myself say to her woulda been even less polite. What was I gonna do? I couldn't force cooperation, not from her. She didn't make it sound as though we hadda be enemies over this, but if she'd gummed up my brain, how could we not be? I—

Say...

"If you won't help me for my sake," I said, "what about for everyone who might get hurt?"

"And why should this harm anyone else, Mick Oberon?"

So I told her about Adalina. All of it. Her bein' swapped out for Celia, bein' raised as human, her slow maturation into somethin' that clearly wasn't. Her exposure to Orsola's magics, her injury and her coma, her awakening at the hands of Nessumontu, her half-awakened screaming—in multiple languages, some of 'em long dead—that she wasn't ready. And of course, what'd happened in the last couple months.

When it was all said'n done, she looked graver than I'd ever seen her. Well, than I ever remembered seein' her. For near ten minutes she sat, thinkin', decidin', and I wasn't near bunny enough to disturb her.

When she was finally done ponderin', I realized she was chewin' on a hunk of meat. I didn't know where it'd come from; she hadn't moved from her makeshift bench. And I *sure* didn't wanna know what it'd been.

It had fingers.

"I will help you this much, Mick Oberon. You have, since you first met this girl, been asking the wrong question."

"Oh? How's that?"

"You have been asking 'what.' You should have asked 'who.'"

I near staggered, as if I'd just taken a poke in the jaw from one of the Firbolg. "Reincarnation? That only happens with the darkest curses, Little Grandmother! Curses like... like..."

Couldn't get it out. Could barely move. I wanted her to foresee what I was tryin' to say, to tell me I was wrong.

Maybe she did the first, but I wasn't so lucky with the second.

What I finally forced out wasn't even a whisper. "The Bereft."

Baba Yaga nodded, once. For all her efforts at sweepin' the snow from her doorstep, it was startin' to fall again, thick and heavy.

You won't have heard that name from me. Won't find it in your legends. But you've heard me talk about the concept, around the edges.

I've told you, the Fae don't make oaths lightly, 'cause there are consequences for breakin' 'em. Sometimes it's a curse. Sometimes it's an emotional stain that turns others against us. Sometimes it's a creature that we can't face, can't escape, that'll do a lot worse'n kill us.

And sometimes, when a broken oath does great harm to one of our own, one of the Fae, they come back. Over and over, to make us—all of us, but especially those responsible—suffer.

Those are the Bereft.

If I'd felt like I was punched a minute ago, now I was back in the Union Stockyards, with phantom claws diggin' deep into my gut—only worse, now, worse ten times over.

Because now, knowin' what I knew, bits and pieces *were* comin' back to me. All those clues Áebinn was shocked I'd missed.

She'd been right. Oh, gods, she'd been right. I hadda find Adalina. Maybe… maybe I even hadda kill her.

She'd woken up before her mind had recovered, before her earlier memories—her past lives—had caught up with her. If they did… she wouldn't be Adalina anymore.

And then I might not be able to stop her at all.

Her appearance. Speaking Old Gaelic. Old Polish. Old Norse.

I knew. I knew, I *remembered*, who she was, who this Bereft had been. Dozens of names, some—when she'd been found, killed, before she could begin her hunt—nobody had ever heard. But she'd had others, and now, in the shadow of Baba

Yaga, I remembered, though the details refused to return, that I'd known her, or known *of* her, in so many…

Jenny Greenteeth, haunter of British rivers. Wąda, sovereign of the *bagienniks*, so-called Queen of Underwater Lawns. Possibly Caoránach, dubbed Mother of Demons, though we were never entirely sure if that creature was really her. And more.

But the one I know you've heard of? Her first and most infamous monstrous incarnation? She never had a name of her own that I, or anyone else, ever heard. She was known, far and wide, only by the name of her son.

As the Mother of Grendel.

That was who dear, confused, innocent Adalina was—or would become. That was what the goddamn Chicago Fae had let loose on the world.

I had no idea where she was. No idea what she'd find herself able to do, or when the curse of her past would catch up to her, turn her into a monster worse than any Unseelie.

I knew only one thing. I still had no memory of it, couldn't have told you *how* I knew, but I felt it. From deep in the past I couldn't remember, from deep in my soul. This was my fault. Because somehow, sometime, so many centuries ago…

I'd created her.

# A BRIEF AFTERWORD

So, first things first. The whole vampiric watermelon/pumpkin thing?

Yeah, he wasn't lying to you. That really is a genuine myth. Obscure, but genuine. It traces back to a particular branch of the Romani in the Balkans. Feel free to look it up.

But the main reason I'm writing this afterword is to talk about mistakes.

I make them. I do a lot of research for these books, and I try to get everything just so, but things still slip by me. The use of pink as a girl's color in *Hot Lead, Cold Iron*—it was considered more appropriate for boys at the time—or the use of "Ms." as a title in *Dead to Rites*. It existed, but it wasn't in common usage. You know, little stuff like that.

But the one that bothers me, and the one I'm discussing here, is *fata*.

As you may have noticed, Orsola uses that term to refer to Mick a lot in *Hot Lead, Cold Iron*, but she doesn't do so in this book. That's because, between the two, I've spoken to a native Italian speaker, and I've learned I used the term incorrectly. It doesn't mean "Fae," as I thought it did, but refers more to a female sorceress or witch. Worse, it's become something of a pejorative in modern times for referring to effeminate men.

Obviously, I can't go back and change *Hot Lead, Cold Iron*. But as I won't be using it moving forward, I wanted to explain the inconsistency to readers who may pick up on it, and to apologize, however unintentionally, for the use of the slur. *Mea culpa*.

# FAE PRONUNCIATION GUIDE

Áebinn [**ey**-b*uh*n]
*aes sidhe* [eys shee]
*bagiennik* [**baig**-yen-nik]
*barbegazi* [bar-buh-**gey**-zee]
barghest [**bar**-gest]
*bean sidhe* [ban shee]
*benandanti* [ben-ahn-**dahn**-tee]
*brounie* [**brooh**-nee]
*cu sidhe* [koo shee]
*dullahan* [**dool**-uh-han]
*dvergr* [**dver**-gr]
Elphame [**elf**-eym]
Eudeagh [ee-**yood**-*uh*]
Firbolg [**fir**-bohlg]
*ghillie dhu* [**ghil**-lee doo]
Goswythe [**gawz**-weeth]
Grangullie [gran-**gull**-ee]
*haltija* [hawl-**tee**-yah]
Ielveith [ahy-el-veyth]
*kobold* [**koh**-bold]
Laurelline [**Lor**-el-leen]
Luchtaine [**lookh**[1]-teyn]
Lugh [**lugh**[2]]
Oberon [**oh**-ber-ron]
*phouka* [**poo**-k*uh*]
Raighallan [**rag**-hawl-**lawn**]

Sealgaire [sal-**gayr**]
Seelie [**see**-lee]
Sien Bheara [shahyn **beer**-*uh*]
Slachaun [**slah**-shawn]
*sluagh* [**sloo**-ah]
spriggan [**sprig**-*uh*n]
Tuatha Dé Danann [too-**awt**[3]-h*uh* de[4] **dan**[4]-*uh*n]
Unseelie [**uhn**-see-lee]
*vuoren väki* [vour[5]-ren va-kih]

[1] This sound falls between "ch" and "k," as in the word "loch."
[2] "Gh" pronounced as "ch," but more guttural.
[3] This "t" is *almost* silent, and is separate from the following "h," rather than forming a single sound as "th" normally does in English.
[4] Strictly speaking, these "d"s fall somewhere between the "d" and a hard "th"—such as in "though"—but a simple "d" represents the closest sound in English.
[5] This is a rolling *r*.

# ABOUT THE AUTHOR

When Ari Marmell has free time left over between feeding cats and posting on social media, he writes a little bit. His work includes novels, short stories, role-playing games, and video games, all of which he enjoyed in lieu of school work when growing up. In addition to the **Mick Oberon** series, he's the author of the **Widdershins** YA fantasy series, *The Goblin Corps*, and many others, with publishers such as Del Rey, Pyr Books, Wizards of the Coast, Omnium Gatherum—and, of course, Titan Books.

Ari currently resides in Austin, Texas. He lives in a clutter that has a moderate amount of apartment in it, along with George—his wife—and the aforementioned cats, who probably want something.

You can find Ari online, if you're not careful.

Website: mouseferatu.com
Twitter: @mouseferatu
Facebook: facebook.com/mouseferatu